Guilt on the lily

The letter Richard Patton receives has taken so long to reach him that any urgency would seem to have resolved itself. When he phones to enquire, this turns out to be true. The sender has been murdered.

This, in itself, would not have been enough to take him back to his home town but the young woman's death has left behind a disturbing chain of events, which involves past colleagues. Richard feels he must try to help them, if only to square his conscience. Returning, though, presents difficulties. Old enmities are aroused as he becomes involved in the, as yet, unsolved murder. His presence is resented. Yet his efforts not only uncover the background facts of the death, but also a personal hatred that has grown into paranoia.

Very soon, he realises that what he has uncovered has brought his wife, Amelia, into very real danger, and when another tragedy occurs he is painfully aware that he might have averted it. He is by now too involved to withdraw from the situation, and only one event can free him from the web in which he is caught.

Roger Ormerod's twenty-seventh novel of suspense – as compelling and carefully constructed as ever – builds to a dramatic finale, confirming the opinion of Harriet Waugh in *The Spectator* who wrote: 'He ranks among the few English crime writers who can still construct a traditional detective novel in which the ending does not come as a wet squib.'

Also by Roger Ormerod

GUILT ON THE LILY

Roger Ormerod

Constable London

First published in Great Britain 1989
by Constable & Company Limited
10 Orange Street, London WC2H 7EG
Copyright © by Roger Ormerod 1989
Set in Linotron Palatino 10pt by
Redwood Burn Limited, Trowbridge, Wilts
Printed in Great Britain by
Redwood Burn Limited, Trowbridge, Wilts

British Library CIP data
Ormerod, Roger, *1920–*
Guilt on the lily
I. Title
823'.914 [F]

ISBN 0 09 468810 9

This book is dedicated to Eileen Dewhurst, who pointed out that *Face value* could not be the end of it.

My thanks also go to the author of the play for allowing me to reveal the plot of *I'll go along with that*, and for his explicit breakdown of the emotional conflicts involved in it.

R.O.

1

It's no good telling me I shouldn't have gone back. I knew. But I had served that town for twenty years, right through from Constable Patton to Detective Inspector – yet I had left it in an atmosphere of acrimony and distrust, even hatred. I could never forget that look of white, intense dislike on the face of WPC Marjie Crane.

Now I was settled at The Beeches, Boreton-Upon-Severn, allowing the atmosphere to seep through me and feeling the contentedness creeping into my bones. I could be happy there for the rest of my days, I had decided. Yet behind it all there was a haunting feeling of uncompleted business. Foolish, I kept telling myself. But Amelia and I had spent over a year hunting for somewhere to settle, before she'd inherited this house. And what had we been doing in that time? Chasing around, that was what, and if that wasn't a subconscious attempt to flee from the inevitable, then fate was only playing its usual tricks.

It was March. I was in the terraced rear garden, which slopes down to the river, pruning the hundreds of roses, as instructed in the book. The Severn was running high, bustling noisily round the bend below me, so that I barely heard Amelia's shout.

'Richard!'

I paused and straightened, looking back and up towards the house. She was standing at the top, waving something.

'Richard – the post.'

Our morning delivery was always late. I would normally have timed my break for the pot of tea that would be waiting, and by then the post would have arrived. So it was unusual for Amelia to call me. Due to the cunning and complex paths that had been fashioned in the slope, it was quite a walk back up to the house, and not to be embarked on for one single letter. But this was what she seemed to be waving.

I removed my old tweed hat and waved it in compliance, then set off back to the house.

'What's all the fuss?' I said, reaching her and breathing heavily. She simply handed it to me.

What was unusual about it was that it had been chasing after us for four months, to Devon, then all round Wales, when in fact we had been at The Beeches since November. Which was the date cancellation on the stamp. November 16. Later, that became important. It had been a Monday. The time of the cancellation was 7.30 a.m.

My original name and address were almost buried beneath the various forwarding addresses. It had been posted in my home town. I could see that Amelia had realized this. Looking up from it to her face, I could also see it had not pleased her. Her lips were thin and her eyes troubled.

I took it inside to the kitchen, where Mary Pinson had tea waiting. She is not truly our housekeeper, as she has a legal right to live there, but she acts as though she is. She had obviously sensed that something was amiss, and her eyes darted from one face to the other.

I opened it and sat. I stirred my tea absent-mindedly, and slid out the letter inside. It was one single folded sheet. The writing was round and immature, but clear. The sender's address was in a wealthy location – Lower Bracken, Manor Park Estate.

14 November

Dear Mister Patton,

Sergeant Brason gave me your address, but doesn't know if you are still there. It seems you might help me, though I don't know how. It is not a police matter, I am told.

Somebody is playing tricks on me. On Monday my car was stolen, but it was standing outside the house next morning. On Tuesday my camelhair coat went missing at a caff. On Wednesday it was left inside my car, but my shoulder bag was missing from the seat. On Thursday it was hanging on the gatepost. Nothing gone. It is driving me crazy. Today (Saturday) my car has been stolen again. It is driving me crazy.

If I do not hear from you, I must assume you think me silly

and hysterical, like the police do. Yes, they do. Please help me.
Yours
Linda Court

My first thought was: Brason. Tony Brason. He'd been on my conscience since I'd last seen him. I had treated him badly, there's no getting away from it, but I'd desperately needed somebody who would offer a false theory. At the time, I'd been convinced I had probably ruined his career. Yet . . . Sergeant Brason now, it appeared. So perhaps I had not.

I had sent him one of our change of address cards, although he had no reason to feel anything but distaste at the very mention of my name. There had been a reason for that: it had seemed important to let everyone know where Amelia and I had gone. To demonstrate it, in fact.* So now, was he using this as a means of striking back at me? If so, it was very devious.

I passed it to Amelia.

'Tony Brason,' I said, keeping all emotion from my voice. I had read it three times.

Amelia whispered: 'Yes.'

There was plenty of emotion in that one word. She'd said it on an indrawn breath. Her hand on the table was clenched into a fist, and for one moment her eyes closed in pain. 'You treated him disgracefully, Richard.'

'But for you, my dear.'

She sighed, and bit her lower lip.

'It's dated November,' I commented. 'Whatever was going on, it's probably been cleared up by now.'

She shook her head. 'But you'll need to find out.'

I glanced at Mary, who was sitting there quietly, warming her hands, as always, round her cup. There was concern in her eyes. She realized that this was something that cast a cloud, whatever it was. She nodded, purse-lipped. It had to be disposed of. I smiled at her.

'Perhaps I'd better give them a ring,' I said brightly, implying that a ring would see an end to it. Amelia nodded. I said: 'Only be a minute.'

Then I went through to the front living room, where the phone was, and where the gloom still hung heavily in spite of our efforts to brighten it up.

*Face Value

9

After looking up the town's dialling code, I got the station immediately. The Station Sergeant's voice . . . I thought I knew it, but couldn't add a name.

'Can I speak to Sergeant Brason?' I asked.

'I'm sorry, sir, but Sergeant Brason's still off work.'

Still? 'It's Ted Carter, isn't it? This is Richard Patton, Ted.'

There was a second while he decided his attitude. Then: 'Hello, Mr Patton. How are you?'

I was 'Mr' I noted, when I'd always been Richard. 'Quite well, thank you. And you, Ted? The family?'

'All fine, thanks.'

'Good.' The ice was not melting, so I plunged on. 'Can you give me Tony's home number?'

'Oh . . . it's DC Brason you want. You said sergeant. That's his wife. I think Brason's in the CID office. I'll put you through.'

There was a click, a buzz, then the familiar voice. 'CID. Constable Brason.'

I took a breath. 'Tony, it's Richard Patton.' All bright and friendly, as though we'd parted bosom friends.

'Yes,' he said. 'Ah. Hello. What can I do for you?'

There was something in his voice I couldn't understand, a suggestion of relief, of hope. Still trying to be cheerful, I went on: 'What's this about a wife? In the force, too. I didn't know. Sergeant, I understand—'

He cut in, his voice crisp. 'You'd know her, Mr Patton. She was Marjie Crane. Remember?'

Oh Lord! I thought. Yes, I remembered, her face flashing up with its usual disturbing clarity. Outside the house, Amelia's house that had been, after Marjie had heard me cutting Tony down to size and destroying his immature authority. I had looked out from the window, watching them all leave. Marjie Crane had been driving for Chief Inspector Donaldson, and she'd looked back, her face white and bitter. That was explained now. She and Brason!

'Yes,' I said, no light in my voice now. 'I remember. She made Sergeant, then? But she's off on leave, I hear. Sick leave.' Still, Ted Carter had said.

'She's been off for three months now.' He cleared his throat, but it didn't help. 'A kind of nervous breakdown. They say. She's under treatment . . .'

It was impossible for him to maintain his unemotional tone. His voice was breaking. I plunged in, to give him time.

'Tony, I've had a letter. It's been chasing me for months. Somebody asking for help . . . some silly business about things being stolen and returned. But it was a long while ago – '

'November.' No hesitation. He knew.

'Yes, November, and probably it's all finished with now. So I wondered . . . any information you can let me have . . . though it seems it was your wife this woman spoke to. A Linda Court. Know anything about it?'

The sound he made could have been a laugh, but if so it lost its way. 'Yes, I know about it. It's the reason Marjie's sick. Blames herself. When was this letter posted, Mr Patton?'

'The cancellation's Monday the sixteenth of November, early.'

'Then it must've been posted late on Saturday evening.'

'Why d'you say that?'

'She died later, that Saturday night.'

The phone made the little ticking noises the line always makes. Through it, I could hear him breathing. He was waiting. For what? For me to say: thank you for letting me know – goodbye? I spoke very carefully, picking my way tenderly through the words.

'And Marjie blames herself for that? But surely – '

His voice cut in. 'Linda Court was murdered, Mr Patton. And Marjie had treated it all as a practical joke.' Then he suddenly burst into a stream of words, like the collapse of a weakened dam. Outrage, despair, pleading – they were all there. He was close to a breakdown himself. 'So there's nothing here for you, Mr Patton. Nothing you can pick at and dissect. Nothing you can see that *we* can't – that I can't. D'you think there isn't every smallest item I haven't gone over and over . . . and over! I'm going insane with this, but I don't need you sticking your nose in and telling me how it's done and saying what I've missed. Because I've missed nothing. Marjie blames herself. There's nothing I can say to her. Nothing. I've said it all. So what d'you think *you* can say, Mr Patton? There's nothing here for you.'

'Isn't there, Tony?' I asked, but I wasn't sure he'd heard. The phone was dead.

I stared at it, then slowly replaced it. I tried to remember every word he'd said in that final torrent. He'd begun by talking about

11

the murder of Linda Court, but he'd finished by talking about his wife. There was nothing I could do for Marjie, that was what he'd said. But hadn't it been a challenge? He had been bright and intelligent when I knew him, and he was now under pressure, but he'd failed to comfort Marjie by producing some evidence to indicate she was not to blame. Had he been hinting that I might? A fresh approach, a new eye on the scene. Surely he was not so desperate as to defer to the experience of someone who had tricked him and denigrated him!

Surely he wasn't asking for my help with his wife!

As I walked slowly back to the kitchen, I realized he hadn't told me whether they'd made an arrest for the killing of Linda Court.

In the interval another pot of tea had been brewed. Mary Pinson took one look at my face and murmured something about cleaning in the hall, but I said I would like her to stay. A special relationship had been maturing between us; I didn't think we should keep secrets from Mary. Amelia, her eyes on mine, nodded absently. Mary was about to learn that Amelia had been a suspect in a murder case.

I told them what Tony Brason had said. To Mary, I had to explain that Tony had reason to hate me (and why), that even my friend, Sergeant Ken Latchett, had been uncertain of our future relationship. And as for Chief Inspector Donaldson . . .

'So you're thinking of going back,' said Amelia miserably.

'Yes.' I'd seen a slim chance of helping Tony Brason, and of repairing something.

'Alone?'

I looked down at my cup. 'I think it would be wiser.'

'We ought to be together.'

'A united front?' I raised my eyebrows at her, probing for a lighter mood.

'Something like that.'

'It'll be a prickly business,' I decided. 'They'll toss the book at me. You wouldn't like it.'

'I don't like it when we're apart.'

'I know. Me neither.'

She was silent for a moment. 'You'll not be interfering with their murder case?' she murmured.

'It's probably cleared by now.'

'Even so . . .'

I knew what she meant. DCI Donaldson would run me out of town. I grinned at her. 'Would I be so foolish?'

'Yes. I know you.'

'If I go – '

'You've already decided.'

'I'll go to try to help Marjie Brason. I liked her. A quiet, sensible woman. A good officer. After all, she made it to sergeant.'

She gave me a twisted smile. 'And is it usual for good officers – sergeants – to have nervous breakdowns? Or do they fall out long before they get to be sergeant?'

'Ah, I see what you mean.' And indeed, that had been worrying me a little. 'But woman officers are a special case . . . and don't start throwing your equality at me. The men have their own fallback. They can be rough and tough, and rely on the rule book. Like automatons. But the women have more sympathy and understanding in their make-up. They have to learn not to feel it, or they get too involved. Perhaps for Marjie it's been like that. She's a sergeant. By this time, she'll have learned to control her emotional involvement. Maybe she controlled it too well. Maybe, if she'd used more understanding, she could have saved that young woman's life. Or so she believes, I suspect.'

I was tentative about this, trying to build logic without any foundations.

'Young woman?' Amelia asked. 'What gives you that idea?'

'Somehow the name sounds young. Linda.'

She frowned, pinning the letter to the table with a forefinger. 'And I wonder why she put *that*. Why did she write 'Today' and than add 'Saturday' in brackets? She'd dated the letter. It *was* a Saturday, I've checked. So why put Saturday at all?'

'And now you've got me thinking about her death.' I grinned at her. 'I told you it'll be difficult.'

She shook her head into an auburn swirl. She was not disagreeing, merely commenting. Two vertical lines appeared between her eyes.

'I'll get on with the roses,' she offered. 'We've left it a bit late as it is.'

'You'll need some thick gloves. They tear you to pieces.'

'I'll do some of it, while you're away.'

'Away?' I laughed at her. 'It's less than thirty miles from here. I'll be commuting, as they call it these days.'

She nodded solemnly. 'That's just it. Commuting. You make it sound like a full-time job.' She turned to Mary. 'You'll see. I know him. Once he gets involved . . . '

I pushed back my chair and reached over to kiss her forehead. 'I'll just drive over and see Marjie Brason, and that'll probably be the end of it.'

'There's confidence for you! One visit, and you're expecting to clear up the whole affair.'

'No. I'm expecting she'll tell me to go to hell.'

She came out to watch me back out my Triumph Stag, then waved as I drove round the half-circle of drive. It was a gesture usually reserved for the parting of a warrior husband to war.

This could well turn out to be true. My rather abrupt departure had been based on the feeling that a few minutes of mature and composed thought would have led me to a change of mind. Certainly, Brason would not be expecting me, and would not be surprised if I did not appear. The writer of the letter was dead, and could no longer be helped. So what the devil was I doing, driving rather too fast down the hill into Boreton?

I knew very well what I was doing. I was setting out in search of a salve for my bruised conscience. As simple as that. It was a purely selfish expedition.

It turned out to be thirty-two miles on the clock, and I was drawing into the outskirts of the town in fifty-five minutes. This is a bad direction from which to arrive, if you want a true impression. For a hundred years this town had thrived on industrial production, but in recent years it has all died away. The heavy-industry factories have failed, partly because of ancient machinery, partly from an inability to compete, partly from a reducing demand. I'd watched one complex after another closing down, silent and sad and decrepit. Huge open spaces appeared, and scrub grass and pools were flourishing in their place. The new industrial site was barely making its presence felt. It is a depressing drive into the town from the east. If I hadn't already been feeling low, this would have set it off.

The town centre itself is not inspiring, but I noticed new shops opening where empty fronts had stared sightlessly when I was there. A good sign. It was Wednesday, the big shopping day of the week. The streets were full, in spite of a chill drizzle that I'd run into in the last few miles. It would have been hopeless, I knew, to find space in any of the public car parks, even in the multi-storey only a hundred yards from the police station.

I had driven directly there by instinct. How many thousand times had I headed straight for it, and for my office? But I had nowhere else to start, and it was with a jolt of surprise that I realized we were still occupying the same red and hideous Victorian building of my time. *They* were occupying, I mean. A new glass and chrome building had been well on its way to completion when I'd left. I was wondering what had happened to it as I turned into the official parking patch beside the old building, and stopped the car with its nose facing the side door.

Here there was plenty of room. I cut the engine, filled and lit the meerschaum pipe Amelia had bought me for Christmas, and waited.

The CID offices had always overlooked the parking area. I would have been noticed. It was not the same Triumph Stag as I'd had then, but it was a Stag, and I was associated with such a car. Who would it produce? Brason? My old friend Ken Latchett? Even, perhaps, Chief Superintendent Paul Merridew, my former sparring partner? We had struck sparks, like a hammer and an anvil, though who was which I'd never decided. Whatever it was, it had worked. Something had always been fashioned. We had not been personal friends, but had not been enemies. I had an idea I might find an ally there, but wasn't banking on it. I hoped I wouldn't need one.

The side door opened, and a man stood for a moment in its shadows. Then he advanced into the drizzle. He was trim and slim, moving with stiff and upright inflexibility, and still had the moustache, trimmed in a military style, but the sideburns that I recalled had now gone. His only concession to the weather was his crisply correct trilby hat, which could have been intended to hide the thinning patch in his hair, or perhaps to shield his horn-rimmed spectacles. Detective Chief Inspector Donaldson.

What I have to say about Donaldson could well be biased, because of our former relationship. My last case as Detective Inspector had broken wide open only three days before my retirement. Donaldson had been my replacement, but he'd been drafted in early, to take over the murder enquiry. Continuity, you see. He'd also been given promotion on the transfer, to DCI. I was retiring as Inspector. That hurt, but it was Donaldson who resented me, not the other way round. It had been his theory, involving Amelia, that I'd needed to destroy before the end of my last day of duty, and it was Brason's impetuous enthusiasm I'd used to destroy it.

Donaldson had no reason to like me. Considering it had been his first case in this district, quite the opposite. Now he advanced unhurriedly towards my car.

I opened the door, got out, and stood facing him. My pipe was in my teeth, clenched firmly to prevent any hasty words from my side. He stopped, sliding his hand into his right jacket pocket in a gesture of casualness. It indicated his unease.

'This is an official car park, Mr Patton,' he said calmly.

'I rather hoped to be considered a life member' I took out my pipe and smiled past it.

His lips twitched. 'A lapsed member, I'd have said. But use it by all means.' His left hand gestured around vaguely, indicating the acre or so of spare space. 'Just as long as your intentions are not official.'

Then, surprisingly, he removed his right hand from his pocket and stuck it out at me. He was offering to shake hands!

I took his hand. I'd never have expected such a thing to happen. Now I saw that his face seemed thinner, his eyes more deeply sunk.

I smiled. 'Official? Heavens no. You'll have cleared the Linda Court case ages ago, I'm sure.'

He snatched back his hand as though I'd burned him. 'By God!' he said quietly. 'You touch that case, Patton, and I'll have you inside.'

'You mean you haven't?'

But he turned on his heel and marched away.

2

I reached inside the car for my anorak and the tweed hat, slammed the door, and ostentatiously locked it. There was a face at the window upstairs, at what had been my office. I thought it was Ken Latchett and grinned upwards, received no response, so I turned away and walked out into the street.

The Rose of Picardy had been one of my favourite pubs, handy for the office and doing a very good cheese and onion sandwich, real Cheddar, not your imitation stuff. I was sitting at a corner table in the snug, a near-empty glass in front of me and not much left of the sandwich, when Ken walked in, glanced in my direction, then went to the bar. He walked over to my corner with two full glasses – he knew what I drank. He put them down, wiped his palms on his flanks, and said: 'Richard! By heaven, it's good to see you.'

This time I received a genuine handshake, and he drew his chair close to the table, his wide face warm with pleasure. To my mind, he'd always been too transparent for a detective, but perhaps it disarmed people into confidences they would not have made to a more stolid officer. There were touches of grey at the temples of his dark brown hair, and his eyes were tired.

'What brings you here? You've left it a hell of a long time. Surely you didn't come just to annoy Donaldson. What really brings you here?'

I slid round that. 'I've been rather busy, Ken.'

'I heard.'

I raised my eyebrows. 'Oh?'

'Is she well? Are you happy?'

'Yes and yes. And you, Ken? Using my old office, I see.'

'Inspector now, Richard.'

'Congratulations.'

'Not so quick with your congrats, please. I'm working directly to Donaldson.'

I raised my glass and drank deeply. Put it down again. 'Ah!

His grin was twisted. 'Exactly. He's a perfectionist.'

'No harm in that.'

'Perfection in approach, perfection in treatment, perfection in reporting, perfection in . . . oh hell, in everything except getting out on the streets and digging up results the hard way.'

'Hmm!'

'The cleared-case percentage has gone up.'

'Well then . . . '

'But not the ones that matter.' He brooded into his glass. One murder is a case. One pocket picked is a case.

'Such as the Linda Court case, I gather,' I suggested quietly.

He raised his glass an inch, and thumped it down again. 'Oh hell, Richard! You're not interested in *that*?'

'Only peripherally.'

'You and your big words! I suppose that means yes?'

'It means no, Ken. I've heard about Marjie Brason. There was just a possibility . . . you know . . . a possibility I might help her and Tony.'

He cocked his head. 'I can see why you might grab at the chance.' Always quick, was Ken. His eyes were now bright. 'Does Tony know?'

'Well . . . ' I considered that carefully. 'Let's say he might not be surprised. The trouble is – I know absolutely nothing about it.' I raised my eyebrows in query.

He glanced at his watch. 'Hell, Richard, it'd take hours. The Linda Court file's an inch thick.'

'An outline. Something to start from.'

'I ought to get back.'

'A slave-driver, is he?'

'He's like a machine. Drives himself, and expects everybody else to do the same.'

I remembered Donaldson, that night we wrapped up the Amelia Trowbridge case, alone in the office Merridew had lent him, bent wearily over reports, reading, checking, inflexible. 'Yes, he would,' I agreed 'A summary, Ken. Please. Just to see if there's anything in it.'

'Marjie's involvement?'

'The lot.'

'So you *are* interested.'

'Background, Ken, background,' I said soothingly.

I couldn't remember Ken having looked so worried. His nerves were stretched, though he was trying to act unconcerned. But it had been too long. Our time together was in the past, and he couldn't recapture our mood of airy freedom. There had never been anything we kept from each other. But now he was protective, even secretive. When he began to speak his eyes were down, watching his fingers turning the empty glass. His voice was unemotional, but he spoke rapidly.

'Linda Court was twenty four. Unmarried. A model. Not one of your slim, superior beauties. Five feet six, and a bit hippy, in

18

fact. It was hands she modelled. She'd got beautiful hands. Travelled to Birmingham mostly, but London sometimes. Modelled gloves and rings and watches. That sort of thing. If you see a hand in a telly advert, raising a glass of champagne or a hair spray, it's probably her hand. Nothing more. Nothing beyond the elbow. Nothing to tell you the sort of person she was. But frankly, Richard, from what we've dug up, she was a right bitch.'

'Plenty of enemies, perhaps?'

'Some.' He shrugged. 'But about Marjie. She was Station Sergeant that week. It all happened in a week. On Monday afternoon, Linda Court's car was pinched. Obvious guess: joy-riders. Marjie put it in the book and said give it a couple of days . . . '

'What shift was this?'

'Two till ten. Linda came into the office at about 2.30. The following morning, she phoned in to say it was standing outside her house. Then it was a coat, which turned up. Two more visits to the station, seeing Marjie each time. It was getting to be rather a bad joke. Then a shoulder bag, which turned up – '

'Left hanging from the gatepost.'

'If you know, Richard . . . '

'Sorry. I only know bits. The car went again on the Saturday, I understand.'

He blinked at me suspiciously and grimaced. 'How d'you know all this?'

'I'll tell you afterwards. She came in on the Saturday?'

He nodded. 'It's in the Incident Book. Five-twenty. She'd parked her car and locked it and had the keys in her hand. She was almost in tears, said Marjie, frustration I reckon, because Marjie had told her off for not having locked it before. Linda couldn't understand how it could've been nicked, so Marjie told her all about hot-wiring and shorting-out the starter, just to take her mind off it, sort of. And Linda walked out of there at around 5.40. Marjie was sure it'd turn up. And it did.'

'When? Where? I said it quickly, because he'd consulted his watch again.

Ken sighed. Perhaps, in the telling, he'd hoped that something he'd missed would rear up and bite him, but it hadn't.

'We reckon she set off for home. Not a taxi – we checked. The bus schedules . . . well, she lived out in that estate of Colonel Forrester's, you know it.'

'Manor Park Estate. Yes.' It was not on a direct bus route, as people living out there always used cars, and would be shocked to hear of any suggestion otherwise.

'We checked. Taking a 37B, and walking the last bit – and all the way through that estate . . . they're in the furthest property from the gatehouse . . . she couldn't have got home before seven. An hour and twenty minutes. I timed it myself. In her high heels, maybe a little longer.' Now his mind was involved; he was no longer rushing it. 'She must have thought to look for it where she'd found it the previous time, which was in a sort of cul-de-sac outside the drive. It would've been very dark, but she found it all right. She must have gone to it and opened the door, leaned in to get inside and run it into the drive, and when the inside light went on somebody smashed the back of her head in with a chunk of tree that we found nearby. And it *had* been hot-wired. The wire and clips were still there.'

'Still there . . . '

'The bonnet catch had been broken open.'

'Had it?' I thought about that. 'I wonder why.'

'Whoever pinched it couldn't find the bonnet-release knob.'

I shrugged. 'And the door? Had *that* been levered open? You said Linda had locked the door.'

'You know damn well these people can open a car door with a wire coathanger.'

'Yes. You remember Charlie Bright?' I played with the pipe, twisting it in my fingers. 'He showed me how. Got into my damned car while I watched him. That's not the point. Linda's car had been parked . . . where?'

'The multi-storey car park, just along from our place.'

'Right. Ideal for a car thief. It'd be dark in there, so he – or she, of course – would be able to open the door without much trouble. But the bonnet-release would be in there – right by the driver's knee, usually.'

'Might not have spotted it.'

'What was the car, anyway?'

'An Allegro. Richard – '

'I suppose the bonnet-release was working? I suppose you checked?'

He slapped down his palm angrily. 'Richard, you're bloody

well doing it already! You're not my boss now. And you're not interested in the murder. You said you're not.'

'Sorry, Ken. I'll get 'em in. You're still on – '

'No! I'll have to get back.'

'Something pleasant waiting, is there?'

He shook his head in exasperation.

'Or something unpleasant here?'

'You come here . . . and in ten minutes you're picking holes in what I've done.'

'I'm trying to find some way of persuading Marjie Brason that she's got no reason to blame herself. That's all.'

'A damn funny way of going about it, then.'

'I've got *no* way of going about it. I'm feeling my way. Ken . . . the post mortem? What did it give you?'

'How d'you mean?' He relaxed enough to feel in his pocket for cigarettes, but he was suspicious.

'Time of death.'

'Oh . . . that. She wasn't found until the next morning. Go there yourself, and you'll see why.'

'I might just do that.'

'It was a cold night, damp and misty. Any time from five the previous evening till about midnight, they said, but we know she couldn't have got there until sevenish.'

'She could've got a lift in a car.'

'We advertised. Nobody came forward with information. And nobody saw her on a bus – before you ask. So . . . after seven and before midnight, say.'

I thought about it, filling my pipe, staring down at it. I wasn't going to be able to hold him for much longer. We were still friends, but I was outside it all.

'Could probably have been later than seven,' I told him at last.

'Now what?'

I produced the letter from my inside pocket and handed it over.

'That's what's brought me into this. It has a Monday morning post office cancellation. If she died Saturday evening, then she must have taken time out to write that before she started off home and found her car and got herself killed. Get my point?'

He didn't answer. He was reading it carefully. When he looked up, his eyes were bright, his expression all eager intensity.

21

'I got it this morning,' I told him, then I nodded, smiling at his enthusiasm, nodded to encourage him.

He said: 'She took time out to write you this . . . '

'So she left Marjie at the station and went, say, to a post office, if there was one open, or somewhere else she could write it. Did she have paper and envelopes with her? Did she buy some specially? How much time did it all take?'

'Yes, yes.' His face went blank. 'Contents of shoulder bag,' he said, recalling it from his memory. 'No. No, nothing to do with writing in there. No paper, no envelopes. No pen. I'm sure of that.'

'Then I've brought you a clue. A fresh clue. Aren't you pleased I came, Ken?'

He reached over and grabbed my arm, and was half on his feet. 'Donaldson'll go mad with joy.' He laughed. I was glad to see he still could.

'Isn't it worth a bit more information?' I asked.

He slowly lowered himself again. 'Such as?' The suspicion flickered back.

'Names and addresses of the people who disliked her, and who might have killed her.'

'No,' he said.

'A sight of the file – '

'For God's sake! Are you crazy, Richard?'

I smiled at him. 'Sneak a few photocopies, say. Or some spare official photos, if you can.'

'I thought you said you're not interested!' he said tersely, controlling his voice. 'You jump about. One subject to the other. Marjie one minute, the murder the next.'

'They're linked. Besides – I *wasn't* interested in the murder – but inside a few minutes I spot a point you haven't checked.' I grinned at him. 'Oh, a very minor point. Breaking the bonnet catch could have several explanations. But I did spot it, so now I'm interested.'

'Richard . . . please . . . go home and forget it. Donaldson'll go spare, even knowing I've told you this much.'

Now it was my turn at the arm gripping. It was to detain him. 'Ken, you told me that Linda was a bit of a bitch. I know the type. A bit empty-headed, probably completely involved with her own interests. And in that letter she tells us something else. She left her keys in the car the first time it was stolen. So Marjie probably warned her about it. But the next time anything happened she'd not left the keys in, but she probably hadn't locked the car. We know that, because her coat was found on the car seat and her shoulder bag was taken. So I bet Marjie warned her about that, too. Then, the second time the car went, Linda actually locked it and brought the keys along with her. It took a while to sink in, didn't it? She couldn't have been very bright.'

He grunted at his beer. 'What're you getting at?'

'She wasn't the sort of person to go straight from the station, write a letter, and post it that evening. She didn't *know* she was going to be killed, and she says herself she wasn't sure the letter would reach me. She would've put it off, to be done some time over the weekend. So ... inconsistent behaviour. Always interesting, that. I'd like to know what prompted it, Ken.'

'And you intend to find out?'

'I thought *you'd* give it a thought.' I released his arm, finally allowing him to leave, but he hesitated.

'I'll try Donaldson. We'll probably try to trace the paper in town ... ' He waved the letter.

'It's common enough.'

'And other things.'

'Of course,' I agreed.

'He'll want to thank you.'

'I can just imagine. You run along, Ken. Work to be done.'

'And you, Richard? What're you going to do?'

I shrugged. 'Wait for things to happen.'

I watched him leave, and very nearly called him back. But I'd only have made things worse. After a few minutes I followed him, got my pipe going, and went for a tramp around the main square. I'd always hated that gangrenous statue in the centre, still did, which was no more than a reminder that I was back.

I'd known it was a mistake to go back, and so had Amelia.

It was almost as though I'd plunged once more into the old life, but with a net hung tantalizingly between me and the action. And I had no claim to the action any more. It had run away with me. Sparked by Donaldson's opposition, warmed by Ken's renewed friendship, I'd come alive, eager and anxious to get back in there with all cylinders firing. So I'd had to be clever! That tiny point about the broken bonnet catch – it *was* tiny – I'd built on it. I'd wanted Ken to see I was the same old Richard. Vanity.

So . . . for just a few minutes my brain had clicked into action. The bonnet catch, and then the bit about Linda Court acting out of character by sending the letter that very evening . . . inconsistency, I'd called it. Of *course* inconsistency is interesting. It's what makes people fascinating. But it didn't have to be given great weight.

I did my fourth circuit of the square, chiding myself on my eager intervention. All right, so I'd had to display something – but to myself, myself. It'd been a mistake to spread it around.

And now? Did I have to pursue this business of helping Brason's wife, just because I owed him something? Did I owe *Marjie* anything? Did I want to help her?

Perhaps, perhaps. Put it on a personal basis, that I'd liked her and therefore wanted to help, then what did I get? I *had* liked her. She'd never worked directly with me, but her cheerful face and solid common sense had helped the day along, whenever we'd exchanged a word. I thought of her now. I tried to think of her now – and didn't know how ill she was. Did I care? Yes, I decided, I cared. So . . . what could I take to her? A friendly face, however battered, encouragement from my years of experience? You can't deny my experience.

I lifted my head. I was outside the Midland Bank. They'd had the building washed. It didn't look much more inspiring, but it indicated somebody cared. The drizzle had eased. The clock in the tower of the Mountford building indicated it was nearly three o'clock. So they'd got it going again; it checked with my watch. I stopped to hammer out my pipe against my heel, forgetting for a moment that it was a meerschaum, filled it, and walked back to my car.

Everything was all right. I could go on with it, as far as Marjie was concerned, with a clear conscience. It wasn't, after all, a simple exercise to clear a dusty corner of my conscience. I stepped forward with more confidence.

You will see from this that my logic is not necessarily logical.

I slid my key into the door lock. Yes, I *had* locked it, as I thought. But I'd left the passenger door unlocked, obviously, unless Tony Brason had been using his own wire coathanger on it. He was waiting for me, sitting and staring blankly forward. I slipped in beside him.

'Tony. I'm glad to see you.'

He turned to face me. I recalled him as having an open and friendly face, full of life and eagerness. None of it was there now. His mouth was stern and his chin stubborn, his eyes haunted. There was an attempt to keep his hands clasped stolidly in his lap, but his fingers twitched and his shoulders moved restlessly. When he spoke, it seemed he'd rehearsed what he intended to say, over and over until it had lost all its colour and was dead grey.

'You shouldn't have come here, Mr Patton. I didn't ask you to. I don't want you here.'

Then he looked away, missing the smile I managed in response.

'I didn't really come to see you, Tony. Thought I'd have a word with Marjie.'

'No. I'm not having you do that.'

'A friendly face,' I suggested. 'I'll offer her a friendly face. An old colleague. Wouldn't that help?'

'Friendly!' he gave an empty bark of sarcastic laughter. 'She hates you.'

I gave it a second or two. 'Because of what I did?'

'Yes.'

'Got it from you, has she?'

'What?' It brought his head round again.

'The hatred. Has she got it from you?'

'Me?' His lips curled into a smile, an apology for one. There was contempt in it, for himself I realized when he went on, for what he would consider a weakness. 'Not from me, no. Oh, don't make any mistake, I hated you at first. I'd made a fool of myself, and you'd led me into it. It was what you'd wanted. Yes, it was!' As though I'd denied it. Perhaps I'd shaken my head. 'But I'm no good at it. Can't keep it up. No, I don't hate you, Mr Patton, haven't done for ages. But Marjie . . . ' He stopped, then turned to stare out of the windscreen again.

'Yes?' I asked quietly. 'Marjie.'

He shook his head, and looked down at his hands. 'It was just after you finished . . . well, I'd been trying to persuade her to come out with me, and suddenly she was all over me.' He turned to me again. There was gentle humour in his eyes now. 'Damn it, I didn't stand a chance. We were married before I knew what was happening. But . . . you see . . . '

Again he found difficulty in going on. He fingered the walnut of the dashboard.

'Oh hell,' he said. 'Why should I tell you this?'

'Because I'll be out of your life again in no time at all,' I suggested. But I don't think he heard.

'She's intense,' he said fondly. 'Emotional.'

'I remember.'

'She hated you for what you'd done to me, but hers went on and on, getting stronger and deeper, while mine just faded away. I didn't *want* it to fade away,' he observed thoughtfully. He was putting it into words in an attempt to clarify it for himself, not for me.

'I reckon it made me uneasy. She seemed disappointed in me, because I didn't care tuppence any more for Richard Bloody Patton, as she called you. It got between us, somehow. Not something you could catch hold of, nothing we could discuss between us, just a feeling. Oh, I'm not making this clear.'

He was miserable that it wasn't becoming clear, when saying it out loud should have done the trick. I helped him along.

'She'd also feel something between you, I'd guess. And like you – nothing she could tie down. But one thing would be clear to her, that the wretched Patton creature was to blame.'

'Yes. Yes, I suppose so. Whatever it was, it made her hate you more.'

'What an ogre I am!'

'It's not funny.'

'Sorry. Of course not.'

'So I'm not going to let you see her again. I daren't. She'd go completely off her head.'

Completely! Did he mean that she was very close to that point? 'If you say not, Tony.'

'I do say not.' He seemed relieved that we didn't have to fight over it.

'But she *does* need help?'

'She's getting it.'

'Such as?'

'She's on anti-depressants.'

26

I grimaced. 'Not doing much good, though, from the sound of it.'

He thumped his knee. 'She's like a blasted animated doll.'

'They treat the symptoms, not the cause,' I commented, somebody having told me that. 'And the cause is that she believes she was responsible – in part anyway – for the death of Linda Court?'

'She thinks,' he said dully, 'that she should have seen past it, and realized it was serious. What she ought to've done, was put it in a report, and got some action on it.'

'Everything's clear, with hindsight.'

'You've got all the clever phrases on hand, haven't you!' He turned and glared at me. The light was going, so I didn't get the full effect of it.

'It's a fall-back,' I admitted. 'For when I get stuck.'

'Well, if you're stuck, and I'm stuck, that's the end of it. So why don't you go home, Mr Patton! I'll work something out.'

Then he got out of my car and slammed the door with unnecessary violence.

'Or I will,' I said, but he couldn't have heard. Just as well, I suppose, because I had no course of action in mind.

When he'd disappeared into the building, I got out of the car again, locking both doors this time, and went to find a phone box.

3

These days they're not so much boxes as cubicles. This one hadn't been vandalized lately, and I got through to Amelia. I gave her a quick run-through of my lack of progress and said I might be home later than I'd expected.

'What I want to do next has to be done in the dark,' I explained.

'Don't tell me,' she said, with a hint of mischievousness in her voice. But also with much more doubt.

I hung up, and went for a pot of tea and an omelette, to keep me going. It was quite dark when I collected the Stag from the police yard. Somebody – Ken, I guessed – had left a parking ticket under the wiper.

The weather wasn't exactly right, but close enough. In November it had been damp and misty. Now it was damned wet and the visibility was bad. But I needed no signposts to guide me to Manor Park Estate.

It's three miles out, on the western edge of the town, and had originally been the property of Sir Guy Forrester, who had probably seen the days when the house was swarming with servants, when there were full stables and hostlers, and carriages up the drive for the county balls. Unfortunately, Colonel Gerald Forrester had inherited it in another era, when two hundred enclosed acres of parkland and a twenty-bedroomed manor house could be nothing less than a pain in the neck. His father had already sold all the family's useful valuables, the china, the furniture, the paintings. There was nothing facing him but death duties, which were going to cripple him, and it's no good mentioning the possibility of turning it into a pleasure park, because we'd got one of the largest in the country only fifteen miles away. It was enough to drive a normal man to suicide.

But Colonel Forrester (Ret'd), DSO, CBE, MRCVS, was made of sterner stuff. Hadn't he had complete responsibility for the whole of the army's livestock for over fifteen years? He cast his thoughts around, and his mind recorded the fact that a motorway spur was under construction only a few miles away. He pointed out to his many friends on the council, and to the various appropriate authorities with which he had influence, that the town would soon become an overcrowded shortcut to the motorway from the adjacent road north – that a bypass road was indicated. No . . . was critically necessary. He indicated that this would most conveniently be sited to the west of the town, and offered up two or three fields from a farm he happened to own, as an inducement.

I was there when it all went through. The rest of Forrester's farm was then diverted from being sacred green belt to consecrated building land, and a housing estate was built. It was a medium to expensive estate, for those of the middle executive who would be attracted to property so convenient to the motorway. It was barely noted that Forrester had acquired a large shareholding in the firm that eventually built the estate. He made a small fortune on that, but not enough to clear his indebtedness to the Inland Revenue. They breathed in, absorbing his profits, and forcibly out again, demanding more.

It was then that Manor Park Estate became a feasible proposition. Forrester also breathed in, and out forcibly. (But hadn't he had quite a bit of practice with this – all those pills?) He breathed out forcibly on the planning authority, who had to agree that Manor Park was now completely surrounded by non-green belt land. Permission was granted for Forrester to sell land on his own estate for building.

But these were not to be the quarter-acre plots that satisfied the young up-and-coming executives on the new estate outside his walls. These were to be five acre plots in landscaped woodland, secluded and complacent, as befitted the mature, arrived, top executives. The MATES. Twenty only, the specification demanding a building cost of £250,000 each, minimum. And who got the contracts for construction? Forrester's firm, that's who.

He was therefore left with his Manor House in 100 acres, and a lot of spare spending money. The Inland Revenue breathed in again, for the last time, and he was still left with a lot. I expect he's on the list for a knighthood. Possibly he's even in line for Chancellor of the Exchequer.

I had never been inside the grounds. There hadn't been anything particularly illegal happening there, apart from courting couples sneaking in with their cars. But now they had a murder. I wasn't sure of my welcome at the gate.

I needn't have worried. There was no gate at the main entrance, just an inviting opening surrounded by the gatehouse. That's the only way of describing it, because the gatehouse is one building each side of the entrance with a joining arch above. I drove in beneath the arch, beneath the present resident's living room, no doubt. This building, too, had been tarted up as a high-class residence.

Just inside the grounds was a simple notice: PRIVATE ESTATE. Very private. There was a two-and-a-half-mile wall around it, six feet high and built of sandstone blocks, with that one main entrance, and a minor one that used to be used by tradesmen. No guards, no barbed wire, no prowling Rottweilers. This was seclusion and class.

A hundred yards inside, I drew in and cut the engine, and sat absorbing the silence.

There had originally been only one drive, up to the Manor House, and it was still there, turning up and away to my right.

But twenty new residences demanded twenty drives and a network of approach roads. These had been provided, with proper metalled surfaces, but in a discreet manner. The main accesses were curved gently, with no kerbstones, but with wide grass verges, these flanked by ancient and honoured trees, dripping now and near-naked in March. Evergreens supplemented them. From the main access roads, minor ones turned away, and from these the individual house drives again turned. It was impossible, from any point, to see one's neighbours, or even see the chimneys unless you ventured along the drives. Each resident could claim his own private park. At corners, and at the centres of long unbroken runs of tarmac, streetlamps glowed. None of the modern harsh blue or sickly orange lamps, but gentle and soft, and purely decorative. Rarely would anyone wish to walk through the estate. You could walk your Dobermann to exhaustion in your own grounds.

I sat, lit my pipe, and allowed the atmosphere to soak in. Ahead, misted through the drizzle, one of the streetlamps beckoned. Trees sighed and dripped. After a while I was aware of the drip-plop from their branches. No wind stirred them. The silence clamped down.

I started the car and moved on. A discreet 15 mph seemed appropriate and adequate. At side turnings, signposts indicated names that meant nothing to me. Four-quarters Lane. Friday Acre. Occasionally there was an entrance drive and its gateway. There was no standardization to the gates, and I'd heard it was the same with the houses. Mock Tudor, neo-Regency, Victorian gloom, modern sprawled bungalow. What did it matter that it was a glorious hodge-podge? No place was visible from another.

I had a name and a clue. Lower Bracken, and located at the far end. The suggestion in the name was of a low elevation, and the far end meant I should just keep going.

It would've been easy to get lost. After a while, everything seemed to be the same: tarmac, green verge, opulent growth. Trees loomed up, in places closing in above me, and receded. Streetlights barely gleamed through the drizzle. As I lost the light from one, the next one spread a pale curtain ahead.

I climbed for a quarter of a mile, then I was easing down a gentle slope. Always winding. I saw no house lights, no cars, nobody. Lower Bracken. I had come over half a mile from the top of the rise, with no apparent end to it. Lower Bracken. My eyes searched for the sign.

It was set back a little to my left, so that I nearly missed it. My dipped heads indicated a mass of yew and cupressus, cut back in curves to embrace the entrance gate, which was open. The sign, Lower Bracken, was also set back. Ahead of me, the tarmac seemed to continue onwards, but the trees encroached closer, there being no more grass verge. I got out and tramped over the grass opposite the gateway. It squelched, but seemed firm enough for the fat tyres of the Stag. I backed her in beneath the trees, cut the lights, and got out through a tangle of branches that shook water down my neck. I emerged with my torch in my hand.

I had met nobody, and didn't want to. I would be asked my business, and the answer would've been difficult.

First, I explored the drive to the house, curving away. Somebody had hated straight lines, probably the Colonel—no straight lines on horses. I kept the torch well down at my feet, until I saw the bulk of the house ahead. I couldn't detect more than an outline against the faintly orange sky, but it seemed to be one of the Georgian reproductions. One window showed light. The porch was dimly lit.

I discovered, later, that Linda's mother was Judge Hilary Hope-Court, a high court judge, in front of whom, if I were Linda's killer, I would not wish to appear. Her father had last been seen tramping into Kurdestan. He'd been on one of the unsuccessful attempts at an Everest assault, and possibly hadn't been able to live with a wife who'd insisted on retaining her maiden name. The judge's brother lived there, but was incapable following a stroke, and there was a live-in nurse. Not much to come home to for Linda, she of the perfect hands and the rest of her thus unattractive in contrast. 'A model, are you? Fancy that.' And the disbelieving eyes considering the unlikelihood. Perhaps she'd had reason for raising a bit of hell here and there. It would be necessary to assert her force of character. She could well have asserted too strongly.

I retraced my steps. The Allegro belonging to Linda, Ken had said, had been left, both times, out at the front. Did that mean the front of the house? In which case, why not simply say: on the drive? I explored.

31

No. I remembered now. Ken had said: in a kind of cul-de-sac, outside the drive. And there it was; I'd already noted it. It was a continuation of the roadway, running past the drive entrance but not going very far. I walked slowly along its middle, fanning the torchlight from side to side. As I've said, the grass verges ceased at that point. The tarmac was just about two cars in width, and finished after fifty yards, becoming no more than a gap of woodland ride, its surface soft pine needles. In less than a dozen more yards it narrowed to walking width, where the growth had closed right in.

This must have been all that was left of the original tradesmen's entrance.

I stopped, put off the torch, and looked back. I couldn't see the nearest streetlamp any more, the trees behind me closing in above my head, and even leafless they provided a heavy barrier. It was a good place for a murder. Leave a car along here, only half a dozen yards beyond the drive entrance, and it would be barely noticeable. Perhaps to eyes accustomed to the dark from a long walk through the park – such as Linda's – it would be detected. The distant lamp could just, maybe, catch a reflection from the rear bumpers.

But now I was considering a murderer who had waited here for Linda, confident enough that she would make her way home and notice her car. It could well have been a long wait, a cold and miserable one. It was not known how late she had died, that night.

I walked back to the Stag and sat inside it quietly, filled my pipe, and groped for my lighter. Then I became aware of a change I could not identify. It could have been an alteration in the sound pattern, something intruding into the dismal hiss of drizzle and the drip-plop from the trees. Or a variation in the shadow intensity. I was very still, attempting to isolate it. Then I saw that somebody was standing a few yards along the cul-de-sac.

There was movement, a pacing backwards and forwards. No torchlight was evident. Someone with good night sight. It moved to the drive entrance and looked towards the house, a shadow, formless. I tried to put a shape to it. Man or woman? Hopeless. Then it moved back into the cul-de-sac and melted into the shadows. Away? Or merely motionless?

After a couple of minutes I had to risk getting out of the car.

Whoever had interest in the site of the murder was of interest to me. The branches moved around me as I slid gently through them. I left the door open. Once out on to the open grass verge I stopped, head lifted, listening. There was the most gentle rustling of disturbed branches ahead. Whoever it was had reached the walkway, and was trying to move with circumspection.

I followed, keeping away from the tarmac, then on to the soft silence of the pine needles, hesitated to allow a gap to occur between us, then moved into the brush myself. I did not dare to use the torch; it would surely provoke headlong flight. But I could afford to lag behind. There was only one path.

When I moved forward it was with an arm raised to protect my face. Wet, dripping branches lashed at me. It didn't go on for long. Suddenly I was out in the open, with naked sky, a brighter orange here because the nearest public highway was close. We were approaching the far edge of the estate.

Still it was slightly downhill, and I was aware of the glow now seeming to be lower, reflected almost at my feet and to my left. Water. Of course, the Round Pond, as they called it, more than a pond, a lake, and not round, haunt of Canada geese and a thousand or so mallards. There was a sound of moving water, and my feet fell on to planks. My hand felt rails. A bridge.

I paused. The far boundary wall was now visible as a sharp, black line against the lighter road beyond. There was a gap in it. The tradesmen's entrance. It would have been abandoned when the bridge became inadequate for the heavier weights of motor vehicles. Beneath me, water rustled. This would be the river, the Penk, entering the Round Pond at one end and leaving at the other, under the road bridge at Kingslake Drive. Now I was orientated. There were lights of an extensive building estate over to my right. That wouldn't be the new mid-executive estate, but what was known as The Dip, a part-council and part-private estate.

I knew where I was, but now that I had more visibility, I had lost sight of my quarry. There was no movement ahead. I stepped forward more briskly, my eyes on the gap in the wall. No movement there. I hurried.

There was a five-barred gate across the entrance, padlocked

33

and with nettles embracing it. I climbed over, and dropped down. Someone stepped forward from my right.

'Why the hell're you following me?' a woman's voice demanded harshly.

Not many women would have waited like that, to confront a follower. I turned.

'Hello, Marjie,' I said.

'I knew!' she cried in disgust. 'I just knew it had to be you. Damn you! Oh, damn you!'

I settled my hat more firmly. Clearly, Brason had phoned her to tell her that I was in town, and equally clearly she'd told him to keep me well away from her.

'Sorry if I scared you.'

'Ha!' she said in contempt of my scaring potential.

'I didn't realize it was you, but naturally I was interested. Somebody at the scene of the murder – I had to know who.'

'So now you know.'

She was in slacks and a red jumper, with a long, black coat over them. There was a nylon scarf protecting her blond hair. By the light from the nearest lamp, I couldn't be sure of her face, whether the shadows carved beneath the eyes and her cheeks were always there. The enlarged pupils, which I could just detect, could have been caused by walking in the dark, or by her anti-depressants. I took this in at one glance. She would not have wished me to stare at her.

'I heard you've been ill,' I said easily. 'I wanted to see you. Chat . . . you know.'

'And if I turn away and start walking, I suppose you'll follow me.'

I grinned at her. 'You could call a policeman.'

She took that with complete seriousness. 'There's a phone just down the road.'

'It's just as you want it, Marjie. You say.'

She looked sideways at me. 'Sod it,' she said. 'I'm frozen.' She wrapped her arms round her body.

'Do this often, do you?'

She shot a suspicious glance at me from under her eyebrows. 'Too bloody often. Can't keep away from the damned place. Sometimes I do miles in the park.'

'I meant the swearing.'

34

Then she laughed, not a good effort, but an echo of what her laughter used to be. The tablets supressed the joy as well as the misery.

'I'm not going to stand here talking to you,' she said decisively. 'Blast you, Richard Patton, let's go home and get it over with.'

'Get what over with?' I asked, falling into step with her.

'The inquisition. The interrogation. Whatever you've got in mind.'

She was walking fast. I wasn't going to get the time to light my pipe. 'It could well be a good spanking, from what I've been hearing.'

'Ha!' she said, again in contempt, then, looking sideways: 'But it's going to be questions.'

'Maybe. Unless you're prepared to tell me all about it without any.'

'About what?'

'You know bloody well what.'

'Now *you're* at it. I know what you mean. Yes. There's never anything else in my mind.'

'Then perhaps we could screw it out and throw it away.'

'I wish it was that easy.' She turned a corner. 'We're along here.'

The Dip estate had been built like a wheel, streets radiating from a central shopping precinct, and others spreading out in bigger and bigger circles. It meant that almost every corner was alike, and residents could drop with exhaustion, just finding their way home. The Brasons had a corner house, half of a semi-detached pair, with a garden fence that needed looking at, and no gate to the short drive up to the wooden garage. You don't expect much from a garden in March, but it didn't look as though the front had been cleared the previous autumn. The grass had not been cut, and hung lank over the single-slab front path, brushing my ankles with wet fingers.

The hall light was on. Inside, it smelt neglected, though there was no physical sign of neglect. Marjie had been home for three months, but in no condition to work up any enthusiasm for housework.

She said: 'Come through into the kitchen. The sitting room's a mess.'

I followed her. The kitchen was large for that size of house, and the fittings modern. There was a smell of cooking that reminded me I hadn't eaten much that day. Something in the oven. That was a policeman's lot, especially a CID man's. Never knew when you'd be home, so it had to be something that could sizzle and wait.

'Expecting him home?' I asked.

'I never know. But he works his head off. Plenty to make up for, with his record.'

That was a dig at me. 'Yes,' I said. 'But he's a good officer.'

She said nothing, getting busy at her stove, slapping on a kettle above the gas ring and searching out mugs. Without asking me, she produced a slab of fruit cake.

She had tossed aside the long coat and the headscarf, and shaken her hair free. In that light, which was soft, white and revealing strips, her face did not seem so harrowed. Misery takes a long while to show; it gnaws away underneath. But there had been a loss of flesh. Her fine bones showed more strongly in her face, perhaps an improvement. But there was no joy in her eyes, only the large, black pupils, and her mouth was set in a firmer line than I recalled.

As she prepared the tea, she chatted. Herself and Tony. I managed, by slipping in the odd gentle question, to clear a point or two that had been uncertain to me. She had known him even at the time he'd been working a country beat, which was when I'd met him. His transfer to town headquarters, and to the CID, had seemed to be intended for them. That, and their mutual hatred for me, had drawn them together, though she didn't put it like that. In fact, she seemed to be steering carefully away from anything so contentious. She had been there, at Amelia's place, when I'd destroyed Tony's precious theory, and then gone on to prove Amelia's innocence.

I thought she was being rather too delicate about it, until she eventually took her seat opposite to me at the table. Then she flicked her hair from in front of her eyes and said: 'They laughed, you know. Somebody laughed . . . at Tony.'

'That's true.'

And yet she'd said it calmly. I'd expected, from what Tony had said, that she would face me with a hysterical tirade.

'Your medication doing any good, is it?' I asked, stirring at my cup.

She laughed. It was a flat, desperate sound, and for a moment she clasped her hands together before shaking her head and forcing them apart.

'They slow my reactions,' she told me. 'I daren't try to drive. They dull all my feelings. I watch old favourite comedies on television, and can't see anything funny. And you're nothing to me now, Mr Patton. Nothing.' She stared bleakly at me. 'Help yourself to cake.'

'Tony said . . .'

'Oh yes, Tony. Dear Tony.' She picked up her spoon and stared at it. 'What do you want me to tell you?'

I wasn't sure I wanted to hear, not now. The whole idea had been to help Marjie, but she didn't seem to need any help, except to be able to laugh at the telly again. Except to be able to hate Richard Patton again.

I helped myself to cake. 'Tell me all you can remember about Linda Court,' I said.

4

She was a police officer, and knew how reports should be presented. I didn't expect to have to assist her. She started steadily enough.

'I was Station Sergeant that week, on the two-till-ten shift. Beryl Tonks was supposed to be on with me, but she went sick, so I was on my own. She came in at 2.30 on the Monday – Linda Court did. She said her car had been stolen. I put it in the book. Place and time and car details. Then I told her – '

'What *were* the details, Marjie?' I cut in.

'You want every little item?'

'Please.'

'I don't understand why.'

'Please. Pamper me a bit.'

She shrugged. Her eyes were beginning to worry me. 'She'd left it for less than an hour in the multi-storey car park near the station. Then she did some shopping. Came back for it. I can't remember the car's registration number. It was an Austin Allegro. She'd left the door unfastened and the keys in the ignition lock.'

'So I suppose you told her off about that.'

'Not as you put it. Gently. She didn't seem too bright. I told her she hadn't ought to make it too easy for them. I said it was probably only joy-riders, in which case it'd turn up again. The ease of it, you see, Mr Patton. Young lads, walking round, looking for something that wasn't going to take much effort – for a quick getaway.'

'Yes. I understand that. Did she?'

She puckered her lips. Her fingers tucked a lock of hair behind her ear, but it wouldn't stay there. 'Not really. As I said, not too bright, I thought. I told her to give it a day or two, and we'd keep a look out for it. You know – the usual. She seemed to think I'd grab a mike and put out an all-cars call.' She gave a little snigger, then put two fingers to her lips.

'So you weren't taking it seriously?'

'No. She wasn't, either. Sort of nervous and tense, but laughed a bit. Then the next day when I came on duty there was a message. She'd phoned in to say her car had been left outside the house.'

'With the keys in?'

'Yes. So I assumed. No reason why they wouldn't be.'

'Left the same place? I mean, the same place as she later died? In that cul-de-sac.'

'I assume so.'

'Assume?'

'She *looked* for it there, the second time it went. Must have done.'

'But that assumption came later, not the Tuesday you got the message?'

'Yes, I suppose.' An edge came into her voice. 'Of *course*. There was nothing to assume before then. You're trying to confuse me.'

I was trying to get a clear picture of her thinking on it. 'So, on the Tuesday, you didn't think anything was strange?'

'Should I?'

'Yes, I'd have thought so. Joy-riders wouldn't have troubled where they left it. And whoever took it must have known where she lived.'

'There could have been an address somewhere in the car.'

'And they thoughtfully delivered it there! Think of the location. Whoever took it there must have had a hell of a walk home.'

'I didn't notice her address, damn it. Not at that time.'

'Not notice it? You must have written it down.'

'What *is* this? An interrogation?'

'Clearing it in my mind. Both our minds.'

'You're going out of your way to show me how wrong I was.'

'If you like. It should've given you at least a hint that there was something strange going on.'

'Well it didn't.'

'You weren't on the tablets then, Marjie.'

'What the hell're you trying to do, blast you!'

'Shake you up a bit. I can't grab you by the shoulders and shake you. I want to show you that you weren't to blame.'

'By proving I was?' she demanded in disgust.

'By digging out the worst, then we'll have got it out of the way.'

She stared at me a full minute, hands motionless now. Then she twisted her mouth into a sour grin. 'Lord, but you're a smug bastard, Patton.'

'Thank God for the tablets. Without them you'd have spat right in my eye. Shall we go on? Can I pour myself some more tea?'

'If you wish.' Which covered both. 'You can't make it much worse, anyway. Tuesday, then. She came in, around four o'clock, to ask if I'd got the message about her car coming back, and to report the theft of her coat, a camelhair thing. She'd put it on the coat–rack by the door in the Regent café in Windsor Street, and hadn't kept an eye on it. I told her there was very little chance of seeing it again. She seemed to think it shouldn't happen to her. Told me her mother was Judge Hilary Hope-Court, with a hyphen, as though that provided her with some special protection.'

'It was probably no more—'

'I know. She'd been brought up in an atmosphere of honesty and a respect for the law. I told her there wasn't much respect for it these days, and said how much crookery we get in this town. She couldn't believe it. I was quite convinced, by then, that one of her friends must be playing tricks on her. She said she had that sort of friends, but I guessed she meant enemies. Professional jealousy, she reckoned. She modelled, you know. Her hands.

39

She always wore gloves, but she wouldn't take them off to show me. I don't know why.'

'Getting chummy, weren't you?'

'She was distressed when she came in, smiling when she went out.'

'But you still weren't worried?'

'I was absolutely convinced, by then, that it was a practical joke. Somebody who must have known her, I mean, the coat taken from a café, and the next day found in her car.'

'We hadn't got to Wednesday.'

'We have now.'

'I was talking about your thinking on Tuesday afternoon. You still hadn't thought about the peculiar bit . . . the car being taken all the way to her place in Manor Park Estate.'

'I hadn't. Not then.'

'Not at all, it seems.'

'You keep niggling at me,' she said, equably enough. Those tablets must have been very effective. I was trying to break through the barrier they'd created, but I wasn't getting anywhere.

'All right,' I agreed. 'Wednesday then. She came in . . .'

'Later than before. Five-thirty or so.' Then, catching my eye: 'All right. Five thirty-three. This time it was to report her coat had turned up. It'd been left on the seat in her car, where she'd parked it.'

'The same car park?'

'No. That cleared patch in Dunkley Street, where the Co-op was.'

'I know it. So once again she'd left the car unlocked.'

She gave me a quirky little grimace. 'She seemed to think she'd done well just to bring the keys with her.'

'But now she was worried?'

'Twanging away, like a stretched elastic band. Tried to treat it as the same old joke, but she was very close to hysteria.'

I fished out my pipe. 'You mind?' She said not, so I filled it, giving myself something to look at other than her face. 'But it quite obviously wasn't the same old joke, was it!'

'No.'

'I mean – there was a lot of work going on there. Her coat taken, and it couldn't have been a casual theft because it was known to

40

be *her* coat. And she must've been followed previously, because it was a different car park. An open one, too. No fishing about in the shadows. And she'd been seen not to lock her car door.'

'It was dark by that time.'

'Not necessarily at the time the coat was returned. So . . . all right . . . then her shoulder bag was taken.'

'You *know* all this!'

'Some. The details are becoming interesting. Go on, Marjie.'

'The coat had been returned – she was wearing it – but her shoulder bag had gone from the passenger's seat. As you know.'

I looked up quickly. She was trying to be persuasive, to go along with how she'd seen it then. She was trying to help.

'So . . . ' I said. 'She went shopping, say, but she left her shoulder bag in the car. Let's assume she had another jacket or coat at the time. Maybe she carried a purse in its pocket. But it's strange, surely, for a woman to leave her shoulder bag behind, and in an unlocked car, when she was going shopping.'

'I suppose. But I don't remember that she actually said she'd been shopping.'

'But you weren't becoming worried by that time? I mean, this had gone far beyond the practical joke stage . . . ' I let it tail off, lifting my eyebrows at her and sticking the pipe-stem between my teeth.

'Yes. I was worried.'

'But not enough to put in a report.'

'I still thought it *could* just be a practical joke. I went as far as getting names from her. People who'd got something against her. You know.' She moved her shoulders uneasily. 'It was more to give her the impression I was taking her seriously . . . Don't you see!' she went on, with a touch of anger. 'It's why I blamed myself. But . . . she didn't seem to want me to do anything. I had to prise the names out of her.'

'Can you remember any of them?'

'She was involved with amateur dramatics. The group was putting on a play that week. At The Prince Of Wales . . . '

'They finally opened it?'

'Yes. But it's not exactly booming. She'd expected to take the female lead. She didn't get it. There was some row with the director – a man called Knowles. Ian Knowles. And there were the three other men in the play. I can't remember their names, now, nor what she had against them.'

'So you gave her another lecture about leaving her car un-locked, and sent her on her way?'

'Not as abruptly as that. She was close to hysteria – overacting the part of somebody who thinks its all a great big joke. I had to calm her down. Then she left.'

'And Thursday?'

'She came in, just after I'd signed on, to tell me her shoulder bag had been hanging on the gatepost that morning. Nothing missing, nothing disturbed.'

'Another trip for the phantom joker, to leave it there! This time, then, it wasn't a phone message?'

'No. She was relieved and happy, as though a great weight had been removed. Wanting to share it. That was it, you see. I got the impression she was sharing it all with me, kind of relying on me to . . . well, help her out, I suppose. She hoped I'd be able to reassure her it'd all finished.'

'And you,' I asked quietly, 'were just as prepared to believe it was finished?'

'I suppose so.'

'But it wasn't. Let's get to Friday.'

'Nothing happened. That was worse, if anything. Nothing happening. I was on edge all that shift.'

'And so . . . Saturday.'

'Yes. She came in. I was shocked at the way she looked. Her face was all twitchy and her eyes bruised, sort of. But she came in laughing. Laughing! Waving her keys in her hand. Look, she said, I locked it, and *still* it's been stolen! Something like that. Then she plonked down on the bench and burst into tears. So I went round and sat by her – '

'Time?'

'Five-twenty.'

'Calmed her a bit?'

'Yes. Then I went back behind the desk and got it into the book. The same car park as the first time – the one just along the street from us. She was jumping from one mood to the other. Scared to death one second, then laughing about what a stupid woman she was, to keep losing her car like that. She just wouldn't believe it *could* be stolen, when she had the keys, so I told her about opening the door with a wire coathanger, and how to hot-wire a car with two dog-clips and a yard of electric cable ... '

'You thought she'd have need of that knowledge?'

'I was trying to bring her down to earth. To her, the impossible had happened. Like magic. I had to make it clear that it wasn't difficult.'

'You know how?'

'I was years on patrol cars. We get to know such things.'

'Drew her a diagram, did you?'

'Sort of. It's simple. Two dog-clips on a length of wire, and connect one to the battery terminal, the other one to one of the end tags of the coil, the one that doesn't go to the distributor.'

'I'll treasure the knowledge. I can see you two bent over the counter, like mechanics planning a robbery.'

'It wasn't funny.'

'No.' I clamped my lips shut.

'She wanted to be sure *anybody* could do it, even one of her friends in the drama group. I felt that. She didn't say it. You could see it going through her mind, though. I decided she was trying to think of somebody she could link it with.'

'You were still clinging to the idea it was a practical joke? If so, it was a very complicated one.'

'It was *all* I could cling to. Think about it – there hadn't been any breaking of the law. Taking, yes, but with obvious intent to return.'

'True.' I nodded. She certainly had a point there.

'And it was too complicated to achieve anything else. It didn't achieve anything.'

'No? Didn't it?' It achieved a murder that hadn't been solved. 'And it was then you gave her my name and address?'

She bit her lip. Looked away. 'So that's why you know so much.'

'She sent me a letter to the old address. I didn't get it until this morning.'

'I see.' Now I'd given her the impression that I'd not come to help my former colleague Marjie Brason, but to find out about Linda Court. I didn't assist her on that.

'Why did you involve me?' I asked quietly.

'Oh ... ' She flipped her hand, shook her head. Hair flew everywhere. 'As I said, she seemed to have somebody in mind as the joker. Then she said she needed help. So I gave her your name and address.'

'Which was engraved on your mind?'

'I had your change of address card with me.'

She carried it with her? 'But why *me*?'

'It was a sort of in-joke. Me and Tony. To remind us. I carried it. To remind me.'

She was now talking as though confused with her own motivations. I levered myself to my feet. 'To remind you that it was Richard Patton who'd finally brought you together?' I asked jovially. 'Me as Cupid! Who'd ever have thought it.'

I looked round to see where I'd thrown my hat. She snatched it up from the sink unit and thrust it at me.

'It was a symbol of what we owed you,' she said, her face now animated.

'I know, Marjie. I was making a joke of it.'

'A rotten one, then.'

'Admitted.'

'If you want to know, we laughed when you sent it. As though *we* wanted to know where you'd gone to!'

'As long as I'd gone?'

'Yes. Yes.'

We stood with a chair between us. I said: 'Apologize to Tony for me – that I missed him.'

'You talk as though you don't understand!' she cried in exasperation. 'When you do.'

'Not really. But I didn't want to upset you. I thought I'd go, while the going was good.' I moved a pace towards the hall, then her fingers were digging painfully into my arm. I turned.

'You *don't* understand,' she said, almost in pity that I didn't.

'Your mutual dislike of me. I can see that. I'll be off—'

'No! You're over-simplifying. It's not so simple. Sit down again. Please sit down again, Richard, I can't talk up to you like this.'

I was Richard all of a sudden. And at last I'd penetrated through the haze of the drugs. Compromising, I hitched half my behind on the kitchen table and swung my leg. Swung the hat from my fingers. She stood behind the chair, gripping its back firmly, perhaps to hit me with it if I played it wrong.

'You don't have to tell me anything, Marjie.'

44

'I do. You especially. Because it was you I hated so much.'

I noted the past tense. 'Not now?'

'I'd known Tony before. Before you came into it, I mean. I liked him. Well . . . you know him. Any girl would. But kind of shy, that's Tony. Not committing himself, you know. Then there was that night, when you signed out with that big scene at her house. Amelia's. That was her name, wasn't it?'

'Still is.'

'And poor Tony! You made him seem such a fool. And I could see through you, and I saw how you'd read him exactly. Too impressionable, that's his trouble. And so sharp, so quick, that brain of his. The snag was . . . has it ever struck you that it's a big liability to have too good an imagination? I bet it hasn't. But Tony . . . he *understands* too easily. Understands other people's points of view so clearly that his own get lost. But here I am, telling you this, and you must have known what he was like, or you wouldn't have chosen him to make a fool of. You *did* choose him, didn't you?'

'Sort of. It was either him or Ken Latchett, and Ken knew me too well, and he'd never have gone for it. I had to have somebody I could sort of feed an idea to, somebody who'd seize on it and enlarge it. As you say, Tony's quick. But I desperately needed somebody, because—'

'I don't want to hear why. The point is that I was so damned sorry for him! What you did was like kicking a puppy to stop it wagging its tail. And *that* was where my mistake came in. I was sorry for him, and hated you *for* him, and it all got blurred from then on. What I thought of him and what he meant to me, that's what got blurred.'

She stopped, and I waited for her to go on. Her eyes were huge. Her warm and emotional personality had pushed its way beyond the drugs.

'It wasn't fair,' she whispered. 'Not fair to Tony. You can't base a marriage on that sort of thing, because it doesn't last. At first it worked. That change of address card came to be a sort of joke between us. When . . . well, when there was a bit of a row brewing up, we waved the card. Richard Patton. It was *you* we were using to hold it all together. It was wrong! Wrong!' she said passionately, gripping the chair so violently that it squeaked on the floor. 'We said one day we'd get back at you. When I gave

Linda Court your address, it was a kind of gesture towards that.'

'I think I can understand that.'

'But *can* you!' she cried. 'It all faded away. It was what I might have expected from Tony, because in the end he seemed to understand why you'd done it. So he sympathized with you, for what you'd done. Typical. But . . . idiot that I am . . . I pretended, and kept it up . . . and for too long. There comes a time. You can feel it. There was a coolness. He didn't want me any more. But, for me, there was no more pity. I don't pity him now. I just ache for him when he's away from me, and slowly he's going away further and further. And I don't know what to do!' she whispered.

'Your imagination . . . ' I tried.

'Don't you think I know!'

'When I spoke to him – '

'You've seen him?'

'Today. He was only anxious that I wouldn't do anything to upset you.'

Blood rose to her cheeks, high spots on the fine bones. 'You've managed that, all right.'

'He didn't want me to see you.'

'To see how much I've changed?'

'I don't think it was that.'

'To see what you've done to us.'

'What?'

'Yes!' she shouted. 'You. Mr Clever-dick Patton. You and your manoeuvring and manipulation. It's all been *your* fault.'

Oh dear, oh dear. She was certainly my side of the drugs now, being able to use multi-syllable words. I tried attack. 'What the hell's my fault?'

'Call yourself Cupid! You didn't bring us together. Leave us alone, and we'd probably have made it. But for the proper reasons.'

'Marjie, I – '

'Don't *touch* me.'

'What can I say?'

'Oh great! Lost for words now.'

'I'll talk to him – '

'Don't you dare!'

46

'I'm sorry – '

'You know. You know now. And what d'you think you can do about *this!*'

There comes a time when you can do nothing else but run. I tried to be dignified; gestured, grimaced, then made my way to the hall. The kitchen door was slammed on my heels, and a couple of seconds later I heard a mug smash. Mine, no doubt.

Before I reached the front there was the sound of a key in the front door lock. I paused, but there was no escape. Tony Brason walked in, saw me, and stood there, one hand reaching behind him to shut the door. The lock clicked home.

There was nothing I could say. He looked past me. 'I thought I asked you not to come here.'

'Just leaving, Tony.'

'How did you know where I live?'

'We met by chance.'

There was still no colour in his voice. 'I warn you . . . if you've hurt her . . . '

I heard her speak behind me, quite calmly, the drugs again in control. 'It's all right, Tony. Don't fuss. Mr Patton was just leaving.'

I smiled at him. 'I'll see you, Tony.' Then I walked towards him, and he stood aside. It was not a wide hallway. We brushed together and I felt his tense aggression. He opened the door.

'I didn't see your car.'

'It's all right,' I assured him.

'I could run you into town.' There was just the hint of a plea there. In spite of himself, he felt we ought to talk.

'My car's within walking distance,' I told him. 'Good night. Marjie – good night.'

My legs were stiff down the path. I walked, not looking back.

Her emotions had eventually come alive, but only when she'd spoken of her marriage. *That* was the mainspring of her depression. She was seizing on the Linda Court case as a subconscious refuge within which she could rationalize the despair of her failing marriage. So where, now, did that leave my involvement? I could no longer claim I wanted to help her over the Linda Court tragedy. I could not claim an interest in the murder itself. It'd been a long day, but I could now see the end of my involvement. Amelia would be pleased.

47

No she wouldn't. She would say I was running away from it, when I'd already run far enough, and yet still hadn't shaken off a feeling of guilt. That guilt was still with me, though in a changed form. I couldn't completely go along with Marjie's claim that I was destroying her marriage, as her reasoning was distorted by her despair. But – to her – it was very real.

Was there any chance, I wondered, that I could assist in any possible way?

Still musing on this, wondering how I could justify – to Amelia, if necessary – any continued involvement, I pushed my way through the bushes and on to the cul-de-sac. I plodded towards my car.

I had not closed the door. I remembered that quite vividly. I'd not wished for even a click from the lock. But now it was closed. My fingers on the handle, I looked round. To my right, a shape detached itself from the shadows.

'What the hell're you doing here?' he demanded.

I stepped free of the branches to face him.

5

There was nothing wrong with his nerve, that he'd challenged me when it must have been clear that I was around twice his weight and four inches taller. It was dark, and it was isolated. Foolhardy would cover it.

'Good evening,' I said.

'Will you please explain your presence here. This is private property.'

I had been using my torch unsparingly on the way back. Now I had it directed at our feet, not wishing to disconcert him by directing it at his face. There was enough reflected light to indicate he was slim and apparently smartly dressed. He was carrying an open umbrella, which dripped between us. It would be, if expertly used, an effective defensive weapon.

But he seemed neither defensive nor offensive. His voice held the rich timbre of self-possession, of a man used to speaking with authority. I could just detect a lean, strong face, graced by a closely trimmed beard and moustache.

I had to wait him out. I needed a lead. He said at last, with a hint of impatience in his voice: 'My wife tells me she's seen someone prowling the grounds. I didn't believe her.'

I flicked the torch back along the cul-de-sac. 'That's where I've been looking.' No lie in that.

'You're a policeman?'

In the shadows he didn't see me incline my head, because I didn't dare to do so. Donaldson would have loved the chance of getting me for impersonating a police officer.

'It has come to my attention that someone *has* been walking in here.' Nicely official, that. 'Did your wife say . . . a man or a woman?'

'A woman, she thought. She had the impression of a long, almost ankle-length coat. I believe they were in fashion – last year, she tells me.'

'And *your* name, sir?' I asked solemnly, to prevent him demanding mine.

'Martin. Rupert Martin. I live at The Swallows, just up the hill from here.'

'Ah yes. Perhaps I'll need to see your wife. I'll say good night, then, sir.'

He took that as a dismissal. I saw his head nod stiffly. Formality oozed from him. He turned and began to walk away up the slope. For a moment I stood and watched him. Had his wife, I wondered, seen Marjie on her wanderings? Or was he another instance of someone who couldn't keep away from the site of a murder? But he hadn't seemed that sort of person; he'd have scorned such morbid thoughts. Besides, it would have been too big a coincidence for him to have invented it, when there was a genuine prowler around.

I climbed in the car, got my pipe going, and started the engine. The dashboard clock indicated 8.15. I got a bit of rear-wheel spin, as I seemed to have backed into a patch of soft ground, but I urged it out. Then I set off for home.

My dipped headlights played on his slim figure, stepping out with a firm stride. He did not turn his head as I swept past. Towards the top of the rise, on my right, the lights picked out a sign reading: The Swallows, and I caught a glimpse, no more, of a woman's face. She was standing in the gateway, no umbrella for her but with the collar of a dark coat turned up high around her neck and a head-covering that gleamed as though it was plastic. My impression was of a round face. Her pallor could well have been a trick of the headlights.

An anxious wife, fearing for her husband's safety? Or fearing for his mental stability, if it had become his habit to visit the scene of a crime? Whatever it was, my impression was of fear.

I drove slowly out of Manor Park Estate, then rapidly to Boreton-Upon-Severn.

'You're late, Richard.' It was no more than a gentle reproof from Amelia.

'I got caught. Plenty to tell you. I hope you waited for me.'

They had. Dinner was ready. I was ravenous.

It had now become routine for the three of us to eat in what had been, before Amelia and I arrived there, very much Mary Pinson's private domain, her kitchen. But the dining room was far too large and gloomy for two to eat in, so it hadn't taken long for Amelia to come to an arrangement with Mary. They shared the cooking and we shared the kitchen.

While we ate, I went through a detailed account of what had happened, slanting it perhaps in my favour, but trying to be impartial. If I stressed anything, it was my reluctant involvement in Tony Brason's marriage. I might as well have spared myself all the agonizing and soul-searching in which I'd indulged. Amelia cut straight through to the heart of it.

'It seems to me that this Marjie was being rather fanciful. Don't be so self-centred, Richard, thinking you're important in someone else's marriage. They're your friends, so naturally you're worried. Quite simply, you're just too lazy to do anything positive for them. Put yourself out for once. And if it's Donaldson you're frightened of, I'll come along with you tomorrow.'

Duly chastened, I said distantly: 'That will not be necessary.'

Accordingly, alone, I set out to do something positive the next morning. Not too early. I had to phone Ken Latchett first, at the station.

'It's Richard, Ken.'

'So I understand.' Said on a sigh, that was.

'You can help me, if you will.'

'You're determined –'

'The file. . .'

'Now, Richard –'

50

'Let me say it. I don't expect to get a sight of it. I'm not *interested* in murder.' A plain lie. 'It's the young woman herself. Linda Court.'

'It's all the same thing, Richard.'

'From Marjie's point of view it's not.'

'And that's your point of view, is it?'

I had to pause there. How to put it? 'Ken, I had a long talk with Marjie yesterday evening. All about what happened that week, you know, at the station, when Linda Court kept coming in. And there's something worrying me.'

'Me too.'

'No ... listen. I can't tie it down, this worry. I'm not getting clear enough mental images. You know me.'

'You and your images!' But a little of our former warm relationship crept in there. It was what I'd always operated on, a clear image of what had happened.

'That's it, Ken. But I'm not getting anything, not from what Marjie told me. It's the actual site of the murder – '

'Now come off it, Richard, please.'

'There's something wrong, and I can't see what it is. Of course, Marjie wouldn't officially go anywhere near the scene of crime. So all I've got from her is hearsay, and I thought – '

'Richard!' he burst in. 'Lay off, will you! You're not fooling anybody. What you intend to do is dip your nose into Donaldson's case. Damn it, you've got him twitchy already. Keep out of it, there's a good chap. He's just aching to get something he can throw at you.'

'Ken, Ken ... it's all right. I'm only trying to justify Marjie's actions. That's all. Nothing else.'

A pause. He was thinking. I heard the click of his lighter, the indrawing of breath and a cubic yard of tobacco smoke. Then he spoke more quietly. 'For your information, Richard, when she's well, Marjie's going to have to face a severe reprimand on this. Maybe she'll find herself back as a constable.'

It was something I hadn't considered. 'And if she'd put in a report, Ken? Don't forget, there hadn't been a positive crime until the murder. So what could you have done?'

Silence.

'Ken?'

'Nothing perhaps. Not in time. But Merridew's niggly on it,

51

pushing Donaldson for a result. You know how it is. Somebody's got to be blamed for something. For the record.'

'And you're still telling me to keep out of it?' I demanded.

'All I'm saying, Richard, is that I can't let you see the file.'

'Did I ask for that?'

'Not in so many . . . then *what*?'

'The official photos of the scene of crime. You know there're always duplicates. Nobody'll miss 'em.'

'You're the living limit. . .'

'There's something wrong, I'm telling you.'

'I'll try. All right. For you, I'll try, Richard.'

'See you for lunch, then? The Rose of Picardy?'

'I suppose so. You worry me, you know.'

'One o'clock?'

'Sure.'

Then he rang off. I hadn't wanted to involve him, but it was either Ken or Tony. And Tony couldn't be approached.

So I drove again towards the police station, but this time went past it, and parked in the multi-storey Linda had used when her car had twice been stolen. I didn't know on which floor she'd left the car, but it didn't matter. They were all the same. Up a curved ramp to one floor, follow the floor arrows to the far end, and up another ramp to another floor. And so on. Seven floors in all. I parked and got out. Even in daylight, I'd needed my dipped heads. It was an ideal place for potential car thieves to lurk. Lots of dark corners, plenty of spare time to operate, and if they were seen bending over a car, so what?

I locked the Stag, and went for a walk round the town. There had been talk of amateur dramatics, and of The Prince Of Wales. I went to have a look at it.

At one time it had been the Queen's cinema, a narrow, poky place, very draughty, which had a distinction in that it had, down each side of the circle, a row of staggered double seats, especially for courting couples. You couldn't see much of the screen from along the sides, but the management knew what they were doing. Who wants to watch the film when you're courting?

They'd knocked it down. For two years there had been a gap-toothed hole between Lloyd's Bank and Boots, then, two streets away, the local live theatre, of Midlands renown, closed due to lack of support. The council took it over, and while they were arguing about what to do with it, a local big-wig got together with some friends – The Friends Of The Stage – and decided to build a new theatre in the gap where the Queen's had been. This local big-wig was Colonel Forrester, whose building company secured the contract.

The Prince of Wales was born. He came down to lay the cornerstone, after Boots had moved to larger premises, and the old Boots was itself knocked down. There was now room for a grand project. The contract was enlarged. Forrester smiled. They installed a rotating stage. There wasn't room for it to rotate fully; it did a half-turn one way, a half-turn back. The auditorium was small, though luxurious. But when I was there it hadn't opened. It seemed that a live theatre was still not a viable proposition. Sadly, the town stared at a closed frontage.

But Forrester hadn't yet cast his last stone. With a knighthood in the offing, he trespassed on anticipated familiarity with that exalted position, and persuaded a knight and a dame of the stage to appear for next to no fee, for an opening performance of *The Importance of Being Earnest*. A married pair of film stars, at present resting and pretending it was from choice, were equally persuadable. And, shortly after I said goodbye to the town so that I missed the opening night, The Prince of Wales was launched in style.

But it was now barely floating. Such theatres do not usually become the venue for amateur groups, yet that had occurred. Or so I'd been told. They must have hired it on the cheap.

Not much had been happening recently. One tattered bill from last November's amateur production still clung to the wall along the narrow alleyway to the stage door. *I'll Go Along With That*, by a local author. First and only production, probably. The cast had been small. I made a note of their names. One woman – Gail Martin. Martin? Could that have been the woman I'd glimpsed in the gateway of The Swallows? Four men. Ian Knowles. He'd already been mentioned, but as the director. Yes, there he was: director and producer – Ian Knowles. Busy man. He'd taken the lead, too. Three other men: Llew Porter, Clive Matthews, Bill Askew. One week. No, less than a week. Tuesday to Saturday. It was on that Saturday that Linda Court had been killed.

But her name appeared nowhere.

On the frontage there were posters advertising a pantomime,

53

which had run from the end of December to, apparently, the end of February. A good run for a panto, these days. But they'd lured a well-known, though ageing, comedian to play the Dame. Since then, nothing, until, in a fortnight's time, the appearance of a pop group.

The booking office was open. I entered the foyer. Discreet bills advertised the Welsh Opera Company for two weeks in April. Not bad. The girl in the kiosk seemed bored. Such lovely eyes to look so blank!

'I'd like to contact Ian Knowles,' I told her.

'Me too!' Her teeth were perfect. 'I'n't he the very end?'

'I don't know. Our interests might not be the same.'

For a moment she eyed me with concern, then she pouted. 'You've only gotta walk round the corner into the pedestrian place, and there he is. The Vortex. He owns it.'

I thanked her gravely and said I'd go and dig him out. She said: 'Lucky you.'

I knew The Vortex. A restaurant. Pseudo-continental. You couldn't see inside from the pavement. The whole frontage was blocked by a display of exotic wine bottles, sheaves of dusty spaghetti, and entwined bunches of artificial grapes. We'd investigated a break-in there. Ian Knowles. (Why hadn't I remembered his name?) He'd lived in a flat above, and had interrupted intruders. There had been blood spattered on the tables and on the floor. Not his. We never got anybody for it, and they got nothing, so it was quits.

Standing in front of his premises, I gradually assembled my memory of him. It would've been five years before. A large man with a large presence and an impressive voice. A foreign cast to his features, but nothing in his accent. Perhaps his mother had been Italian or Greek. There'd been a sense of power and confidence. Supreme confidence. And lurking just behind his eyes there had been aggression. It never got closer to the surface in my presence, I remembered. He had a broad and high forehead, plenty of black hair, but cleanshaven.

I went inside.

It was too early for lunch, and they did not, apparently, serve morning coffee. The lights were discreet, but I could see that the tables were being prepared by three waiters. Close to the door there was a kiosk, inside which Knowles would preside and collect the cash. From the back, beyond swing doors, a radio was blasting out pop. A large, foreign voice was adding itself to the volume. I was therefore not heard.

I approached the nearest waiter and touched his elbow. He jumped. I said loudly: 'Is Mr Knowles available?'

He looked doubtful at first, then he shrugged, managing to direct his eyes towards a far corner. I looked beyond him. Two people were sitting at a table. Morning coffee was available, but only to the boss.

He looked up when he became aware of my presence. Apart from the fact that he was wearing his hair shorter, he seemed barely to have changed. Sitting beside him was a woman, perhaps thirty, slim and proud and dressed in a style that emphasized nothing, but hinted strongly. Seeing me, she looked interested, then a curtain came down over her face, and it said nothing.

'Could I have a word, Mr Knowles?'

'What about?' The voice seemed more harsh, more assertive.

'Linda Court. I believe she was a member of your drama group.'

'I'm up to here with Linda Court, friend. No, you can't. The police have already got the lot.'

'I'm coming at it with an empty mind.'

I'd been watching his expression, his awareness that we'd met, and wondering how long it would take. Then he got it.

'The break-in. You came on that – I remember.'

'Yes.'

He got to his feet. The hand he presented was large and covered with black hair. He made no attempt to impress me with its strength.

'The man they sent on this Linda lark was a complete idiot,' he told me. I took that as a compliment, that I was not complete. 'But there's absolutely nothing. Here. Sit down. Would you like coffee?'

I shook my head, but sat down. We were now a neat triangle. I could not help but include the woman in my appraisal.

'This is Gail Martin,' he said. 'She played the lead in our little production.' The professional false modesty. It meant he'd been damned proud of it. 'We were just discussing our next effort.'

'So soon? I thought you people – amateurs – did about one a year.'

'You've got to plan early. We're wondering about Shaw.'

'Oh yes?' I smiled. Were they up to Shaw? 'It was a success, was it, this last one?'

'We got decent notices.'

She spoke at last, patting the back of his hand in admonition. 'They were very good, and you know it, Ian.' As she turned her head, I was certain she was the woman I'd seen at the gate.

'Well yes,' he murmured. He enjoyed playing this game, demure in order to attract praise.

'I believe Linda Court was a member of your group,' I prompted.

'True.'

He seemed reluctant to go further, but I needed to know Linda Court. Inside out.

'And there was no part for her in the play?'

'The cast was four men and only one woman. Three men, really, because the fourth part was only a small one. Bill Askew got that. Police Sergeant, he was.'

'And the woman . . . '

He squeezed her hand. 'Gail got that part, and she was magnificent. Weren't you, darling?'

He was directing my attention to her, and though he did it smilingly, I had a feeling of underlying cruelty. She blushed, then glanced at me. She was a good actress, though. She managed to cover it with a pout. 'Linda could have done it better.'

'Now, now,' he said, laughing at her. He turned to me. It was almost that he apologized for her modesty. Then he went on smoothly, easily, yet I felt that every word was aimed at Gail Martin. 'Linda would've been perfect for it. She was used to the bright lights and the cameras, but that was her hands, you see. Her hands. You know she was a model?'

'I know that.'

'But this was going to be all of her, and she didn't know what to do with her body. Whereas Gail does, don't you, darling?' I saw her eyes flicker. He smiled. 'The part called for a woman a bit older than Linda. She could do that, though, take on age. The snag was that she wanted to play her as a sexpot. The character was a police superintendent's wife, sensitive, intense, with her nerves crackling, and fighting for her separate personality. Linda wanted to play her as a tart. She *wasn't* a tart. But Linda wouldn't accept direction. I pleaded with her, shouted at her, explained to her. This was during the early rehearsals, you understand. We were using the Methodist Hall. In the end, we had a flaming row, and she walked off.'

'Ian, dear,' put in Gail gently, 'you told her to go to hell and get lost.'

I could see he would be good on the stage. His face was mobile. Every portion of it moved. He registered protest, entreaty and gloom, all in three seconds.

'All right,' he conceded, managing to get gracious magnanimity into it. 'So I was too severe. But I'd got you to fall back on, Gail, my sweet. Reserve. And what a reserve you turned out to be! Mr . . . ' He raised his eyebrows.

'Patton.'

'Mr Patton, you weren't there, or you wouldn't be asking. Let me tell you. Gail'd had only a week or two in rehearsal. It was a difficult part. This woman, the policeman's wife, she'd left him three or four times before. He was insanely jealous, and for no reason. Always he got her back, but his jealousy gradually drove her away again. The play was all about whether he could persuade her to return again and stay. She was fighting him for her independence as an individual. And he . . . oh, you missed something there . . . he was a right bastard. You'd have appreciated it.' His nose quivered. I was expected to react.

'That was you, I suppose?'

He clenched his teeth and laughed through them. Shish-shish. Gail said: 'Type-casting.' Something went wrong with the laugh. I think he choked on it.

'It was,' he went on heavily, 'a complete change of character for me. But I enjoyed the part. Let me explain. It was in three acts. A peculiar construction, really, but it'd been a TV play by a local chap, and he'd adapted it for us as a stage play. We could only do two sets, you see. So I wasn't on in the first act. That was short, only about twenty minutes. The private detective he'd used to trace her, and Gail here. Llew Porter played the private eye. Played it a bit too camp for my liking, but he was *supposed* to get a laugh or two . . . '

'Not like that,' she said quickly.

57

'Gail disapproved.'

'I was supposed to fancy him, damn it. That was the point. What my husband – you – accused me of, other men, hadn't ever been true, and now it was taking place under his nose. Me and the private detective. She had actually met somebody she liked, and the laugh was that her husband had sent him to her. It was subtle. And how could *that* have come across, with Llew playing it gay? I ask you!'

I looked from one to the other. It was in the past, but they still disputed over it. Her eyes flashed, her hands gestured. He went quietly vicious.

'It was a minor point,' he said flatly.

'It was a major issue in the story line.'

'It detracted from the final act.'

'Which you wanted to make your very own!' she snapped.

He smiled at her thinly. '*Our* own, darling,' he remonstrated. 'This third act, Mr Patton, it was a full hour, and all emotional tension. The other two were shorter . . . '

'With me sitting out the second one. Now I ask you!' It was me she was asking, turning to me with one hand fluttering, nearly gripping my arm, and with just a fraction too much agitation in her eyes. Blue, I saw. Unusual with chestnut hair, which seemed to be natural. 'I had the first act, with Llew Porter, working myself into the part – and with him hamming it up with all those tired affectations the gays are supposed to use – and then I had to sit it out, cold, in my dressing room for all of twenty-five minutes.'

Knowles nodded in sympathy. It was a difficulty that he hadn't presented to her himself. 'I know, dear. More than that, even.' He explained to me. 'Two short acts, not much more than scenes, and we used the stage to run them on rapidly, one straight after the other. They were supposed to take place at the same time, anyway, one in the bed-sit, one in the policeman's house. So then we had the big interval before the last act.'

'So I went cold on it,' she picked up quickly. 'I had to hold the part and the mood . . . it was too long. Too long, Ian, I did tell you that. Forty minutes altogether, as good as.'

'Listen to her! Cold, she says. She came on in that third act, and it was like electricity. I could tell. The curtain went up on me, waiting, then she came on with Llew, and neither of us need have been there. There was absolute silence. I'm telling you—'

'That's enough, Ian.'

'She'd got 'em. In two seconds, she'd got 'em, and she held it for a full hour. The act really crackled, the tension building up. And it was Gail here, tense and nervous. You *felt* she was breaking up. At the end, of course, she's lost. That's how it was intended to be. The private eye goes along with it – hence the title – he goes along with what he believes she wants, and it's not. A tragedy. The whole audience ... the curtain came down, that night, on dead silence. Ten seconds. Silence. Then they were on their feet. I've never heard – '

'Just look at the time!' she burst in. 'Rupert said he'd probably phone. I'll have to get back. If you want me, I'll be at home.'

Then, as Gail edged her way out of the corner, saying the last words, her hand fell on my shoulder. I felt her fingers tighten. She was looking at him, but speaking to me.

We watched her walk away. Could Linda have matched that confident and mature swing? I smiled at Knowles. His jaw was set, his lips thin.

'But you still think Linda Court could've done it better?'

He didn't answer the question. 'Her husband doesn't like this acting business.'

'Doesn't he?'

'Now ... what did you want to know?' He was all polite attention.

'I rather think you've told me.' I slapped my palms on the table, easing myself to my feet. 'I'll be off. Got a lunch date. Thank you for your time.'

'Call in again.' But his eyes told me he didn't want that.

I ambled out into the street. She was backing out an Audi 100 from a meter slot along the street. I didn't wave as she went past.

Time to wander back to The Prince Of Wales and check that poster again. *I'll Go Along With That.* Doors open 7 p.m., it informed me. Curtain up 7.30 p.m. The second act, Knowles's first appearance, would have begun at around 7.50. There had been time. Just. I went to meet Ken.

6

He wasn't there at one o'clock. He wasn't there at 1.15. I was on my second batch of cheese and pickle sandwiches, and nursing my second pint, when he arrived just before 1.30. Walking in he raised his eyebrows at me. I shook my head. He collected his own beer, and came over to join me.

'Well?' I said.

'No joy, Richard.'

'Hell.'

'It's your own fault. You've got Donaldson all nervous. He's taken the file into his own office. He's going through it again, in case he can see something we've missed. You've really got him worried, Richard. He thinks you're a genie, popped out of a bottle, and full of magic tricks.'

'Far from it.' But he was rattling on. The interjection didn't stop him.

'That's why I'm late. I hung around, waiting for him to go to lunch, but when he did he locked his door. No go.'

Ken had been taking a big risk for me. I nodded my appreciation. 'Maybe he *will* spot something.'

'Yeah. And what have *you* been doing this morning?' He said it casually, but he was nevertheless suspicious.

'Talking to Ian Knowles.'

'Richard! You promised.'

'Promised what?'

'You said you weren't going to nose into the murder.'

'I'm still not. Getting a background on Linda Court, that's all I've been doing. I noticed something, though.'

Ken was quiet and withdrawn. His enthusiasm for my investigations was nil. 'I'd expect you to. Let's have it, then.'

'It was the way the play was constructed. Knowles wasn't on stage until the second act. Allow twenty minutes for the first, and if the curtain went up at – '

'Richard, I *know*. You're going to say he could've been at Manor Park Estate at the time she died.'

'I was going to say – '

'This is all a waste of time, Richard. I drew up a schedule – you can have a copy of it if you like. The exact times each of the three

60

acts started, who was on stage and at what times. But what's the point in confusing yourself with it all . . . '

'Couldn't I, perhaps, decide what confuses me and what doesn't?'

' . . . the fact is that every one of the cast, four men and one woman, *could* have got away long enough to drive to Manor Park Estate and back again. And not be missed, perhaps. If you don't know, backstage at an amateur production is nothing less than controlled panic. The whole group was involved. And I did a jigsaw puzzle of it, and damn it, any one of the five actors could have sneaked away for a while . . . '

'But the point – '

'And before you think of it, I checked about their cars. That pedestrian precinct, it's thrown open to free parking from six o'clock onwards, and they'd all taken advantage of it, so they all had their cars available.'

'Ken – '

'But if you'd like me to go through it – and if you've got a spare hour or two – I could lay the whole tangle out in front of you, from memory, Richard. Memory. I've been over it so many times . . . '

'You're trying to dazzle me with complexities, Ken.'

He scrabbled for his cigarettes. His beer had gone untasted. I noticed he'd ordered only a half. 'I am trying to impress on you, Richard,' he said heavily, 'that we've gone into it fully. Very fully. It's been four months. There's been time to use a lot of men and effort. There's nothing we've missed.'

It was clear I'd been leaning too heavily on our past friendship. I'd put it under stress. Now, it appeared, I was insulting him by implying a criticism of his professionalism.

'Motives?' I asked quietly, almost miserably.

'Ah yes. Motives. There've been plenty of motives to choose from. Linda didn't make herself popular. The remarkable thing is that I've gathered she thought she was popular. You know the sort of thing, sweeping into any group with the calm confidence that you're welcome. A silly girl with a thick skin. That's what she was, and she went around creating havoc amongst her acquaintances. I nearly said friends. She didn't make friends. There wasn't anything ever done by halves. Love me or leave me. That attitude. And over-sexed. Flaunted it, and used it. Are you getting the picture, Richard?'

'I'm getting a distinct impression of an inspector who's over-worked, and hasn't got much patience for me.'

He gave it a few seconds, then he sighed, and tried a grin. 'I haven't got *time*, Richard. Sorry. Time for you, of course, but . . .' He stopped.

'But?'

He dodged it, shrugging. 'Motive, then. In her profession as a model – this was mainly Birmingham, London and Elstree – she'd picked up dozens of enemies there. Broken marriages, mainly. Short affairs, then she was away, leaving the bits behind.'

'You're bitter, Ken. Don't let it get to you.'

'No. It's Donaldson who gets to me. None of this *means* any-thing to him. But never mind that. All these motives involve people who were too far away to have managed that business through the week, with her car and her coat and her shoulder bag. And don't tell me it hadn't got anything to do with her murder – '

'Of course it had, Ken. You're not drinking.'

'Just lately . . . ' He grinned, almost his old familiar expression of genuine pleasure, ' . . . I've been overdoing it. Where was I?'

'Motives. Foreign and local.'

'Stick to local motives, and it's all involved with the drama group. We tried, but couldn't dig up anything that wasn't. But in that group . . . oh boy, what we didn't dig out! Mostly it was just minor. Except for her fellow actors, we could find nothing that would justify murder, certainly not all the trouble that was taken.'

'Yes?' I encouraged.

'And most of that is putting two and two together. Ian Know-les, now. He'd got a woman friend he was rather serious about. For him, that was unusual, the serious part, I mean. He's about as promiscuous as Linda was. But there was this special woman.'

I realized he was staring at me. He laughed. 'And no, it's not Gail Martin. She finds him a bit of a pain. Never mind who. Linda found out about it, and threatened to inform his wife, and it's his wife who's the money behind him.'

'He's married?' Five years before, he'd been a bachelor, living in the flat above his restaurant.

'Yes. Into money. The restaurant barely pays its way. And how d'you think a small amateur group could find the money to put on a play at The Prince Of Wales? That was *her* money. And Linda, knowing about Knowles's affair, threatened to ruin everything for him if she didn't get the lead.'

'Who told you this?'

'He did.' He glanced at his watch and frowned. 'He gave it as an example of his integrity as a director, that he'd thrown her out and told her to go to hell.'

'And Linda backed off?'

'Apparently. She didn't even stop off on the way home and tell his wife.'

'Stop off?'

'The Knowles live in the gatehouse at Manor Park.'

'Oh Lor'.'

'Yes. Motive, means, and even a knowledge of the terrain. But he had no opportunity. He was there, at the theatre, from 5.30 to the end of the show. The statements prove that. They finished with a party. It went on till midnight. And we've got a whole bunch of witnesses to say he wasn't missing for a minute.'

'All the same . . . '

'You want motives for the rest of the cast?'

'Yes please,' I said meekly.

'Llew Porter, who played the private detective, and Clive Matthews, who was the innocent civilian . . . they run an antiques shop and live together in the flat over it. Llew Porter wasn't really acting when he played the private detective as a poofter. They amused Linda. She was working on Matthews, trying to break them up, just for a bit of sport. And *both* of them would cheerfully have strangled her. Bill Askew, now? He's a furniture restorer, and owns a decent-sized layout. Shortfall of cash, he said. It was temporary, but Linda found out. Said she'd tell everybody – she'd got friends on the local paper. Then he'd get his debts called in. She frightened him. He's fifty, if a day. *He* would've brained her with a chunk of wood, but he'd have chosen it with care, a bit of two–by–two, straight-grained.'

'You're being facetious, Ken.'

'Because I know that not one of these people would've seized on a gap in the production time to drive out to Manor Park Estate. It would have been impracticable, and almost impossible to time it right.'

63

He was looking at me now with his face stern and his expression challenging.

'You're eliminating them? But why, Ken?'

'I'd have thought it was obvious.'

'Tell me why you didn't mention a motive for Gail Martin.'

'Because we didn't find one. Rather the reverse. Linda could've scratched her eyes out for getting that part. And anyway, she's eliminated for the same reason as the rest.'

'You're determined to tell me. All right. Let's have it. Why?'

He paused for a long while, his eyes beyond my shoulder. I'd always thought of him as transparent, displaying his emotions. Now he was worried and embarrassed. I had a feeling what was coming. Abruptly, it seemed to me, he was no longer seized by a feeling of urgency. What he had to say needed consideration, and it had nothing to do with the cast of that play.

'Richard,' he said at last, 'I'm going to trespass on our old friendship. I'm assuming it's still there, from your end. There was a time when I wouldn't have needed to say that. So I'm praying you haven't changed. No, I said that all wrong. You *have* changed, Richard. I know retiring changes people. I've seen it happen. They try to kid themselves they're glad to be out of it, out of all the routine and the pressure of a regular job. They're glad to see the back of it. But that doesn't last for long. It's ingrained in your personality. Like that pipe you keep fiddling with. It's part of you.'

It had abruptly become personal. 'I was happily pruning my roses, Ken – '

'And you can't drop it, can you? All the old habits of dissecting things and trying to make actions logical, and getting a clear picture, as you call it.'

'Habits die hard,' I admitted sadly. But I didn't want anything to die.

'You know what it is,' he said with sudden, bright inspiration, his face lighting up. 'You don't want to let things go, because it's like a bit of you dying. Am I right?'

'It seems such a pity, all that experience going to waste.'

'Yes.' He frowned. It wasn't exactly what he'd meant. 'I've heard you've been using some of your experience since you've retired. With some success, too. All power to your elbow, I say. But don't you think, Richard, that your bit of success might've

64

made you a little over-confident? Frankly, I think you're over-stepping the mark on this one. Most of the work on this case has been mine. You're coming in from outside with the bland, sodding confidence that you can sort it out for me!'

He stopped suddenly, took a drink at last, and wiped the back of his hand across his mouth. I watched him with concern.

'Sorry, Richard. It's been building up. But I want to know if I'm still going to consider you as a friend. Because . . . no, let me say this . . . because a friend wouldn't walk in on my case and try to prove I'm a damned fool.'

'Would I do that? I ask you!'

'You're bloody well doing it. Everybody knows you're in town. It's almost . . . well, almost as though I've got desperate and *sent* for you.'

'Ridiculous.'

'But you're *here*.'

'To help my friends, Tony and Marjie.'

'They hate you.'

'I rather like them.'

'You haven't changed a bit! Still stubborn and pigheaded.'

'Well, thank you. I thought you said we all change when we retire.'

'Not you – oh, not you! And I wish you weren't here. Oh yes, come to visit, as a friend. That's fine. Cath sends her love, by the way, and says when're you going to pop in and see her?'

'I'll have to do that.'

'Preferably on your way out of town.'

I reamered out my pipe into the ashtray. Without looking up, I said: 'Ken, if I come across anything – such as that letter from Linda – I'll come to you first. A promise. You first. But I'm not really looking for anything.'

'I hope not. Everybody with a motive has got a solid alibi.'

I blew through the pipe, and began filling it. 'Except for the ones who might have got away from the theatre during the performance.'

I led him into this, because I knew he'd want to get back to it.

'Don't tell me you can't see what I'm getting at.'

'Frankly, no.' I puffed smoke towards the ceiling. 'Tell me what four months of thought have produced.'

He was not offended. Triumph overrode it. 'Just consider what was done on that last Saturday. Linda's car was stolen, some time before five. It was hot-wired and driven to the cul-de-sac outside her house. It would've been dark by then. Linda came into our station and reported it. We've already agreed she couldn't have got home before seven. Maybe later, if she stopped off to write that letter and post it. Not "if" – she must have done. But she was killed at the time she discovered her car. She didn't find it earlier, or she'd have driven it into the drive. No, it had to be at the time she found the car. It almost seems like part of the pattern, a culmination of what'd been going on through the week. Are you with me?'

'I agree entirely.'

'Then it's obvious that he – or she if you must – would have had to be *waiting* for Linda. Waiting, Richard. They could, any one of those five, have found time to get away for a while from the theatre. But it wouldn't have left much time for hanging about in Manor Park. And don't forget . . . whoever did it, they had to be there when Linda reached her car. How could they possibly have known when that would be? It would've meant relying on luck. A coincidence. No . . . I'm not having it.'

I nodded. It was a point I hadn't seen. The pipe was drawing smoothly. 'I can't argue with that.'

'Well then – as you were always saying.'

'Then you need somebody else with a motive – and no alibi. Somebody who'd got a lot of spare time that evening, and could've done what you've just outlined.'

He finished his beer. 'And a fat chance you've got of finding out.'

'Oh – I don't know. I'm making contacts. Seeing Gail Martin this afternoon, as a matter of fact.'

'Now Richard . . . '

'By invitation.' If a squeeze of the shoulder was invitation.

He pushed back his chair and got to his feet. He was more relaxed, having got his sermon off his mind. 'I wish you luck. Don't forget to pop in on Cath.'

'I'll do that. Oh, and Ken . . . '

He turned back.

'I could still do with a sight of those photographs.'

He laughed, waved, and walked out, leaving me with the gloomy realization that I was making a right fool of myself. I felt like a bookmark, expecting to go through the whole book. Squeezed in, there, I had to wait for somebody to turn the next page. And the book was due back at the library.

I walked out into a dull afternoon, the light already going. Way in the distance to the west there was a line of light under the edge of the heavy cloud layer. I drove towards it. The rain had finally ceased some time during the morning. I headed for Manor Park Estate.

There was a light showing at one of the windows in the archway of the gatehouse. Mrs Knowles was at home. I felt an urge to visit her and chat about her husband, but I had no possible excuse. There is a point beyond which honest investigation deteriorates into plain nosiness.

The lights were turning themselves on along the roadways in the Estate. It was the time when shadows are deceptive, when nothing is either hidden or clear. Only my dipped heads possessed the tarmac, but on the green stretches either side there appeared to be movement and stealth. I couldn't make up my mind whether I would like to live there. Peace and seclusion, yes. But would it not become disquieting?

I drove slowly up the gentle slope to its peak. In the distance, street lights sparkled, and the orange glow clung to the underside of the cloud layer. Then at once I was beneath the trees again, with the darkness each side solid, and if I'd not known where to look I would have missed The Swallows.

I turned in. The curved narrow drive embraced me, but only for the distance required to shield the house from the roadway. Which wasn't far, as it was a sprawl of low bungalow, with the land falling away beyond it. I parked in front. The entrance porch was difficult to locate amongst all the glass and the architectured angles and recesses of the frontage.

With the car lights off, and standing outside on the drive, I stood and looked round. There was still enough light to disclose that the grounds had been landscaped and were already maturing. Unless I was mistaken, there was shortly going to be a grand show of daffodils and tulips under a curved sweep of rhodos.

I discovered the porch, guided by a tiny spot of light that turned out to be a bellpush. Pressure on it also lit the porch and hall, me, and another printed reminder that this was The Swallows, in case I'd lost my way in the grounds.

67

At a sudden thought, I smiled to myself. It was still there when the door swung open. You feel such a fool.

'Sorry,' I said. 'It was just a thought.'

'Oh?' She stood back and aside. 'Am I to be told?'

'I thought . . . with a name like Martin, you should have called your home: House Martin.'

'I suggested that.' She deftly took my anorak and hat. 'But Rupert is humourless. It had to be called The Swallows, for when the Chairman comes for dinner.' She was walking away from me, talking over her shoulder. 'His company, you see. Swallow International.' She led me into the sitting room.

'Ah. They import tea, do they?'

She turned, and was a second late producing the smile. It was stiff. It hadn't had much exercise recently. 'Will you sit down? Can you stay a while?'

I said I could. She intrigued me. I chose a wing-chair upholstered in patterned moquette. It was one of a suite of several such chairs and settees, a lot of furniture, which still seemed to rattle around loose in such a large room. It required two branched chandeliers to mitigate the gloom, and in the corners it needed supplementing with standard lamps. On the tables scattered around there were more lamps. No ashtrays, I noticed, so my pipe had to stay in my pocket. The chair pattern was repeated in the great sweeps of curtain, and in miniature on the wallpaper. An impressive room. That was its purpose. Not to be lived in. It could be repressive. To me, anyway. I like to feel comforted by a proximity of enclosure.

But it was not me it was meant to impress. She moved around it, nervous and taut, touching things, moving vases, finding new vistas in oil landscapes that looked like originals.

I waited patiently. She spoke, eventually, to a case-clock on the mantel. The fireplace was not intended for a fire.

'You realized I wanted to speak to you?'

'I hoped you did.'

'I didn't want you to get the wrong impression . . . '

'I'm not sure I'm entitled to impressions,' I told her.

'But you're from the police?'

'No, Mrs Martin. Put it that I'm an interested party.'

At last she made up her mind to sit down. Another few seconds and I'd have had to stand, myself. She came and sat in a similar chair to mine, but not quite opposite. I had to turn my head. She was wearing one of those loose, one-piece combinations that they call jumpsuits. As I said, there was no intention to impress. It was a plain, dull grey. She might not have realized what it did for her eyes and strong features, how it offset the two red ear-drops at the lobes of her ears and the matching lipstick to her wide mouth, even the matching red of her nails. Might not. It could've been simply that she possessed an instinct for pattern and colour, the jumpsuit being a concession to modern trends and the rest a subconscious rebellion.

'In what way are you interested?' she asked in a formal tone.

'I thought I made that clear at the restaurant. I'm interested in everything I can discover about Linda Court.'

She glanced down at her hands. 'You knew her?'

'No. But I have friends who are deeply affected by her death.'

She gave me a nod. It really meant nothing, or anything you could make of it, but it seemed I'd satisfied her. 'You must have thought it strange, but ... ' She paused. I inclined my head, smiling. '... I couldn't sit there another minute and hear you being misinformed by that ignorant pig, Ian Knowles.' This was said with an unemotional detachment.

She turned her hands over and stared at the palms. Nothing there. She turned them back. The knuckles were a little knobbly and equally uninformative.

I said equably: 'You seemed to be friends.'

'We have to be. He's our producer and director – his wife's our backer – and I'm the chairperson of the committee.'

It wasn't really an explanation, but I nodded. 'And it seemed to me you were going along with what he said. Even encouraging him.'

Her face came up. 'There you are, you see how it is.' There was animation now, her eyes bright. 'It's what he does to people. It's as though he's always on a stage, building up a character. Just try talking to him or listening to him for a while, and you pick it up. You start to be a character yourself, the one he wanted you to be. And then you begin to go along with him. Like a comedian's feed. You know. Am I making sense, Mr ... ' A shake of the head. 'I'm sorry, I've forgotten.'

'Patton. Richard Patton.' I smiled, though what she was saying didn't make me happy. She was apologizing for her weakness, and yet I had not thought of her as weak. I said: 'It seems perfectly acceptable to me, though I haven't had much experience of acting circles.'

'Oh, you'd never believe . . . '

'But I am believing.'

'What it's like, I mean. I don't know how the professionals remain sane. Really I don't. On the stage you're somebody else. It's frightening. It's like being taken over.'

'That's what the play did for you?'

It had been a casual question, to keep things going, but she was considering it carefully, nodding little nods to herself, with her lips pursed. Tiny, fine lines appeared on her upper lip.

'Shall we say I *felt* it?' she asked. I nodded agreement. We would say that. 'But really, the part was me. I'm the same age as the character was supposed to be, and *she* was all tension and crackling with nerves. I can tell you – that was me. It was the first time I'd played a lead part . . . and nervous! I could've run away. That second scene! Twenty minutes sitting in the dressing room, and feeling like I'd burst with tension. Of course, I couldn't *stay* there. Well . . . who could! I went for a walk outside.'

'In your stage make-up?'

'What did I care how I looked! People may have thought I was mad. Well . . . I was. As good as. They said – the reviews we got – they said I was "electric" in that last act. But all I was, when it comes down to it, was terrified. As the character was supposed to be. So it all came out fine.'

We had wandered away from Ian Knowles, but this wasn't an interrogation. She was trying to tell me something. I eased her along.

'But you'd acted before. You must have done.'

'Oh yes. But minor parts. We always stuck to comedy. Difficult to do, they say, though you can relax. But there comes a point . . . how can I explain this to you? A point where having a bit of fun and enjoying yourself begins to slide into something important and serious that matters. And then it's hell.'

'So you were arguing with Knowles about what to do next?'

'Sort of. I was telling him, mainly, that there probably wouldn't be a next, for me.'

'Because you wouldn't be able to face it, if you were again the lead?'

'Perhaps.'

'Now that Linda's gone, you'd naturally take the lead.'

'If you want to put it like that.'

'And you dread the thought?'

'Not if we could stick to lighter plays. I'd enjoy that.'

'But surely, now that you're the leading lady, so to speak, you could dictate the choice. Sort of blackmail him.'

'I suppose I could.' She stared beyond me. The idea didn't seem to appeal. Her face was stony with dismissal.

The idea suddenly came to me that she probably believed I was investigating Linda's murder, that Linda's death had provided her with the culmination of an ambition, to play the lead and to go on doing so – and that I might see this as a motive. At the same time, she was undermining it by stating that she had no wish for this exalted position.

Ridiculous, Richard, I told myself. She hasn't even started yet. There's something else she wants to say.

Her mind clicked back to me. 'But look what happened to Linda, when *she* tried to blackmail Ian.'

7

She really hated Ian Knowles. It was evident in her expression of relieved delight, that I'd presented her with such an opportunity to come out with that line. She didn't strike me as a vicious woman. Strong emotion had forced her to it. She seemed to realize this, and she forcibly freed herself from the mood.

'But seriously, Mr Patton, she *did* attempt that. And a lot of good it did her.'

'I know. She lost the lead. She wanted to play the part all wrong. I've already heard something about that.'

But she was shaking her head. It was doing something strange to her hair, which was set with such a stranglehold that it moved like a wobbly hat.

'No she didn't. Linda – and make no mistake about it – was a wonderful actress. In her own life she played the part of an empty-headed little trollop. But that was an act. She was a scheming so-and-so, but it was deep. All her little acts were superficial.

71

Underneath, she was all serious determination. She knew what she wanted. And she knew exactly how to play that woman in the play. She would *act* it. Not like me. I *was* it, all the nervous tension, all the fighting for her very life – that was me. For Linda, it would've been an act.'

'But I was told – ' Fighting for her very life?

'I know what you were told. Rehearsals. There was something deep between her and Ian. I don't mean just an affair. She'd have flaunted that. No. She deliberately taunted him. It was sort of a challenge, she daring him to take her up on it. She deliberately acted it wrong, in spite of what he told her, and he *did* take her up on it. He threw her out of the show.'

I realized then, that if Gail Martin was to be believed, and she seemed to be telling the truth, that I'd misunderstood what Ken had told me about Ian's motive. I'd thought that Linda had been blackmailing Knowles in order to get the lead. But she'd already got it. It would've been too late to blackmail him over that. She'd got it, and in effect had thrown it away. So what had she been blackmailing him for? Clearly, it had to be something more important to her.

'Linda Court seems to have been very perverse,' I observed. 'She must have known Knowles, what he was and how far she could push him.'

'She did, and she didn't seem to care. There was something deeper between them. But why are we talking about this?'

Because you've led me into it, dear, I thought. 'Because I'm interested in Linda,' I reminded her. 'But it's quite clear that you wouldn't want to work again with Ian Knowles.'

Her face lightened. She was interested in talking about herself. 'I didn't really say that. Now *did* I say that? No. I said I probably wouldn't be going on with it. Not that I didn't want to, because *that* would depend on the choice of play.'

'What, then?'

'My husband doesn't approve.'

'Doesn't he? Wasn't he there every night that week, cheering from the front row of the stalls?'

That drew a wry smile. 'The idea of Rupert cheering is amusing in itself. No. He hates me to go on the stage. He's a few hundred years behind the times, and still thinks of the stage as being home to a lot of indigent rogues and vagabonds. It is undignified, Mr

Patton. My acting reflects on his personal dignity.' She reached up and patted her cheeks. 'He has forbidden me to go on with it.' She smiled. 'He was in Saudi Arabia that week. He chose that week to go so that he would be in no way associated with my indecent antics, as he calls them.'

'Forbidden?'

'Well, not exactly that. He has said he disapproves. He's got perfect confidence that if he disapproves, that will be the last he hears of it.'

'And will it?'

'I don't know.' She thought for a moment. 'If he goes as far as actually forbidding, it might make me angry, and I'd refuse. Then he'd have to back down. His pride wouldn't allow that, so I don't think he'd risk forbidding me.'

She'd lost me a little. I'd met him in the dark, and there hadn't been any sign of backing down, then. 'Saudi Arabia?' I asked, just to keep things going.

'I suggested it myself. He knew I'd prefer him a long way away. But he pretended he didn't realize. He flew out on the Saturday before, and was due back home about midnight on the following Saturday, our last night.'

'So he was home when you arrived here?'

'What?'

'I understand there was a party at the theatre. You would be late getting home.'

'Oh yes. I see. Yes, I was late.'

'And he was home?'

'Yes. And impatient.'

'He didn't ask how it had gone?'

'As I remember it, he complained he was hungry.'

'But he'd have eaten on the plane?'

'Oh yes. He was due in at Birmingham International at around eleven, he told me. Are you cross-examining me, Mr Patton?'

I got a grip on myself. 'No. Sorry. I was carried away.' But I was intrigued with her husband. 'What does he do?'

'Oh . . . his job? He's Overseas Sales Director at Swallow International. They make pumps.'

Pumps? Bicycle pumps? Running pumps? Foot pumps? I said nothing. My expression must have said it all. She smiled, a little pityingly I thought.

'Oil pumps, Mr Patton. It takes pumps to get all that oil hundreds of miles along the pipes in the desert. Big pumps. Expensive pumps. Rupert – give him his due – knows his job. He has authority and confidence and ability, and a seat on the board. But inside, he's a bit of a coward. Never really risks anything.'

I had a mental image of Rupert Martin, in tropicals, fighting a Land Rover across the desert, with Bedouin rebels sniping from the surrounding dunes.

'Did you say coward, Mrs Martin?'

'His idea of high adventure would be to risk the raspberry jam, when he might get a seed under his denture.' And she laughed, a merry tinkle that modulated into a minor key at the end.

I had the impression that somebody had said that to her, probably Knowles. 'All the same, flying abroad all the time, there has to be some sort of adventure in it.'

'Do you think so? Met at the airport by a limousine, airport to hotel, hotel to office suite, limousine again, back to hotel, and so on, until eventually it's hotel to limousine to airport. Saudi Arabia, Iceland, New York, it makes not a bit of difference to him. At his own office in London, he says something and he's obeyed. Of course. No opposition anywhere. He couldn't *face* it. He couldn't face aggression or any serious dispute. It terrifies him, the very thought of it.'

'I must admit I don't understand,' I said. 'Last night, he faced me. He didn't know who I was or what I might do.'

Smiling, she patted a finger on her lips, reproving it. 'So it was you. Well . . . I'd seen *somebody*. I thought it was a woman. He was doing his protective male thing. He would speak to you with authority, and expect you to back down. Expect it. No . . . assume it. Rupert has not the least trace of imagination in his make-up.'

Which would perhaps explain a similar shortage of sense of humour. But what was she trying to tell me?

'So you see, Mr Patton, why I was able to take that part in the play, without really acting. She was me. The superintendent was her husband. He was insanely jealous of her. His jealousy was driving her distraught. She couldn't move, but what he'd accuse her of seeing a lover. She'd left him several times. And he – in the play – used his authority to force her to return to him, when she knew it was going to be the same old torture again. While *she*, risking everything, pretended to an interest in the private detective her husband had hired. No . . . not pretended. That was real for her. But she risked provoking his jealousy by demonstrating his insanity on that subject – and under his very nose! She wanted the private detective to take her away again, out of it. But he didn't see it. That was what the play was about, and that was the reason for our dispute, Ian's and mine. By letting Llew play the private detective as gay, it completely destroyed the meaning of the play. Completely. But all the same, I didn't have to act it. I *was* intense and full of nerves, and I *knew* what it was like to live with an insanely jealous husband.' She sat back. Her lips were pursed, her hands on her knees. So there!

That, then, was what this was all about. Or was it?

'You're saying your husband is a very jealous man?' I asked, very quietly, very casually.

'He's away a lot. He imagines things.'

'You told me he has no imagination.'

She gestured her impatience. 'There are different sorts of imagination. This just bubbles away inside him.'

'But it's quite unfounded, of course?'

That forced her to her feet. I thought, for one wonderful moment, that she was going to get us drinks. It's a useful ploy for distracting attention. But no, she merely circled the chair then returned to it, leaning on the back of it in order to speak down to me. I wondered whether that had been in the play, too.

'You seem to lack imagination as well, Mr Patton. Do you think I can go on and on, like this, and do nothing about it? In cases like this, it's sometimes a good idea . . . sometimes . . . to pretend to an affair. To throw out a challenge – '

'Like the character in the play,' I interrupted in triumph.

'Yes. Yes, if you like.'

'It was you who pointed out the similarity.'

'But I thought of it first. Before the play. I thought that perhaps I would give Rupert something genuine to face. Can you not *see* it? He'd be terrified I'd leave him for this man, because he wouldn't have the guts to try to get me back. So he'd . . . he'd . . . oh, I don't know. But it would shake him up. At least. Yes. Something like that.'

More likely it would drive him to appeal to the authority of the divorce court, hiding behind the majesty of the law.

75

'And that was where Ian Knowles came in?'

'It was foolish of me. Ian was a bad choice. Nobody would ever accept that he could be a permanent lover. But I played at it, tested it out, and experimented with it. And Ian, well he . . . he laughed at me. Oh, not out loud. But I could see he knew and understood, and he played along. But only play. You understand. He mocked me. I could have killed him.'

But it wasn't Ian Knowles who had died. It was Linda Court. And what she was telling me could have no connection with Linda.

'I trust,' I said, 'that your husband isn't due home yet.'

She showed her teeth, but it wasn't quite a laugh. 'No.'

'Then I'm safe.'

'Yes.'

She seemed to be waiting for me to go on, but I could think of no point we hadn't covered. I levered myself to my feet. 'Well, it's been a very pleasant chat, Mrs Martin. But I must be off.'

'Oh dear. So remiss of me. I never offered you anything – '

'It's all right.'

She was making no move to see me out. Her eyes moved away from me, then back. 'Mr Patton, the plane my husband was on was *not* due back at eleven that night. It landed, on time, at 7.15.'

I had to give that a moment's thought. I played for time.

'How do you know that?'

'I checked.'

'Why did you check?'

'Because he was hungry. Coming back first class, he'd have had a good meal on the plane. But he complained he was hungry. It made me think.'

Clever woman. 'So you checked. And found he would have been home at around eight. Why should you be concerned about that?'

'He lied to me, that's why. He let me assume he'd only just arrived, and it was after midnight. He was spying on me.'

'And?' I was not being encouraging. Purposely.

'Mr Patton, I've been indiscreet. Maybe . . . well, shall we say almost certainly . . . I let it go too far with Ian. If Rupert knows . . . I told you, he will not fight his own fights. I may need protection.'

I breathed deeply, in and out. 'For yourself?'

76

'For Ian. I wouldn't want . . .' She left that hanging; grimaced, gestured. It should have been enough, for a man of my imagination. 'You're investigating. You said you're not a policeman. So, I thought, private – possibly. If I could pay you . . .'

I didn't really listen to the rest. She must have been crazy. Just imagine me going along to Knowles and telling him I was his protector. Protecting him from Rupert Martin and his gang of toughs! I nearly laughed out loud. But that wouldn't do. She was now gesturing wildly, and I had to calm her.

'I'll have to give it serious thought.'

'Oh, if you would, if you would.'

'But I do think you might be exaggerating a little.'

'I hope you're right. Do you *have* to go? Let me find your coat. And you had a hat. I remember that. It's been a great relief, Mr Patton, finding someone to talk to. You *will* think seriously about it . . .' And so on.

I found myself on the gravel outside. The porch light went off. I waited in the dark until I could see enough to find my car.

Right at the end it had all disintegrated. And right at the end had appeared the one gem of information. Rupert Martin had no alibi for the killing of Linda Court. No motive, either, it seemed. But *that* was what she had taken so much trouble to get across. That her husband had no alibi, and could have been home, only two hundred yards from the scene of the murder, at eight o'clock to 8.30.

Clever woman, I'd thought at one point. Clever woman, I thought again, as I bumped into my car. Taking my time over it, I filled my pipe, lit it, and filled the car with smoke. I wound down the window. It took a little time to assemble my thoughts on Gail Martin, until I eventually located the underlying impression – fear. It was what I'd thought when my headlights had glanced at her.

On dipped heads, I took the car out of the drive. As the light disclosed the open gates a figure walked across the space. It was a woman, wearing a long dark coat. She glanced my way, giving a little skip to take herself clear. Instead of turning right, back up the hill, I turned left.

She was aware that I was following her, and began to walk faster. I resisted the temptation to put on the main beams; she would feel impaled. But I increased my speed. She broke into a staggering run, weaving from side to side. At this point it became dangerous. She could slip and fall, and with the nose of the car downhill my brakes might not hold quickly enough on the wet tarmac. I stopped, switched off the engine, locked on the hand-brake, and climbed out. She was still running.

'Marjie!' I called out.

Hampered by the long coat, she could not run very fast. Hampered by my bulk and lack of practice, nor could I.

'Marjie, it's Richard!' I cried.

Still she ran.

'For God's sake!' I panted to myself.

I caught her almost at the spot Linda had died, caught her by the arm and turned her to face me. 'What's the game, Marjie?' I asked. 'It's me. Nobody's going to hurt you.'

'Leave me alone.' She was panting. Her face, turned back, just caught a spill of light from my car further up, her lower lip drawn in, her eyes wide. 'Why the hell can't you leave me alone!'

I tried to speak with calm reason. 'It doesn't do any good, this prowling round here. It's morbid. You can't do anything. All you're doing is upsetting yourself.'

'If you hadn't stuck your nose in,' she told me briskly, 'I'd have been on my way home.'

'And back here tomorrow – and the next day?'

She shook her arm free. 'That's my business.'

'Not entirely, you know. This is private property, and you've been noticed.'

'I know the law on trespass. I'm doing nobody any harm.'

'Yourself.'

She took a breath. 'All right! Then keep out of it. Who asked you, anyway? Tell me that. Keep your nose out, Mr Patton. And go your own way.'

I stood and watched her turn, the coat swirling, and disappear into the darkness of the cul-de-sac. A tiny circle of light appeared ahead of her. There'd been a torch in her pocket. Then that, too, had gone.

Slowly, I plodded back up the slope, into my own glaring headlights. The engine made clicking, cooling sounds as I approached. I had left the door open, and my hand was on it when I noticed that somebody was standing beyond it, behind the light and not much more than a tall shadow.

78

For some seconds, my eyes still adjusting from the headlight glare, he had the advantage of me. All that I could tell was that his voice contained harsh and peremptory authority, and that his intonation had the clipped precision of an army officer. His first words linked with the impression.

'Do you know this is private property!' He demanded, not so much a question as a demand.

Lord, I thought, they're taking it in turns. 'Yes, I'm quite aware of that.'

'You're trespassing on enclosed grounds.'

'I've been visiting a resident.'

'Hrrmph!' he said in disgust.

Now he was becoming more clear. I moved round so that the light was behind me and we were at the same level. He topped me by two inches, which took him over the six feet mark, but I had to take into account his tweed hat and the fact that he had his head back in an attitude of deep offence. A short raincoat covered a tweedy-looking suit, and he was carrying a walking stick in his right hand. There was no impression that he needed it for assistance. He probably slashed at things on his way past, but at that time it was slapping continuously against his right leg in imitation of a riding crop. At his left foot sat a spaniel, which gave the appearance of being more friendly.

It didn't take much detection skill. 'You'll be Colonel Forrester.'

'This property is mine, and you're trespassing.'

'I've done no damage. There's no legal offence involved, unless you order me off and I refuse to go.'

'Tscha!' he said, a bark like a heel hitting a parade ground. 'A barrack-room lawyer. I've met your sort.'

'And I was just about to leave, anyway,' I told him politely.

He might have been deaf, because he went on as though I had not spoken. 'I've been getting complaints. Prowlers. You fit the description. Explain yourself.'

'I've done so. I've been visiting. If you'll just allow me . . .'

'You were chasing a woman. I saw you. I've a good mind to . . .' He stopped, coughing. I realized it was a damp night for a man of his age – I could now see he was at least seventy. Dewlaps wobbled as he spoke. What had he been about to say? Teach me a lesson? Give me a damn good hiding?

I had no intention of explaining my position further, whatever his authority. I'd told him the truth.

'If you'll stand clear,' I told him, 'I'll back round, and leave.'

He teetered back on his heels and showed me his dentures, glinting weirdly in a reflection of the orange sky, then he turned abruptly and began to walk steadily away up the slope. The spaniel trotted at his heels. Perhaps he was going to fetch a pack of foxhounds, I thought sourly, and his voice drifted back.

' . . . that'll teach the bastard a thing or two . . . ' He was talking to his dog.

I got in the car and cut the lights down to sides, saving the battery, and fumbled for my pipe. I'd left it in the ashtray. A pipe relit is never the same. I felt in a poor mood, and reached for the ignition key. It wasn't there.

For a moment my mind went blank as I tried to remember what I'd done with it. Then I knew. I'd left my keys hanging from the ignition lock. There was only one answer: the old fool had taken them.

I could have hurried after him and demanded their return. I could have spoken of theft, as it was. But he need only deny it, I realized. I couldn't call him a liar, because someone else might just have managed to get there before him. I couldn't knock him down and search him. He had deliberately intended to cause me trouble, leaving me stranded there, which was a prime example of inverted logic. It hardly assisted my early exit from his private and secluded property.

What he had no way of knowing was that I'd recently received a lecture on hot-wiring a car, and from the very woman he'd seen me chasing. As though I needed a lecture!

The snag was, when I came to examine the problem closer, that any equipment I possessed for doing the job was in the boot, which was locked, and he had the keys. I searched in the back of the glove compartment and found my extension lead and inspection lamp. It was intended to plug into the cigarette lighter. But what I wanted from it was a length of wire, and I had my pipe-reaming penknife in my pocket. With the door open to operate the internal light, I cut off a yard of wire, and stripped bare about three inches each end. Then I yanked at the bonnet release next to my right knee, and got out to look at the job.

With the bonnet raised and my torch balanced on the cylinder head, I twisted one end of the wire round the live terminal of the battery, then turned my attention to the coil. It had two protruding tongues of metal, each bearing a clip and a wire. One wire went to the distributor head. Ignore that one. To the other I fastened the spare end of my yard of wire.

Strictly speaking, I could have done it firmer with a pair of pliers, but they were in the boot. I now realized the practical advantage of having sprung dog-clips on each end of the wire. They would clip on firmly and quickly. There are sparks, you see. There *were* sparks. Nothing troublesome, because this was only twelve volts, but it sparked and it crackled, and it burnt my fingers. I ran through a few words in my mind. Selected three of the best. Used them sparingly.

I now had to turn the engine over. This can be done by shorting the starter motor terminals with a screwdriver, but mine was locked in the boot. It can be done with a push start, but there was nobody to push me. So I engaged second gear with the clutch out and ran it down the slope, which I did happen to have. Towards the bottom, I engaged the clutch. The engine fired.

The whole operation had taken me about five minutes. An expert can do it in half the time.

Using the drive entrance of the Hope-Court residence, I backed round and headed for home.

And there, of course, I couldn't switch off the engine, the ignition switch being inoperative. All it took was a yank on my bit of wiring, tearing it free, but I wasn't in the sunniest of moods when I went into the house.

'Had a good day?' Amelia asked, ignoring my expression.

I told her what sort of day I'd had.

'Poor dear,' she said. 'Never mind, you've got a spare set of keys.'

'That's not the point.'

The two women looked at each other. 'Let's have it in detail,' suggested Amelia, because she knows how I like to talk things through.

So I did that, and it helped. I had, I realized, a good excuse for going back the next day. I would visit Colonel Forrester and demand the return of my keys, and an apology. Nobody would be able to say I had no right to be in the town. Not even Donaldson.

8

On this point my confidence was misplaced. I drove at a reasonably sedate speed, because I wanted to think up something useful to do while I was there. But nothing came. I seemed to be at a dead end, as far as information was concerned, and neither Tony Brason nor Ken Latchett had shown any inclination to help me. Even the person I was supposedly trying to help, Marjie, had rejected my assistance.

So I drove into Manor Park Estate with no more than a short and brisk visit on my schedule.

The old drive to the manor house, as I've mentioned, was still there, and could not be missed. It curved away, soon after entering beneath the gatehouse, to the right, and having been in existence long before the other approach roads, was of a different surface. Of no surface at all, really, having been hammered into a solid, but uneven, surface by a hundred years of traffic, from ironshod to rubber-shod wheels. Along here, too, there were no trimmed grass verges, and the trees pressed in closely. It had promised to be a brighter day. Beneath the trees, there was no evidence of it.

However, there had long ago been a clearance of trees closer to the house. I came out from beneath them to see the drive continuing in a sweep round the hillside. The house was set high, but not at the top of the slope, a stand of conifers beyond shielding it to the north and east. The open views would have been magnificent, though it did seem, from the narrowness and obscurity of the windows, encroached as they were by insidious creepers, that it might be difficult to see any view at all from them. The building was of a grey stone, the roofs peaking steeply in odd and random directions, and the chimneys, in a design like twisted barley sugar sticks, tall. There would no doubt be a downdraught from those shielding trees.

The drive ended in a wide stretch of gravel. The front entrance was imposing, consisting of a Gothic archway in descending perspective, with a solid dark oak iron-studded door set back in its shadows. I got out of the car and looked round. The vista was all I'd anticipated, and more. Crows circled, crying defiance, above the trees. In the far meadows a horse was galloping, the rider too small at that distance to identify. The only other sign of life was an inanimate Vauxhall Belmont, parked a little way away.

I entered the porch and sought out a bell-push, the old bell-pull lever clearly having retired.

The young woman who opened the door could have been a servant, or a granddaughter. There was nothing in her dress to give me a clue.

'I would like to see Colonel Forrester,' I said.

'And you are?'

'The name is Patton.'

'Ah yes. He's expecting you.'

He would be, no doubt, but not by name. I hadn't offered it to him.

The hall repeated the Gothic theme, beams peaking over my head. The stairs opposite must have been there a couple of hundred years. To my left was an ornate mirror, to my right an antique hallstand that included an umbrella stand. His stick was in it. Also, on its surface, was resting my bunch of keys.

'Mine, I think,' I said, picking them up.

She did not object. 'If you'll come this way.'

There were passageways, just beyond the welcome mat, in both directions. She turned right. I followed. 'The weather's improving, I believe,' she remarked. I agreed that it was. Doubtless, I decided, Colonel Forrester was preparing his apology. If he'd found out my name, he'd at least know my intentions were honourable and my presence on his property bore no illegal undertones.

'In here, if you please,' she told me, opening a door on the left.

It had closed behind her before I realized that the Colonel was not alone. He was standing with his back to a huge, empty fireplace. Sitting, relaxed in the corner of what would have been called a *chaise-longue* when it was made, was Detective Chief Inspector Donaldson.

And he was smiling.

It struck me that I had never before seen Donaldson smiling with any indication of pleasure. I wasn't sure it was an improvement. It was certainly ominous.

The spaniel came across the room to investigate my trousers. I carried the scent of our boxer, Sheba. I bent and fondled his ears.

They love that. He wagged his tail. I had one friend in that room, anyway.

I straightened slowly, giving myself time to assemble my attitude. Casually, I looked round. It was a quiet, sad, and well loved room, its panelling nutty and ancient, thus matching its owner. He was at home there, but not, at this time, completely relaxed. His fingers twitched and his eyes would not meet mine. I saw, now, that he could have been older than I'd guessed. Everything about him sagged, his shoulders, his worsted grey suit, the pouches beneath his eyes, his cheeks, his lower lip, the skin at his neck. He seemed feeble and simple-minded, and yet this could not be so, the way he'd manipulated his way out of his financial situation.

'I see you've got your keys,' he said at last. His voice shook.

I inclined my head, not helping him out.

'I owe you an apology. It was an unconsidered action. I'm sorry if it inconvenienced you.'

His teeth had difficulty with the long words, but that was the way he'd prepared it, so that was the way it had to be said.

Donaldson attracted attention by stirring slightly. It occurred to me that he was a younger version of Forrester. There was the same military doggedness, the same steely hard will towards self-survival. To each of them it would appear that the world was full of predators, each determined to destroy him. They would recognize each other at once, for what they stood for. They would be as one.

And yet, from what followed, they had not apparently met before that morning.

'Let me explain, Richard,' Donaldson said, making it plain that this was to be all chummy and relaxed. 'The Colonel, afraid that he'd been a little severe with you, phoned his friend, who happens to be our Chief Constable, for advice. You'd challenged him on the law of trespass, as I understand it, and the CC, probably not knowing the answer . . . ' Here he permitted himself a rumbling chuckle. ' . . . called Merridew, who referred it to me. I phoned the Colonel, and we thought it best that I should be here when you came. As I was sure you would come, Richard. And here we are.'

'Here we are,' agreed Forrester.

'So we're here,' I said. 'I've got my keys, I've heard an apology. Any reason why I shouldn't leave right now?'

'I thought we'd have a quiet talk.' Donaldson moved his hand in a gesture embracing the ambience of the room. I set off on an amble round, absorbing it physically. 'Somewhere quiet and unofficial,' he continued. 'Restful.'

Crossed polo mallets were mounted above the fireplace, surrounded by sepia photos of suitably dressed officers. Crossed, rusty-looking pig-stickers and shotguns were on each side of the windows. A number of glass cases containing large, stuffed fish, which forever regretted one vital error, decorated the other walls. It was a room of peace and non-violence.

'No feeling of . . . shall we say . . . animosity, Richard?'

He spoke of it as a thing of the past. I paused in front of a pedestal, on which was the bust of a Roman. Perhaps a Roman vet? Brutus? The old man was nodding benignly, Donaldson waiting for a comment.

'I appreciate the thought behind it,' I told him.

'I could've had you in the office,' Donaldson decided, as though he'd just thought of it. He fiddled with his shirt cuffs. 'But we wouldn't have wanted that, would we?'

'I can't say I'd have minded. I've spent many happy hours at the station.'

'Have you?' His eyebrows shot up. 'Have you, now?'

'Perhaps you'll like it better when you move to the new place.'

He frowned, realizing I was deliberately digging at him by ignoring the point he wanted to make. I thrust my hands into the jacket pockets of the blue suit I'd put on, to convince the Colonel of my solidity and worth. I grinned at him, drawing him into a conspiracy against Donaldson that he didn't wish to share. The Colonel blushed, his cheeks actually flaring. 'Well . . . damn it,' he said in embarrassment.

'Colonel Forrester very kindly suggested we could meet here,' Donaldson pressed on with determination. 'Where it need never be known we've met. The Colonel can keep his mouth shut . . . '

' . . . leave you alone if you like . . . hrrmph!' he grunted.

'It's fine with me,' I told him. 'By all means stay.' I beamed at Donaldson. 'I could well need a witness.'

'Hardly for what I've got to say.'

'That bad, is it?'

'I meant it will not be necessary,' Donaldson said, a litle more sharply.

It confused Forrester. 'Go? Stay? Anything you say, old chap.'

'Oh, stay!' Donaldson gestured with impatience, forgetting whose house he was in. Then, realizing he was losing control of the conversation, he gave himself a few seconds. 'I didn't want to meet in the saloon bar of one of your seedy pubs,' he told me, using a phrase he'd clearly prepared and didn't want to waste, playing for time.

'Of course not.'

'I've been going through the file, Richard. Minutely. In detail. Coming back to it after a short space of time, I find, gives one a fresh slant.'

'I've found that very true.'

Encouraged by my agreement, he swept on with more confidence. 'You'll realize, I'm sure, that I wasn't overjoyed when you reappeared on the scene.'

'I got that impression.'

'It seemed to me you intended to involve yourself in a case over which I have complete control.'

'The intention was not to interfere with what you're doing.' Oh, to hell with all this formality, I thought. 'I had the idea I might be able to help a couple of my friends. Your case didn't mean all that much to me. Why should it? Why should you jump to the conclusion that I wanted to interfere? Because you were scared I *would* interfere, and think of something you'd missed! You're not that important to me, Donaldson. If I found out anything, just by chance, then you could have it. Didn't I hand over that letter from Linda, the same day I received it? So why are you in such a tizz . . . '

'Heh!' he said. 'Easy. I wanted this all friendly and reasonable, a little chat.'

I shrugged. 'All right. So I'll tell you what I've been doing. I've been talking to people. There's no law against talking. Nobody has to discuss anything with me, if they don't want to. Tell me the harm I'm doing. Tell me.'

'Shall we say . . . ' He stared at the ceiling. 'Imagine I'm pursuing a certain line of enquiry. I'm not saying I am, but assume so, for the purpose of this discussion. If you, in your talking – as you call it – put the wrong question at the wrong time to a specific person, you could in practice warn him – or her – that *we* might be coming along to ask the same question. And then they'd have time to prepare a different answer.' He was smiling. He knew very well he had a good point.

I tried to recover the initiative. Forrester was looking at me with a speculative eye, which had no sign of the blurring of age. 'But they talk to me, Donaldson. I'm finding this out, and it surprises me. They talk more freely to me because I'm *not* a policeman. Things are said. Facts come up that can be checked. Not by me, perhaps, but by you people. No question of them taking time to prepare different answers. They couldn't change facts.'

'Give me a for-instance,' he challenged.

'All right. Did you know that Rupert Martin did not fly back very late that Saturday night, from Saudi Arabia? His plane got in at around 7.30. It's a fact that can be checked.'

I could see by his expression that Martin had not even entered into his investigation. He recovered well, though. 'And it's a fact,' he observed sourly, 'that you've kept to yourself, intending to continue your enquiries into *my* case.'

'No. I discovered it yesterday afternoon.'

'But I don't remember any message that you'd phoned me.'

I hadn't done so. The information had been intended for Ken. 'The information would've reached you.'

He flexed his lips. 'I'm a bit sceptical about that.'

'Please yourself.' Which was a bit weak, but all I could think to say.

'Oh, I intend to, believe me. I want to tell you, here and now, that I want you out of this town and out of my investigation. I don't want your help, Patton.'

It was what I'd needed to keep me going. Opposition. Orders.

'Very well. I understand. It's what you want. It'd be a fine world if we all got what we wanted.'

'And a finer one if some of the people who want things did something about getting 'em, instead of dreaming about it and waiting for it to be handed over. You've got to fight for what you want in this world, Patton. I had to fight. D'you know what I wanted most, when I was fifteen? Go on, guess.'

His pride had entered into it, his self-justification. 'A train set?' I suggested.

He smiled bleakly. 'I wanted – God help me – to be a police-man. But my father wanted me to go to college and get a degree. I was too young to oppose him – '

'And did you get one?'

'I did. A double-first in sociology. And then I was old enough to go for what I really wanted, and I can tell you, that degree's helped me no end in the force.'

He didn't realize that he was contradicting his own creed. It was I – and countless others like me – who'd had to fight our way up from the ranks, with no degrees behind us. 'So he was right, after all.'

'If you want to see it like that.'

'He provoked you into putting up a fight for what you wanted, and probably for what he did, too.'

He grimaced. 'Hardly. He was in the city. But he *did* teach me to fight. For what I want. And I want you out of this town. Today, Patton, for good.'

He was offering me a fight. I could've hugged him. The en-thusiasm had been dying. But why get me here in order to say it? I pushed him a bit further, to see how far he would go.

'And if I don't? I've got friends in this town, in no way connected with this case. Can't I visit them? Are you going to have a police car following me everywhere? Am I to have my shoulder tapped if I go anywhere near anybody at all? "Move on, sir, if you please!" What say I pop into Ian Knowles's restaurant for a meal? Are you going to have me tossed out on my ear? You know you can't do any of these things, not without facing a charge of harassment. So maybe I want to buy a plank of wood from Bill Askew. Wouldn't it be strange if I didn't have a word with him about his part in the play! And if I hunted for something in the shop that Llew Porter and Clive Matthews seem to run, well ... I'd have to speak to somebody. Or perhaps you're going to have the places bugged!'

'That's enough!'

But I was working up a righteous wrath. 'And if, when I'm doing my casual talking, I should come across something rele-vant to your case – am I going to think: No, mustn't tell Donald-son, he wouldn't like the interference! Damn it all, man, it probably needs only one tiny fact to clear the whole thing. Don't

Damn it all, the man was paranoiac. 'I'm not laughing, and you're wrong. The case was solved.'

'But not closed.'

'Heh!' said Forrester. 'What's this? I'd better go and see – '

'It's all right,' I told him. 'Nothing secret. A man was found dead in a cottage from gunshot wounds. A shotgun. Donaldson, here, formed the idea that Amelia Trowbridge had killed that man. I was able to prove that she didn't, and that somebody else had. Donaldson has been unable to arrest that person. As simple as that.'

'Oh well . . . rather . . . yes,' said the Colonel.

'That lady, Amelia Trowbridge, is now my wife,' I amplified.

'By jove . . . yes,' he said, brightening.

'And the file,' said Donaldson, slipping in discreetly, 'is now very much alive. Thanks to your intervention, Richard. I now feel that something is expected of me. So I've been re-reading the file. In detail, and with an open mind, coming at it afresh. And d'you know what I've spotted?'

'Not until you tell me.'

'Your theory – that wonderful theory that you produced, that night at her house – it's not as solid as it might be. There are aspects that might well be reinvestigated. We did not . . . and this I found strange, Richard . . . we did not have Amelia Trowbridge in at any time to conduct a full interrogation. I think that could now be rectified. And whereas, at the time, until midnight that day, you were a serving officer, and could hardly have been excluded from any interrogation, now you are not. Do I make myself clear?'

And if *that* had not been rehearsed, I'd throw in the towel. 'You make it very clear.'

'I believe you're now settled, so it's unlikely you'll make a run for it.'

'Very unlikely.'

'So I'm not proposing to make any rash or premature moves. In fact, I feel that if you were to leave town now, this morning, and not show your nose again, it's all likely to go quiet. Richard Patton will no longer be in town. I'll be able to slot the file away again in pending, and everybody will forget about it. Including me.'

'I hear what you say.'

91

'So we're agreed?'

I was having difficulty in speaking. My mouth was dry and my teeth seemed to be sticking to my teeth. 'I agree to one thing, Donaldson. You make one move to harm my wife, to harass her, to . . . to do anything to her, and by God, I'll kill you.'

'Here! I say!' said the Colonel.

'As he's my witness,' I said, pointing at him.

Donaldson stretched his lips sourly. His eyes went blank. 'But you're leaving? For good?'

The man was a fool. Didn't he understand? 'Go to hell!' I shouted, though it came out a little hoarsely.

I got out of the house, though I couldn't remember the way. My keys would not find the ignition lock. I sat, trying to force myself into calmness, then managed to fumble tobacco into my pipe and light it. A pipe helps. It reintroduces you to your personality.

Calm at last, I started the engine and swung round on the drive. Donaldson was standing in the open doorway, watching me leave.

On the way home, there was time to marshal my thoughts on it. By the time I turned into the drive at The Beeches I'd discovered that I still had a smile, if I tried hard enough. It was there when I walked into the kitchen.

'You're back early,' said Amelia, a hint of suspicion in her voice.

I dangled the keys. 'Got 'em. And an apology.'

'And the rest?'

'Oh, nothing more to be done there,' I said. 'It's finished, love.'

Then I went up to change, because I couldn't stand the look in her eyes, and because the jacket suddenly felt tight around my chest.

9

I might have known I wouldn't get away with it that easily. Over lunch, she demanded everything in more detail.

'You didn't just march in and demand your keys,' she decided. 'And he didn't just say sorry, here they are. You've been away too long for that. I know how fast you drive, Richard.'

'I was taking it steadily, coming back.'

'And why was that?'

Because there had been times when I couldn't see the road. 'Just thinking.'

'About what?'

And so on. My wife would have made an expert police interrogator. Besides, when she feels it necessary she plays disgracefully on the fact, which she knows well, that I hate to tell lies. I try never to. I succeed when I'm talking to her.

She had me trapped, and it all had to come out. During the telling, her questions gradually became less eager, and eventually ceased. At the end, she was watching me with huge, aching eyes, and the only colour in her face was her lips.

'Poor Richard!' she murmured.

'Eh?'

Mary Pinson had been listening to all this, not before aware how notorious were the people now living with her. Finally, she burst out: 'That horrible man!'

Now I could manage a laugh. 'He's only doing his job, as he sees it.'

'And your friends?' Amelia asked. 'Tony and Marjie.'

'Marjie can work it out herself, without my help. And marriages *do* fail.'

'Without your help.'

'Now . . . Amelia. Besides, I'm not sure I've got any right to interfere.'

'Oh, for heaven's sake!'

'Not as things stand. With you, my dear.'

She looked down at her hands, then up again, raising her chin. 'So we'll leave it there?'

'I think we'll have to.'

It was a miserable afternoon. I tried to get on with the pruning, but kept finding myself with the secateurs perched over a rose I'd just finished. It was a relief when Amelia called me from the top. The light was going, anyway, so I wouldn't have to track all the way back.

'Telephone,' she said, when I got close enough.

'Couldn't you . . . '

'He said it had to be you.'

'Who said?'

'Your friend, Ken.'

'Ah!'

We trooped together through the house, to the room with the phone, which would be the living room when we got it more cheerful. I hadn't wanted Amelia to accompany me, as clearly Ken had not heard that I was no longer involved, and it would require a little diplomatic discussion with him. But she was determined to be in on it.

'Ken?' I said. 'Sorry to keep you waiting.'

'I've been looking round town for you, Richard. Listen—'

'Have you spoken to Donaldson?'

Amelia wasn't simply listening to my end, she was now standing close enough to hear both.

'Not today. He was out all morning, heaven knows where.'

Richard did, too. 'Where are you?'

'At home. I took an hour or two off. Privilege of rank. Do you want to hear this?'

'Say on.'

'I've got 'em, Richard.' The triumph in his voice warmed my ear. 'He was out, as I said. I tried a few keys. After all, I *am* his inspector, so I've got a right to the Linda Court file. I've got copies for you of most of the official photos, and photostats of all the statements we've taken.'

'Oh . . . ' I cleared my throat. 'Fine.'

'Cath says come over, and you can have dinner with us. Seeing I'm home early, you might say. She's here now . . . '

'Richard! It's been ages! You must come. Bring your wife . . . '

'I don't know . . . Cath . . . '

Amelia clamped her hand over the mouthpiece. 'Yes!' she hissed.

'Richard?' asked Ken. 'You there?'

'I can't,' I whispered to Amelia. '*You* certainly can't.'

'Richard?' Ken insisted.

'I certainly can. And ask him to invite Donaldson, if you like.'

'Richard? Are you still there?'

Amelia took the phone from my hand. 'It's Amelia, Ken,' she said. 'We'd love to come. Richard can hardly wait to see what you've got.'

'As soon as you can, then?'

I grabbed it back. 'Ken, hold on . . . '

'Yes!' Amelia's voice was a sharp and crisp directive to me. Only twice have I heard that tone. The first time was when she told me we were to be married.

'Ken,' I said quietly, 'we'll be very pleased to come. We'll be there in . . . what? A couple of hours.'

'You lovely man,' put in Cath, and she hung up.

I replaced the phone slowly. 'Now look what you've done.'

'You can't go on dodging the situation.'

'Do you imagine Donaldson was just playing with words?' I demanded. 'I was *there*. I could see his face. He not only meant it, he was looking forward to carrying it out.'

'We'd better go and get ready.'

'You're not taking it seriously,' I accused her.

'And you're not taking it logically, Richard. Think. You told me that you had a feeling . . . '

'My feelings!' I said in disgust.

' . . . that something was wrong. About the part Marjie had in it, and the way Linda died. All right. So you wanted photographs. Get a clear mental picture, you said. And now – we go there and you get a picture, and maybe some useful thing will come out of it. If it does, you could well have something encouraging to tell Marjie, and it'll be over. If your interest is only in that.'

'Oh, it is.'

'And if you don't see anything, then there'll be nothing more you can do, and it will still be over. So, in either event, it'll be a quick in-and-out, and Donaldson need never know.'

But she was only trying to polish a very rough possibility. Donaldson, I was now certain, was unstable, and there was no point in considering his reactions in any logical way. And he *would* know. I felt that.

We were on our way an hour later. Amelia had taken immense trouble, I think to impress Donaldson, if it became necessary. The Latchett residence was on the eastern side of the town, so that no detours needed to be made. It was straight through the devastated industrial district and into the former working-class suburb.

It was a street of Victorian red-brick terraced houses, built solidly, squashed in tightly, and three storeys high. There was a lick of gentility in Ken's street, hinted at by the front downstairs mullioned bay windows, but with no frontages to speak of. There was just room to stand within the openings where the metal gates had been, before the 1939–45 conflict took them as war effort. There was no parking space. In the days the streets were laid out, no one could have envisaged the residents with their own private carriages.

The street was now lined with such private carriages, all with their nearside wheels up on the pavement, and I finally managed to park a hundred yards past the house. When we'd walked back, Ken had the front door open.

'Saw you drive past,' he said. 'Murder, ain't it!'

I don't think he and Amelia had met more than a couple of times, and then it had been officially. Nevertheless, he took both her hands in his, held her back so that he could look at her, then kissed her on the cheek.

'You're looking splendid, Amelia.'

She smiled. 'Richard's told me all about you.' She could hardly return the compliment with sincerity, because Ken looked worn and tattered. But he was still the ladies' man, though his pleasantries contained no background intention. Cath was his woman. Always had been. You could feel it in his attitude when he took us through to meet her. They had no children. Cath used to say: 'Who needs children when they've got Ken?' But it was always said with a shadow behind the eyes.

At one time I'd rather fancied Cath, back in the days when I was working a beat, but like a fool I introduced her to Ken. No chance for me then. She and Amelia seemed to get along fine. Contrasts, I suppose. Amelia is short, sturdy, dark hair and dark eyes, all nervous energy, and Cath nearly as tall as me, angular and brittle, outspoken, slim, and going rapidly grey.

'You two men,' said Cath, 'can go into the front room and have your bit of a conference. We've got things to talk about.'

The house was built one room behind the other. No hall; one room opened into the next, with the stairs inset in the wall from a door in the middle room. In the front – where *had* Ken obtained all the Victorian rubbish to make the room feel at home? – Ken waved a bottle of sherry at me, I nodded, and he pointed to the large manila envelope on the richly ornate sideboard.

'I got what I could,' he said. 'It's the marrow out of the file. Most of the rest is routine reports. See if it helps, Richard.'

I sat on his musty settee, facing a low table that had had its legs cut down – not accurately; it wobbled – and spread it all out.

There were photocopies of statements made by Linda Court's associates, even the ones she worked with and for and against in Birmingham and London. I gave these no more than a quick glance. Ken and his mates had established that none could have carried out the necessarily complex performance with the car, the camelhair coat, and the shoulder bag, which had taken quite a chunk out of the week leading up to Linda's death.

There were also statements made by her associates in this town, which of necessity, because she seemed to have no close friends, were her colleagues from the drama group. Twenty-three of these, because the investigation had been thorough.

Ken put a glass of sherry on the table surface.

'You'll see, when you get time to go through 'em in detail, that not one of them could've got away from that theatre long enough to have *waited* for Linda to get home. Not unless it was sheer luck. There's a cross-mesh of linking check-ups, one person for another. I've included a breakdown layout of who saw whom and when. There're no gaps, Richard. It's watertight.'

I took his word for it, putting the statements aside. The photos, that's what interested me. They were eight-by-sixes, flash shots in colour, one or two of them slightly imperfect from a stray flare or reflection. Which was why they were spares, and why I had them before me. The mute testimony of a vicious crime.

'Sharp and clear,' I said.

'Good man with a good camera. The top one's exactly as we found things.'

As it would be. A permanent record of the scene of the crime.

I was looking at an Austin Allegro, facing right in the picture. With flash pictures the light fades rapidly with distance, but I could just see that the other side of the car was hard against the shrubbery. I already knew the scene was the cul-de-sac outside Linda's home, so the shrubbery was the boundary. It was a two-door saloon. The driver's door was wide open.

She had been about to get in the car, bent forward. Blood was detectable on the back of her head. She had fallen face forward on to the driver's seat, her arms spread, one hand flopped over the steering wheel. Hips and legs were outside the car. Her left leg was twisted awkwardly.

There were several close-up shots of her head and the wound, then there was one of her right foot. The car keys, with leather tab, were lying on the ground just outside the car, beside her foot.

Another shot, of a length from the branch of a tree, close-up, a white ruler beside it so that the diameter could be seen as two inches, this diameter being at the point where blood showed on the bark.

The next print was of the same length of wood, but from further away, so that its distance from the car, about six feet, could be seen.

They would have got these shots before they moved in closer. The meticulous care in covering every possible aspect of the scene was evident. Patience and detail; the CID officer's watchwords. I was now getting my clear picture, but nothing was happening.

A picture from the front of the car. It told me nothing, though it indicated the buckled metal where the bonnet lock had been broken. Another picture from the front, but this time with the bonnet raised. There was no tingling to my spine, no prickling of the hair at the nape of my neck. Nothing.

The camera had come in close, then. There was a half-downwards shot of the engine compartment. It clearly showed the hot-wiring, the dog-clips screwed to each end of the wire, and clipped as I'd done it with my own car, one to the live terminal of the battery, one to the tag on the coil.

The wrong tag.

Slowly I put the prints down on the table, and sat back. 'You didn't tell me that, Ken.'

'What?'

'You said the hot-wiring was still there. I assumed you meant it'd been left behind, unconnected. But it's still connected, and what's more, to the wrong tag on the ignition coil.'

'I don't see . . . ' He stopped. I sat back and took a sip of sherry, waiting for him to get it. 'But that doesn't fit at all,' he decided. 'It doesn't make sense.'

'Got a magnifier?' I asked.

He went across the room and found a magnifying glass in a cupboard drawer. I took it, and bent over the print. Just to be certain.

'Yes, that's definitely the wrong tag,' I decided.

'But it wouldn't even *run* like that!' His eyes opened wide. 'Ye gods!' he whispered.

98

'Who arranged for the car to go to forensic?'

I knew how it would've been: the ME coming to pronounce death, and to give a reasonable approximation of the time of death, the wagon coming to take the body to the pathologist for a post mortem examination, a possible identification made – her shoulder bag was shown to be on the passenger's seat in one of the photos. Perhaps Donaldson would have come along, then drift away to leave it to Ken. It would be getting light. Eventually, they'd have to take the car and the residual evidence (the length of tree branch and anything else they might find on the scene) to forensic at County HQ.

'I think Tony did all that,' said Ken. 'I had to contact her mother, the judge. She was at Stafford Crown Court for the week.'

'Let's ask him.'

The phone was handy on the window-sill. Ken dialled Tony's number from memory, and when he got the ringing tone he handed it to me. When he eventually answered, Tony seemed short of breath.

'Mr Patton. Sorry, I was out at the gate.'

'Just a little point, Tony. Was it you took the Allegro to forensic?'

'Not took it. They sent a low-loader, and winched it on. Blood-stains inside, see, and possible prints.'

'Yes, of course. So you wouldn't know . . .' I paused, not being able to imagine how he could know what I wanted.

'Know what?'

'If the battery was flat.'

'Oh – I know that. The lights were switched to parking, and there wasn't a glimmer from 'em. Wouldn't be, would there, if it'd been there all night?' He was impatient. 'If it matters.'

'It matters, believe me. Is Marjie there, Tony?'

'Why the hell d'you think I was out at the gate?' he said tersely. 'She's not here. I've been home an hour, and she's off on one of her blasted walks.'

But I was in a position to pronounce an end to all that. 'I've got to talk to her. Can we come over? Ken and me.'

'I suppose.'

'Right.' I hung up. 'Ken,' I said, 'that car could not possibly have run, wired like that. And there's no mistake. Here – you

99

haven't got a car maintenance manual around?'

'One for the car I had before. Thought I'd do my own work on it, but I'm no mechanic.'

'It doesn't matter what car, the wiring systems are all the same on these older ones.'

He eventually ferreted inside a cupboard and found it. We studied the wiring diagram. It was as I'd believed: the tag to which the dog-clip had been attached was connected to the contact breaker points, and from these straight to the earthing connection. If the points happened to be closed – as they usually are when the engine is at rest – it would have produced a direct short across the battery terminals. Which would run the battery flat, exactly as it had been.

'That's it, then,' I said, feeling a great load lifting from me.

'Come on, you two,' said Cath from behind us. 'It's on the table.'

We glanced at each other. Ken said: 'Cath's a marvellous cook.' We could not walk away from it, however urgent I now felt it to be to talk to Marjie.

We ate in the middle room, their living room. The old storage cupboards still filled the alcoves each side of the fireplace. The meal was superb. It was protracted. I sat in agony, mentally urging it onwards, whilst having to give full and loving attention to each of the three courses. We reached the coffee stage. Ken and I lit up, me following his lead.

I said: 'If you two ladies will excuse us, Ken and I need to pop along and see Marjie Brason.'

Amelia met my eye. 'Something?'

'Yes, something. It should please her.'

'Then you'd better go,' said Cath. 'We'll be happy enough here.'

We smiled our way outside. 'My car,' said Ken. 'It's nearer.'

I sat beside him. There had been changes. Streets I'd driven along in both directions were now one-way, but Ken knew them all, and could thread his way neatly through the centre of the town. It was now nine o'clock, and the streets were fairly clear. We barely exchanged a word, me putting it together in my mind, and Ken no doubt cursing himself for having missed a point.

But so had Donaldson.

We drove past the gatehouse of Manor Park Estate.

'Who found the body?' I asked.

'Didn't I say? It was Rupert Martin. Very early – about six.'

'What was he doing there at six? A morning stroll?'

'Taking the dog for a walk, before he drove to his office in London.'

Dog? 'He hasn't got a dog.'

'He had then. Had it put down, I believe.'

'What was the matter with it?'

'Nothing. Apparently. I think it was because it began to snarl at him whenever he went near his wife. Or so she said.'

'That could make things difficult.'

So maybe there'd been something in what she'd told me about him.

'A dog or a bitch?' I said.

He glanced at me, laughing. 'I didn't ask. This another of your details, Richard?'

'I don't know.' But a male dog would become protective of a female, if it sensed aggression from a man.

Tony was still at the gate, looking very cold and very white in the orange street-glow.

'Hasn't she come back yet?'

'God, no! It's never been this long. And I daren't go off in one direction in case she comes back from another.'

'Let's go inside,' I suggested.

'How can I –'

'Get you warm, a few words to be said, then we'll all go out and have a look. You know very well she'll be in Manor Park.'

'I suppose.'

'Five minutes only. I promise you.'

He grumbled something, but led the way inside the house, which was itself cold because he'd left the front door open.

'I'll put the kettle on.'

'Only if you want something hot yourself.'

He shook his head.

We went no further than the hall. He was poised, prepared to rush out. A nerve was pulsing in his forehead, and his eyes were wild.

'She'd been getting worse, Mr Patton,' he told me. 'It's the tablets. I told her. Get 'em changed, I said. But she wouldn't listen. I'm going off my head with it. How can I even *go* to work, and leave her . . . I never know, when I come home . . . like now. Last night she locked herself in the bedroom. Oh Christ, I don't know what to do!'

'Perhaps I can help. Listen, Tony. Are you listening?'

He nodded, eyes deep-set and haunted.

'The car was found with the engine dead, Tony. The hot-wiring was still in place, still connected – and I don't think the sidelights were what ran it down.'

Tony was watching my lips, frowning. 'What's the battery got to do with anything?'

'I think we're on to something. Ken and I have been taking another look at the official photos. And d'you know what . . . the hot-wiring was still connected, as I said, but more than that, it was connected to the wrong tag of the coil. That mean anything to you, Tony? Think. Come *on*, Tony, think.'

His eyes cleared. 'It wouldn't run like that. Couldn't.'

'Not only that, but it would also drain the battery. And it *was* flat. What d'you make of that?'

He was struggling to get his brain into focus, beyond the barrier of his worry and exhaustion. 'I don't see – '

I was impatient. I took his arm and shook it.

'Linda Court told Marjie her car had been stolen in town. How *could* it have been, with the hot-wiring done wrong?'

'What're you getting at? Can't it wait? Marjie . . . ' He made a feeble gesture.

'Tony, once that wire was connected, the car wasn't going to go anywhere. Therefore it was hot-wired after it was driven to where it was found, and there's only one way that could have happened. The damn car wasn't stolen at all. It was driven there in the normal manner, the engine was switched off, and the hot-wiring was then connected. There was only one person who could've done that, the person who was told by Marjie, that very same evening, how hot-wiring was done. So Linda Court must have done it herself. She was therefore lying. She was therefore lying about the rest. Her car was not stolen once, let alone twice, her coat was not taken and returned, her shoulder bag was not taken and left hanging on the gatepost. The whole thing was a load of lies. God knows why. It was a trick, and Marjie has not one thing to blame herself for. She was the one being tricked. *That* was what I wanted to tell her, but *you* can, now. When she's home. Let's go and find her.'

'What the hell're we waiting here for?' he cried, and the three of us almost ran from the house.

They didn't give me time to add the very important point: that we still didn't know the time Linda had arrived home. But no one else could have guessed it, either.

10

Once more we used Ken's car. Tony fetched the torch from his, and Ken had one. But I hadn't.

Ken didn't drive fast. There were many detours that Marjie might have taken on the way home, so we paused at each road junction to stare down sidestreets. It was not logical that she would have diverted, but we all knew that, for Marjie, logic was no longer relevant.

We parked opposite the five-barred gate and climbed over it. There was nothing but blank darkness ahead, no pin-point of light that would indicate her presence. This, and the gatehouse the other side of the estate, were the only practical entrances. So far, we had this one covered.

Tony led the way. He was too eager and anxious to be leading, but at this stage Ken said nothing, pressing at Tony's heels and preserving his own batteries. I, torchless, trailed behind. By the time we reached the bridge I realized that there would have to be a certain amount of organization involved. There was really no point in my joining one of them, as two would be no more use than one, with only one torch between them. It would also be necessary for the others to split up, so some method of signalling had to be arranged.

At the far side of the bridge I halted and said: 'Here, hold on. We'll have to make arrangements.'

Tony said something that sounded impatient. Ken said that I was quite correct.

Up to this point there had been only one possible approach for her, but from where we were standing there was open grassland in each direction, reaching back to where the trees and under-growth began. We had no certain knowledge that Marjie, in her travels, kept to the park roadways. She could well have walked the riverside bank, up-river, or the lakeside bank to our right.

'What say I wait here,' I suggested. 'You two could cut through to the cul-de-sac, then a bit further on you'll have to split-up yourselves. She'll have to come to the bridge, so if you miss her I'll be able to intercept.'

'We'll need a signal,' said Ken.

'How about this?'

I put two fingers in my mouth and produced a shrill whistle. Two whistles. In the still, damp and heavy night, the sound would travel a long way. I got an echo from the facing trees. They tried it. Successfully. It was a long while since either of them had carried police whistles, and they were not equipped with two-way radios.

'Two whistles,' I said, 'means I've found her. Then we all meet back here.'

'Let's get on with it,' Tony grumbled. He had no patience for organization, and it must have been sounding, to him, like an official search. Which was a little premature.

They set off. I stood at what would be Marjie's approach end of the bridge, stood with feet apart, lit my pipe, and waited quietly for my eyes to adapt completely to the dark.

As they did so, I gradually became aware of the night sounds reassembling themselves around me. The river, recently re-freshed by the rain, seemed to be more urgent in its travel be-neath the bridge. I could detect the suck and gurgle as it dispersed its flow into the lake. There was the rustling and chuckling of wildfowl further away on my right, a sudden splash and flutter of disturbance, then silence again. Way ahead I heard the sounds of Tony and Ken calling to each other.

I could now detect form in the trees ahead, at the top of the slope. Form, but no movement of shadows. Some minutes had passed since I'd seen any flick of light from either of their torches. There was one more distant shout, then silence again, but there had been no whistled signal. Away to my left there was a sudden scream, an animal sound, then the night was silent.

I could not see the Hope-Court residence. The assumption had

104

been, from its location, that it would have an open view over the lake, but I could see no lighted windows.

Irked by the lack of action, I turned and strolled back over the bridge, the ancient, wet half-logs slippy beneath my feet. There was enough width for a motor vehicle, but the entire structure was wood, the guard rails themselves being trimmed slim poplars, no doubt. I wondered whether it was a preserved monument, jumped up and down to test its solidity, peered at my watch, and remembered I was wearing the non-luminous one. It was a guess that they'd been gone for twenty minutes. I lifted my head and sniffed the night. A smell of old, wet wood and of wildfowl, and the faint tang of pine.

In the centre of the bridge I stopped. I leaned back against the guard rail, my elbows on top to support me. My left elbow met nothing.

I turned, and felt along carefully. The gap was about three feet. The breaks felt sharp and fresh. I flicked on my lighter, but it didn't help much, except to confirm that the two points of break were new and clean.

I stood back. The implication was unpleasant. I could see nothing of the lake but a dark surface. Quickly, I returned to the end of the bridge and again looked back. The orange streetlight glow was now reflected in the far rim of the lake. I retreated backwards up the grass slope, moving sideways, experimenting until almost the whole of the far hundred yards of the lake now presented a flat reflection of orange.

Where the river surged into the lake it had cleared itself a moving channel, but in less than twenty yards the placid bulk of the lake absorbed it. To each side of the central flow there was a backwater of current, in which debris had collected. By positioning myself I could consider at least one half of the foam-flecked surface this presented. There were portions of tree, plastic bags, beer cans half submerged, the detritus of our tidy society trapped in the backwater. There was also a large, dark shape, which, as I stared and tried to maintain a clear focus on it, resolved itself into a black, spread coat and a blob of floating hair. No pink flesh was visible, no face, no hands. She was lying face down.

I put two fingers into my mouth and whistled twice. It is impossible to impart urgency into a solitary signal. I did it twice more, then I ran back across the bridge, my feet uncertain on the slimy wood.

The idea was to find my way along the lake bank that side, to see whether I could reach her. As I recalled it, the hundred yards or so of wild ground between the lake and the wall contained nothing but scrub. It was, in fact, mostly nettles and dead bracken. I waded through this, my arms held high. From this side, there being no sky-glow to reflect on the surface, all I got was an unbroken black, and I very soon lost touch with where to look. Lifting my eyes, I saw torchlight break through the trees opposite, so I struggled back.

Ken was the first, for which I was thankful. I met him on the bridge.

'What is it?' he demanded. 'Where is she?'

Not saying anything, because I couldn't trust my voice, I took the torch from his hand and swept its light along the guardrail. The gap told its own story. Then I redirected it across the water. The floating body was not drifting, but it rocked a little. Ken whispered something viciously obscene.

She was ten feet from the bank. It was not going to be easy to bring her in. Behind us I heard a shout. Tony's light bobbed towards us as he ran down the slope.

'Marjie? Marjie!' he shouted.

We stood and waited for him, Ken's torch now directed at our feet. I still held it, so it fell to me to break the news, which I did with its rays. Tony made a sound as though somebody had punched him in the stomach. 'Oh God! Oh God! Oh God!' he said softly.

But it didn't go away.

'I'll get down to the car,' Ken said quietly into my ear. 'We'll need help here. Can you handle him, Richard?'

I nodded. Tony was now silent. His own torch had taken over, as though he dared not remove its light. The spray of illumination wavered around her.

'Accident, Richard?' Ken asked, so quietly that it barely disturbed the air.

'Seems so. It'd be more kind.'

Ken went to call in for assistance. I stood beside Tony, and he said nothing. There are appropriate words that can be said at such times, and there are times when words are appropriate. This situation seemed to fit neither. We stood close together, and did not exchange a word, not exactly silent because Tony was making noises in his throat.

Ken came back and drew me aside.

'There'll be a team here soon. You take my car, Richard, and tell Cath I'll be late. You know the drill. She'll want to come back – for Tony. Tell her no. I'll try to get him involved with the routine. It's the only thing. You know that.'

He was now the officer-in-charge, and there was no doubt who was handing out the orders. He gave me his keys.

'Your car?' I asked. 'And you?'

'I'll get a lift home. Whenever it is. See you, Richard.'

'I'll be in touch.'

'Accident,' he said. 'I'll see it's brought in as an accident.'

We both knew that there could be a suggestion of suicide.

'Yes,' I said, and I walked away, my legs aching.

There were blue lights flashing in the distance when I drove away. No sirens. There was no desperate hurry.

By a miracle, the space Ken had been using was still vacant. I manoeuvred his car in with difficulty, there was so little space, and when I'd got that done I saw that Cath was already at the front door.

She looked from me to the car, back again, and asked: 'Ken?'

'He's detained, Cath. There's been an accident. Marjie went into the lake at Manor Park.'

'She's . . . ' Her hand flew to her lips.

'Dead. I'm sorry. You must have known her.'

She backed away from the door, and as I moved to go past, her face crumpled as it hit her.

'Marjie! Oh no! No!'

She brought her hands up again to cover her face, and supported herself against the wall. I shut the door behind us with my foot. She was sobbing. 'Cath!' I said softly, and I put my arm around her shoulders.

For a second she responded to the pressure, and I thought she was going to fling herself into my arms, but then she straightened, stiffening her shoulders.

'I'm all right, Richard.'

'I'll get Amelia . . . '

107

She sniffed, but her throat was still congested when she spoke. 'Wait. Richard . . . *he's* here.' She clutched at my arm.

I looked at her in surprise. Her eyes were wide, and what I saw in them was trepidation, almost fear.

'Who's here?' I asked gently.

But she was nodding, and I knew suddenly, from her expression, whom she meant. She had read my mood, and knew I was close to an emotional explosion. Still her fingers were painful on my arm. Donaldson. And he was sitting in there that very moment, talking to my wife. Questioning, probing, dismembering. It had seemed, from the moment that I'd seen Marjie's dead body, that I'd been possessed by a tight and baffled anger. I'd found something, and Marjie had been snatched from me before I could get to her with the pleasure of imparting it. I'd found it, but too late. The anger was at myself, for not having realized how wrong it had all been, and earlier. I had managed to contain the anger, but only by subjecting myself to a stiff and formal discipline, as though any abrupt movement would spill it over, and I'd be lost in stupid, impotent fury.

And now this! I felt it churn inside me. There was even a hope, which I suppressed at once, that I might find Amelia in tears, so that I'd be justified in a physical attack.

Cath must have seen the intention in my eyes. I shook her hand free, but still she stood in front of me.

'I've been with them, Richard, every minute.'

I breathed deeply, twice, then went to open the communicating door into the living room.

They were sitting there, side by side on the settee, Donaldson gesturing with a cigarette, and he must have said something amusing because my wife was laughing. Not at him, but with him. I could have told her that this was the softening-up process, that if I'd not appeared at that time he would have chosen his moment to pounce. In practice, it did win him a small victory.

'What the hell's this?' I demanded, fracturing the mood.

Amelia's eyes were startled. 'Richard!'

He was rising slowly to his feet. This he managed to do lithely, with no apparent effort, when I would have needed a hand to the settee arm. 'Ah, there you are,' he said smoothly, a smile on his lips but not confirmed in his eyes. He was furious that I'd returned too early. 'Your wife and I – '

108

'Didn't I tell you! Didn't I warn you!'

Already I found myself in the wrong. It is always dangerous to lose control of your emotions.

'We were having a pleasant chat, Richard,' Amelia told me with a warning tone in her voice that I should have heeded.

'So I see.'

'Cath has been with us every minute.'

'I did say that,' murmured Cath from behind me.

But my eyes were fastened on Amelia's. 'He wouldn't have dared to speak to you without a witness,' I told her.

'Come now, Richard,' said Donaldson, without any hint of anger. 'This won't do, you know. If this was anything in the way of an interrogation, you know I'd have had to do it at the station. It came to my attention that you were in town. Again! I wished to meet your wife, after this length of time. There is no more to it than that.'

Only because he hadn't dared, only because this wasn't a sufficiently unnerving setting, only because it would have been clear to him that I was due to return at any moment. So he'd been playing himself in, ensuring that if he needed to pounce on her in future, and in earnest, she would go with him into the trap with a calm and even friendly confidence.

I could not explain this to Amelia. It was clear she did not understand my attitude, and that she was already believing I had exaggerated the menace Donaldson could represent.

It was an agony to produce a smile and toss it at him.

'If you say so,' I assured him stiffly, 'then it must be so.'

'Latchett's not with you?'

'It's what I came to tell Cath. He's been detained. While we were out, we came across a drowning incident. A body in the lake at Manor Park.'

'Foul play?'

'It doesn't seem like it. There's a broken rail on the bridge, so it could have been an accident. But I think it might be a good idea if you went along there. The death of a police officer.'

His head lifted. 'Who?' he demanded.

'Woman Police Sergeant Brason.' Amelia gave a little gasp, her eyes big. 'Not a CID officer, so not one of yours, but as a courtesy, perhaps . . . '

I was being, frankly, sarcastic on purpose, not liking the way he'd initially failed to respond. If it wasn't foul play, he wasn't interested. But now he was.

His eyes went cold, and one hand came up to smooth his lapel. I'd challenged his professionalism.

'Latchett's there?'

'Sent for a team.'

'I'd better get along.'

'Yes. It's quicker to go to the rear entrance of the park, in Courtney Street.'

'Thank you.' He turned with exaggerated courtesy to Amelia. 'I must rush away. I'm sorry we were interrupted, Mrs Patton. We should talk again, some time.'

Amelia was plainly confused by the criss-cross of emotions involved. She had seen him change abruptly from a charming and amusing companion to a bitter and saddened policeman, his officialdom shaken by his concern. I hadn't expected this commitment. He thrust past me with impatience.

I went after him, and halted him before he got to the front door. 'There's something else.'

He swung round. 'More important?'

'Possibly.'

I went across to the table on which the photographs and photocopies still lay, and picked up the one showing the hot-wiring still connected.

'I told you I'd let you have anything I come across,' I said flatly. 'I've come across this. You'll see the hot-wiring's still connected. I'm told that the battery was flat.'

'So?' His eyes lifted to mine, and they were empty.

'Think about it. Look at it through a magnifier. If it tells you nothing, then ask Inspector Latchett.'

He took the print from my fingers, went to the door, and slammed it behind him. It is not polite to slam somebody else's front door.

As I turned away, I realized bitterly that I'd betrayed Ken's trust. If I'd not been so eager to gain a point over Donaldson, I wouldn't have produced the photograph, but left it to Ken. Now Donaldson would know that Ken had been working with me, and behind his back.

We sat, Amelia and Cath and I, around the gas fire in the living room. Cath had not recovered from the shock of Marjie's death, and at intervals Amelia went and made tea, and we talked it through.

We could not leave Cath on her own, though she would be used to waiting into the middle of the night for Ken's return. We sat, and tried to keep to generalities, but the topic kept drifting back to Marjie and Tony, and their marriage.

Cath and Amelia were on the settee, me in the facing easy chair. It was a long while before it became clear to me that Amelia was referring the conversation less and less towards me. I was seeing more of her shoulder than of her face. Because it was clear that I knew more than either of them about the marriage under discussion, I occasionally slipped in a comment. Although Cath would then glance at me, frowning perhaps because she didn't agree with my opinion, Amelia simply waited for me to finish, not turning towards me.

At the times when Cath, asserting her rights as a hostess, disappeared into the kitchen, Amelia sat quietly, her eyes down at the fingers in her lap. We waited for the time when it would be reasonable to leave. As far as I was concerned, that time had long passed.

Ken phoned, somewhere near midnight, and Cath came back from the front room to say they'd taken the body away, that Ken was now at Tony's place, and he'd be home when he was satisfied Tony was fit to leave. It seemed a signal for our departure. Amelia rose to her feet, smoothing her skirt.

There were no platitudes that exactly fitted the situation. We said good night quietly, then walked up the street towards where I'd left the Stag.

Still Amelia was silent.

A mile clear of the town, she led in gently. 'I can appreciate that you were upset at seeing him there, Richard, but that doesn't excuse your appalling manners.'

'The situation was not what you think, my dear.'

'I know what the situation was. I was involved in it, and had been for half an hour. Cath was with us, and she could tell you that Mr Donaldson was no more nor less than the senior officer of her husband, paying a social call and being polite . . . '

'I could tell you . . . '

' . . . and charming.'

I was silent as the wet tarmac whined beneath the tyres.

'Richard?'

'If I say one word, it'll put me in the wrong.'

'And please let's have no self-pity. You *were* in the wrong.'

I sighed. 'You can't imagine the background of the situation.'

'But I can.' And now her voice held a bit of a snap. To imply a weakness in her imagination had been a mistake. I decided to remain silent, to see how it developed.

'Do you realize, Richard, that the whole business about Mr Donaldson – everything I know about him and your relationship – has come from you? Think back. Have I really *met* him? He was no more than a police officer to me. But you've made him a rounded and complete person, in my mind. You, Richard. You've presented him as a stiff and inhuman puppet, with no emotions other than his resentment of you. He hates you! That's been the theme. And yet, when I meet him myself, in circumstances where you couldn't influence my opinion –'

'Now hold on,' I cut in quickly, sensing the way things were heading.

'Oh no! I will not hold on. All you want to do is throw in some more of your vicious remarks about him.'

'Vicious!'

'Yes. Arising from *your* hatred of *him*. Not the other way round.'

'You couldn't have been listening.'

'It was clear from what he said . . . *do* watch the road, Richard . . . from what he said it was clear he has the greatest admiration for you –'

'Christ!'

'And profanity won't help you. It's got to be said. Just think back. You said he resented you, from the time when you undermined his theory that I was a murderer. His first case! But Richard . . . it was your *last* one. And he'd been sent in to take charge of it. And he'd taken your job with a rise in rank. And I've never realized! All the while, it's been you who've resented *him*.'

'What nonsense!'

'You're driving too fast, Richard.'

She didn't mean that I was driving dangerously, but that I would get us home too quickly. Mary had not seen us in dispute, not in such serious dispute, certainly. Neither of us wished to upset her. I slowed. I did better than that, I spotted a parking lay-by ahead, and drew into it. With the engine cut and my window an inch wide, I took my time in filling my pipe, even though I was smoke-dried and had no intention of lighting it.

'I can see he's completely bamboozled you,' I said at last.

'Not so.'

'He's presented you with an image of a Chief Inspector Donaldson who doesn't exit.'

'Are you telling me I wouldn't have been able to see through that sort of thing?'

I would not normally tell her such a thing. She would have spotted it in a second, at any other time. The surprising thing was that she had not. Amelia is always so perceptive. Donaldson, clearly, had driven himself to a superb effort.

'Amelia, I think you already realize he was putting on the best act of his life.'

'That's a very smug thing to say.'

'Is it?'

'Calmly assuming you know what I'm thinking.'

'You told me yourself, in effect. Remember? You said you were thinking that I've built up a background of hatred for this man, simply because he took over my job.'

'With promotion. Which wasn't offered to you.'

'It was a bit of a jolt, I must say. But not as bad as you make it sound.'

'I don't make it,' she said with forced patience. 'Mr Donaldson appealed to me . . . '

'Appealed?'

'Appealed to me to do my best to persuade you . . . well, to get you to understand . . . that you have nothing to dislike him for. He's always been willing to be your friend . . . '

I reached forward and started the engine.

'Richard!' My interruption had been graceless.

'Let's get home. I'm tired.'

'And leave it unfinished?'

I said nothing. I was too startled by the realization that Donaldson, too, had been so perceptive. He'd given the impression of possessing no imagination or understanding, relying on routine and paperwork to clear most of his cases. Now this! He had seen how he could strike at me most effectively. I'd made it very clear that I would not allow him to harm Amelia. That had told him what she meant to me, and how he could best strike me a telling blow. And he could do it by being pleasant to her, so that I had no appeal against it. He was simply using the hatred he'd generated himself to undermine our marriage. And so far, it seemed to be working.

'It isn't unfinished,' I assured her, accelerating through the gears. 'It's over, done, kaput. I wasn't telling any lies when I said my main concern was Marjie Brason. *Main* concern, my dear. Of course I was interested in the murder, but not interested enough to interfere deliberately. Now Marjie's dead, so that's the end of it. There's no reason we need ever meet Donaldson again.'

'No?'

'Unless you really want to, of course.'

'Why should I want to?' I could hear the uncertainty in her voice.

'Because you found him so charming and appealing.'

I glanced sideways momentarily. I was taking a risk, hoping the pleasantry would break through the mood, with the chance that the mood might sour the pleasantry. But I caught the flicker of her smile.

'I didn't say appealing, Richard.'

'I thought you did.'

'I didn't fancy the moustache.'

'Ah!'

We laughed moderately. It wasn't the end of it; it hadn't died. But the sting had been drawn.

She was silent. I concentrated on the road, and on the one important fact that she had missed: that I'd let down Marjie Brason because I hadn't tried hard enough. Accident, they were going to say. Accident, hell!

Savagely, then, I drove on, and in this mood could again turn my mind to Donaldson. It always surprises me that anyone would *dare* to intrude into anyone else's marriage. This must surely be the filthiest blow that can be administered. But . . . for a senior police officer to have risked it! He, of all people, must have known that this is one of the prime motivations for murder.

I decided that it was a good thing we need never meet again.

11

A small coolness hovered between us for the whole of the following week. An outsider would probably not have noticed it. Mary Pinson did, and said nothing, merely expressing her opinion with a worried frown. But I would not consider her to be an outsider.

On the Saturday morning a week later, Amelia and I were working together on the terraced garden. The weather had changed, and we were revelling in a spell of sunlight, quite warm on that south-facing slope. It had become obvious, in the past few days, that the garden was going to prove too much, even if the two of us could guarantee to work together on every suitable day. The weeds were growing faster than we could pluck them out. Sheba, our boxer, watched our every move, but could offer no assistance. The question of employing a full-time gardener was naturally raised, so we broke off for a stroll along the river bank to discuss it, downstream to where Sheba's friends, the otters, usually fished and played.

She no longer goes in to swim with them, having learned that they play rough and have sharp teeth. So she stands on the bank and barks.

It was when she ceased barking, tensed, and growled, that I knew the game was over. She was looking beyond us, back along the river bank.

'Easy,' I told her. 'Friend.'

Boxers have a disadvantage in that they have no tail to wag and they always look miserable. Ken doesn't worry about outward appearances, and has a naive faith that his friendliness will rebound. He crouched, and she ran to him. After allowing himself to be slobbered all over, he straightened, and grinned at us.

'Some place you've got here, Richard.'

'It's not strictly mine. Amelia's.'

'And how are you, Amelia?'

She raised her cheek. He kissed it. 'It's good to see you, Ken.' Even if he was a reminder of unpleasant things. 'You'll stay for lunch, of course.'

'I've already had my orders. Yes, I daren't sneak away now. How far is it possible to walk along the river?'

'We haven't checked, yet.'

'Let's try it, shall we?'

In certain circumstances, Ken likes to walk while he's talking. It means that he neither wishes his expressions to be analysed, nor wishes to view the effect. I glanced at Amelia. She shrugged, and then frowned. We began to walk. He didn't know, but we would shortly be trespassing on some else's territory, but no one as touchy as Colonel Forrester. We could not always walk three abreast, so from time to time I fell back. Sheba enjoyed it immensely. I was nervous. The lead-in of small talk I found nerve-racking.

'Cath all right?' asked Amelia.

'Fine, thank you.'

'You must bring her along for a visit, now you know where we are.'

'I'll do that.'

We strolled on. A bit more fill-in, then Amelia casually said: 'And Tony? How is he coping?' As though this wasn't what we all wanted to get round to.

'He's pulling round, I think. I'm not giving him a spare minute to brood over it.'

'He'd be entitled to compassionate leave,' I pointed out, not to be excluded completely from the conversation.

'He refused it, Richard,' he threw over his shoulder. 'Care to sit a bit on this tree trunk?'

'We often do,' Amelia told him.

He sat between us. The river flowed at our feet, and the nearest traffic was a mile away. Sheba went off to explore. Placidity enwrapped us.

Into this, Ken dropped: 'Tony was all right till the inquest.'

'They brought in suicide?' I'd worried that they might.

'No. It was adjourned. For further enquiries.'

'Oh,' I said.

'It was the post mortem that really upset him,' Ken went on.

I turned and stared at him. 'Post mortem? For a straightforward drowning?'

'That's the trouble. It's not straightforward. The ME noticed an abrasion on the back of her head. The water's quite deep under that bridge, Richard. The river was in full flow. We couldn't find anything beneath the gap in the rail that might've inflicted it.'

'Hell!' I said.

'So we had a post mortem examination, and it seems she was struck from behind. She was dead before she reached the water.'

There was a long silence, into which Amelia said: 'Poor Tony.'

'Exactly,' Ken agreed, biting on the word.

'It's murder, then,' I said blankly, trying desperately to sort out my attitude to this possibility.

Ken didn't answer. He sorted through pockets until he found his cigarettes, and offered one to Amelia. She shook her head, giving him an empty smile. I lit my pipe. Amelia said nothing.

'I'm having trouble with Donaldson,' Ken went on at last. 'After you gave him that photograph – '

'Sorry about that. I was mad at him.'

'No harm done, really. It cleared the air. We had a stand-up row in his office. Oh, don't worry about it, it's been on the cards for ages. I think he's going round the twist, frankly. He accused me of breaking into his office, and I shouted at him that he'd got no right to lock the file away where I couldn't get at it. I thought he was going to explode. And then, quite abruptly, he was dead calm, almost polite. He'd stared at that photo for ages, and couldn't see what it meant. He didn't know about hot-wiring. I had to explain. He had to *ask* me. It drives him insane, just the thought that anyone, any time, can make a logical deduction before he gets to it. A megalomaniac, that's what he is. I looked it up,' he said proudly.

We ventured nothing. I dared not glance towards Amelia.

'I think I'll have to resign,' he said eventually.

'Oh, surely not!' Amelia burst out.

'Richard's lucky to have got out of it. In time.' He turned to me. 'He's never forgiven you for that first case of his.' He turned to Amelia. 'Your case, love.'

'Yes,' she agreed. 'I know the one you mean.'

'But not resign, Ken. A transfer perhaps,' I suggested.

'It'd be running away.'

'And what would resignation be?'

'A gesture.'

'Rubbish! He'd love that. When?'

'I was only thinking about it,' he said morosely. 'In any event, I couldn't go yet.'

'What's keeping you?' I can be persistent when I try.

'I can't go before I've sorted out the murder of Linda Court and the murder of Marjie.'

'It isn't your case. It's his.'

'And d'you reckon he stands a chance!' Ken said violently, tossing the cigarette end in the water. 'He's gone crazy. Didn't I say? Wild ideas. Can I tell you?'

It was what he'd come for. I smiled to myself, and Amelia said it for me. 'Isn't that why you came, Ken?'

He grinned at me. 'A sharp woman you've got here, Richard.'

'Don't I know it! Go on, let's hear it.'

So he told us.

'He's going at it all wrong. Just because both crimes were committed in Manor Park, he's assuming they've got to be linked.'

'Within a hundred yards of each other, Ken! And their meetings at the station that week.'

'Yes. That's clear. What I mean is that he's going at it backwards. Link Marjie's with Linda's, and that's okay. Link Linda's with Marjie's, and there's something wrong about it. No, I'm not going crazy. Hear me out. We're getting nowhere with the Linda Court case, so Donaldson, all clever and going by the statistics, concentrates on Marjie's killing, and comes up with the fact that most murders are domestic – in the family. Working from that, he takes a good long look at Tony – '

'What!' said Amelia, who, for once, was a second behind my own thoughts.

'Tony Brason,' Ken stated again. 'Grieving husband.'

I stared sightlessly at my pipe. 'And I suppose he pointed out that Tony has not been grieving as much as he might have done.'

'He did. But for Tony it's all inside. That's why I'm worried.'

The deeper the grief the thicker the camouflage.

'He said this to you, Ken? To you alone? Has any accusation been made? Any talk about statements?'

Ken got up and kicked at a stone, which plopped into the water. Then he turned, facing us, and thrust his hands into his trouser pockets.

'It's all been implications and suggestions. Little chats over lunch in the canteen.'

'With you?' I asked quickly.

'Yes. It's gone no further yet. I didn't even realize what he was getting at, not for a while, and not until after I'd told him too much. I mean – it didn't seem unusual that he'd be concerned about Tony, and asking about his marriage. But that wasn't what he was getting at. Oh no. Mind you, it's all . . . what's the word? Ephemeral, that's it. He's scared of sticking his neck out, that's what it is. The pressure's on, you see. The powers-that-be expect action. And he daren't move, in case he puts his foot in it.'

Amelia looked at me for guidance, but I wasn't going to commit myself until I knew more.

'Has he said anything definite?' she asked. 'What *did* you tell him, Ken?'

'That his – Tony's – marriage had been rocky lately. That's all. He was on it like a shark. There's only one reason for rocky marriages in Donaldson's book. Another woman. Infidelity.'

I groaned. 'Donaldson?' I asked. 'Is *he* married, Ken?'

'Yes. I thought you knew.'

'And what about *his* marriage?'

'It wouldn't *dare* to sail anywhere near any rocks.'

'So . . . ' I said. 'Having decided Tony must've had a woman tucked away somewhere, how did he link that with Linda? . . . Oh, good Lord! Don't tell me that.'

'But I do. Oh, he hasn't said as much. Hints, though, on where our enquiries ought to be heading and who we ought to be questioning. Richard, we don't get any of the old lark, you and me throwing it at each other in The Rose, and seeing what comes out. You'd think everything's a blasted secret. Paranoiac, that's what he is. I looked that up, too.'

This time his grin was weak, a feeble thing. Amelia, who had obviously been considering what he'd been saying about Tony, smiled at him encouragingly.

'But, Ken,' she said, 'isn't that very silly?' We both looked at her. Unabashed, she went on: 'If this ridiculous theory is based on the fact that Tony was having it off . . . ' She touched her lips. 'Having an affair with Linda, then the moment she died there'd be no more trouble for their marriage. I mean, Tony wouldn't want to kill Marjie unless Linda was still alive, and there in the background.'

Ken looked uneasy. It wasn't his theory, and he was ashamed that he might be called on to justify it. I winked at him. He'd said it himself; a sharp woman, my wife.

'Well, yes,' he said. But . . . you see . . . ' He paced a few yards along the bank, then back. He seemed embarrassed.

'Look,' he admitted. 'I thought this next bit out myself. Don't think I was happy about it, because I was working against Tony. But I could feel Donaldson working round to it, and I had to try and get there first. If only to be able to destroy his theory – you get what I mean. But the hellish thing about it is that the more I think about it, the more it fits, in some crazy and revolting way. And Donaldson'll get to it any time now. Make no mistake about it, he's got a brain, if he can only control it. Brilliant, in patches, but then he gets obsessed, as though there's a block there, some-where. Once he gets the idea, he'll have Tony in the interrogation room, and that'll be it. One dose of Donaldson at his most vicious, and you'd admit to raping the milkman.'

'He means me,' I murmured to Amelia. 'Why don't you stop wandering about, Ken, and sit down.' He did so, leaning forward and staring in misery at his toes. 'Let's have it,' I encouraged.

He lifted his shoulders, then let them drop. 'This Linda Court. You'll have found this out, Richard. She was a flighty bit of flibbertigibbet, and she was twenty-four. They go on so long, playing the field, that sort do, and there comes a time when somebody special comes along, and it seems time to think about settling down. Tony could have seemed like something special, in contrast to her associates in the advertising world. Say she decided she wanted him, as a husband. She wouldn't let it worry her that he was already married. On the contrary, it'd add a bit of a kick to it. And perhaps Tony, if you can imagine him interested at all in such a young woman as Linda, perhaps he wasn't as serious about her as she was about him. His marriage might've been a bit rocky, but it hadn't sunk. Maybe he backed off, and if you do that to the Lindas of this world you're in trouble. She'd expect to do the dropping, not be dropped. So . . . what would she do? She'd apply pressure, that's what. She was good at that. If that didn't work, then she'd go as far as trying to break up their marriage more directly. And *this*, let me tell you, is where I don't like the theory one little bit. You see, it explains that week of the play, her actions and what she did, and there's nothing else I can imagine that does. And damn it, the whole thing fits too blasted well.'

I'd never encountered a police officer so annoyed with his own theory. For a moment I didn't think he was going on. I urged him gently. 'Let's have it, Ken. Get it out of your system.'

'Well . . . who was Duty Sergeant that week? Marjie was. And Marjie, having a policeman husband, would probably describe to him the details of this strange woman, and what was happening to her. But Tony, listening, would see it all in a different light. He *knew* what Linda was doing. When he was trying to shake her off, she'd invented all those things she was complaining about. She was using them to get close to Marjie, and friendly with her. It was Linda's threat, indirectly aimed at Tony. The implication was that it would go on and on, until Linda would do something terrible that'd ruin their marriage completely. Something like telling Marjie about this dishy copper who'd gone crazy for her. You know. And Tony would have had to listen to all this from Marjie, until he'd realized he had to do something positive about stopping Linda.' He paused. It wasn't finished, though. 'And Tony . . . ' He sighed. ' . . . was on a rest day that Saturday, while Marjie was stuck at the station till ten that night. He could have done it, you see. He could've waited for Linda in that blasted park, and nobody know about it.'

I glanced at my watch, almost an instinctive gesture not to continue to watch his face. 'We ought to begin strolling back,' I said. 'Mary'll have it on the table.'

Amelia heaved herself to her feet, brushing bits of bark from the behind of her slacks. 'Is that the end of this wonderful theory, Ken?'

He looked a little peeved that we didn't seem to be taking it too seriously. 'There's more,' he claimed.

'I trust you haven't gone and persuaded yourself it's true.'

'I thought I made it clear – '

'Of course you did,' she assured him, patting his arm. 'And it's not the end of the story, is it?'

'That's the ghastly thing about it. You're forgetting – there's Marjie's death, too.'

'Now you really *are* getting into fantasy,' she told him. 'Don't you think so, Richard?'

I admitted it was a bit far-fetched. But I knew she was only prodding at Ken, provoking him into taking it as far as it would stretch, so that we'd all see the strength of it before we set about breaking it.

'So tell us why Tony would want to kill Marjie,' Amelia prompted.

He rubbed his fingers through his hair. 'That's when it gets even more weird and frightening. The same fact – Marjie being a policewoman and on duty that week – can be used to show why she might have had to be killed. We don't *know* what was said between those two women, because they're both dead. But Linda might have gone too far with Marjie, and told her just a little too much . . . '

'As you did with Mr Donaldson?' asked Amelia, in all innocence. 'When you talked about Tony.'

'Like that.' His voice was tight. 'Just like that. Suppose Linda said too much, and by the end of the week Marjie had got a good idea what all those visits to the station were all about. They were about Tony. And then Linda died. *Then* . . . Marjie would have the horrible suspicion that Tony had done it. That would explain why she went off sick, and all her morbid depression. It'd explain what she was doing all the time, wandering in the park. She was a good officer, Richard. It was a job she wanted to do, and which she knew she could do well. She believed in what she was doing and why.'

'All that claptrap about protecting the peace and safety of the community?' I asked idly.

'That! Yes!' I'd annoyed him. 'She'd have to decide what to do about it. Maybe turn him in.'

'Her own husband?' Amelia was shocked.

'It's been done before,' I told her. 'That Chief Super, Norwich way. He turned in his son for a mugging where an old lady was stabbed to death.'

'Oh!' she said.

'And Tony would be watching her watching him,' said Tony, 'until he couldn't bear it any longer. So he waited for her at the bridge . . . and afterwards went home, until it was time to send for a search party.'

'And *we* turned up,' I said.

We had arrived at the foot of our terraced garden. A pity it wasn't showing much at that time. Angrily, I pounded up the winding slope, well in the lead.

'Richard?' Amelia called after me.

I waited until they caught up. 'Just think how it would've

been,' I told them, 'if we'd got there earlier with that lovely hot-wiring theory. In time to tell it to Marjie, I mean. Wouldn't it have been great? If there's anything at all in that damned theory, it would've been a confirmation of what she'd been guessing, which was that Linda had been lying about it all. Maybe, who knows, Marjie would have come out with all her sick and scared fears there and then – and she'd bloody well be alive now.'

Amelia stopped, facing me. 'But it's only a theory, love.' She turned. 'Isn't it, Ken?'

'It's only a theory,' he admitted wearily. 'But won't it be fine if Donaldson gets round to it!'

'As a theory, it stinks,' I told him.

'D'you think I like it?' he demanded.

'No, I'm sure you don't. Oh hell, let's go and see what Mary's got for us.'

What she had prepared was trout, with a very succulent sauce, and for a while I was engaged too intricately with bones to listen to the table chat. Ken had come to see whether I could dig a hole in that fine theory; I hadn't any doubt about that. Yes I had. Cancel that. Amelia had called me smug, so I had to watch it. Ken had come, guided by a memory of the times when we'd thrown ideas at each other, clearing our respective minds. He'd come to air his grievances over Donaldson, and share his concerns.

Satisfied with this, I dug into ice cream, and Amelia was saying to him: 'But you'll know what to tell Mr Donaldson, Ken, if he comes up with a daft idea like that.'

'That's the trouble, I don't know. I hoped Richard could think of something.'

You see . . . no rest from it.

'I'm out of it, Ken. Not involved any more.'

'A crack somewhere,' he suggested. 'Something I can get a lever in, that's all I need.'

'I can't think of anything, off-hand.'

'You're not *trying*,' Amelia accused me.

I rubbed my face, hoping for inspiration. 'There was one small thing,' I conceded.

'There!' She thumped me on the shoulder, and Ken demanded: 'What?'

'We were going to put an idea to Marjie, to prove to her that Linda had been telling lies all that week. Remember? I had it all

123

worked out, based on the hot-wiring. It was feasible. Even better than that. But there was one thing I was hoping Marjie wouldn't bring up. There was a good chance she wouldn't, because it was unlikely she would know about it. And that was the letter Linda posted, addressed to me, and which took four months to arrive.'

'I don't remember,' put in Ken, 'that you even mentioned the letter. I can't see what it's got to do with that theory, though.'

'It didn't fit in, not click-click-click, into place. All we needed, at that time, was to show that Linda'd been lying. No explanation as to why. Just that she was lying, and had rigged it all herself, No . . . rigged is the wrong word – she wouldn't have needed to rig anything, only imagine it. Until right at the end, with the hot-wiring. So Marjie would've been prepared to accept what we told her, so long as she didn't know about the letter. Why did Linda send it? That's the problem. It's too far-out for her to have expected it'd back up her lying. Too remote. So the letter was a weakness in the story we had for Marjie. Nothing more than a weakness, though.'

Amelia frowned. 'I don't see what you're getting at.'

'Look at it in the context of what Ken's been telling us. Now we get some sort of a crazy reason for the tricks Linda had been playing. She was – we're expected to accept – using it as an excuse to see Marjie pretty well every day that week at the station, to get close and friendly with her, and to use that to scare Tony to death, and maybe force his hand. Even if you accept *that*, there's no logical reason for her sending the letter. In no way would it help her to put pressure on Tony, even if she ever got a response to it. Throw *that* at Donaldson if he produces the idea, Ken. See if he can fit *that* in.'

He stuck out his lower lip and glowered, not at all the reaction I'd expected. 'The trouble is, Donaldson's apt to ignore details that don't match his ideas. He wouldn't be interested in fitting it in.'

'It's not a detail, damn it.'

'All the same, you don't know him. No, Richard, you don't. Not as I do. I've worked with him. Tried to. Worked under him, rather. He's in charge. I do what he tells me. My suggestions get slipped under the blotting pad.'

'Then I don't see – '

'There's only one thing that'd mean anything at all to him – I'd

124

have to come up with a solution to the murders. Both of 'em. And how the hell can I do that if I spend all my time chasing around to add to his wonderful paperwork collection?'

'I see.' I saw only too well. But he had only Tony to worry about, whereas I had Amelia. 'Can't see how I can help you there, Ken,' I said, shrugging.

'Didn't I hear somewhere . . . you're finding that people talk to you? More than they would if you were still a copper.'

'I said that to Donaldson.'

He rubbed the back of his neck. 'He must've passed it on.'

'Ken, I've got personal reasons – '

Amelia interrupted. 'You men! Missing the obvious.' She looked from one face to the other. 'It all happened in the week of the play. Linda should've been in it, and she wasn't. Whatever went on, it has to be connected with the drama group.'

We'd already decided that. 'Even so . . . ' I said.

Ken pointed out: 'They're all excluded. Alibis. Richard'll tell you . . . '

'Then alibis must be broken,' she decided.

Ken and I looked at each other.

'And don't you see,' Amelia went on in triumph, 'one of the group . . . wasn't he something to do with woodworking?'

'Bill Askew,' said Ken. 'He's a furniture renovator.'

'There you are, then,' she told me. But *where* was I? 'Isn't there one of our dining room chairs with a loose leg? And there was mention of two men running an antiques shop.'

'Llew Porter and Clive Matthews,' Ken supplied, prepared to sit back and watch it happen.

'And we were thinking of brightening up the living room,' she reminded me.

'With antiques? We could stock a shop, ourselves.'

'All the same, we could *look*. And wasn't there a restaurant . . . '

'The Vortex.'

'What a romantic name! We must visit it, Richard.' She sat back. 'Nobody can object to us shopping. Not even *him*. And we have to eat.'

Keeping my face stern, I smiled to myself. I hadn't told her the details, but she might just as well have been in Forrester's trophy room with me.

'What you expect from me – ' I began. But it was no good at all.

She swept on: 'What day is it? Saturday? We could come on Monday, Ken. And talk, Richard. You're so good at it. Something's sure to come from it.'

And with that I couldn't help but agree, though I didn't say so.

Ken seemed a little more cheerful when he left. 'You'll be in touch?' he asked me.

'I know where you live, Ken.'

He smiled, he nodded, and he drove away.

'Now look what you've done,' I said. 'And there isn't a chair with a loose leg.'

'Now don't be difficult, Richard. You can easily fix that, surely.'

I spent Sunday fixing it.

12

Bill Askew had his premises down an alley called Mortice Lane (so the business could have been in existence for a long while) which is just off Gospel Street, where the defunct GWR used to have a station. There was plenty of parking space, as the old railway loading yard was now deserted.

We were using the Granada, experiment having shown that the chair wouldn't go in the Stag's shallow boot, nor fit behind the two front seats. I got out, and stared across at the partly open gates, on which I could just read Furniture on one and Restorers on the other. I lifted the chair out of the back and we walked with it into the yard.

It was different from what I'd expected. There was more wood than a restorer would seem to need, and all stacked inside open-sided sheds with corrugated iron roofs. Each layer was separated by an inch from the next. It was more like the yard of a timber merchant. At the far end was a workshop, wooden, which itself seemed to be in need of restoring from newer stock in the yard.

We approached. A high-pitched whine from inside indicated that there would be no point in knocking, so I pushed open an inset door, and we walked in.

A smell of wood, resin and glue greeted us. It was a clean smell, wholesome. The whine of a three-foot circular saw seemed to cut into my brain. I stood. Amelia flinched, and took a pace backwards. The large and rotund man working the saw was sliding a length of wood through the teeth. His head was low, judging the exact cut, his fingers lovingly handling the wood, and only fractions of an inch from its whirring menace. I felt the skin prickle on my neck. The piece of wood seemed ridiculously small for the size of the saw blade. I felt I dared not move in case I distracted him, and had to catch one of his flying fingers.

A young man in jeans and a T-shirt, with a white apron protecting his front, was gently and tenderly running a tiny plane along the edge of a larger length of wood, standing at a side bench under one of the windows.

The working space seemed very extensive for only two workers. Benches lined it. On their surfaces, standing beside them when whole but mostly dismembered, were portions of furniture. Here a chest of drawers, there the drawers from it. A sideboard, with its carved back leaning against it. A folding table – I think it was a table – in such a demolished state that it was difficult to recognize, other than the fact that it did fold. I would have hated to come in here and see my precious antique torn down to basics like this.

As would be our chair, I realized.

It was the young man who first noticed us. He put down his plane, then, to my horror, he walked over to the man at the saw and slapped his shoulder for attention. Perhaps he was used to it. He merely raised his head, and miraculously, because I didn't see him touch a switch, the saw began to run down, the whine dying like an ambulance disappearing into the night.

He straightened, nodded to us, and lifted a portion he'd cut from the length of wood, turned it critically in his fingers, put it down, and at last advanced on us.

This would be Bill Askew, who had played the police sergeant in the play, and had therefore, according to my schedule, been on stage from 7.50 to the end. He had a cheerful air of bustle about him, although his work, I had gained the impression, was clearly taken at an unhurried pace.

'Mr Askew?' I asked. 'Good morning. I thought you might look at this for me.' I thrust the chair at him.

He took it from me, but didn't at once give it much attention. He said: 'I'm sorry I can't offer your good lady a seat. Not one fit for you, ma'am.'

127

'It's all right,' she assured him gravely.

'We're not equipped . . . ' He left it uncompleted, but his eyes had been twinkling. He at last looked at the chair. 'Hello!' he said. 'What've we got here, eh?'

'I don't really know what it is,' I admitted. 'But it's got a loose leg.'

He moved back and placed it on a bench. Then he called to the youngster. 'Come over here, Kevin. Tell me what you think this is.'

He came over. I could see now that they must be father and son, sharing the same eyes, an element of wry humour in them. Their view of the world probably brought them into contact with only its better productions; they could allow themselves a laugh at the rest. Kevin looked at it, peered at it, rubbed his hands down the seat of his jeans, and bent to look under it.

'Eighteenth-century?' he asked. 'Early nineteenth?'

'Unless it's a reproduction,' Askew said lugubriously.

'Nah! Not it!'

Askew turned to me. 'Rule one,' he told me. 'Never admit you don't know what you've got.' He turned to his son and thumped him on the shoulder. 'Rule two,' he told him. 'Never suggest it could be an original.'

'It's not really what I wanted to know,' I said. 'I've come to see if you can repair the leg.'

'Well yes. But you never know, I might want to make you an offer for it.'

'Then why, in that case, are you telling me this?'

'Because, if it's an original, I couldn't afford what it's worth, and if I paid you what I could afford, I'd be cheating you.'

'Ah!' I glanced at Amelia, who pouted. 'You know what it is, then?' I asked him.

He grinned, tapped the side of his prominent nose, and said: 'Never trust anybody who says he knows before he really looks.'

'I won't. In future.' Presumably that was rule three.

Then he got down to it. Every inch of our chair was examined, underneath, the joints, the seat, the fretted back support. His son watched patiently, chewing a match. I assumed that smoking inside there was prohibited.

Askew replaced it on the bench. Stood back. 'A pity about the leg,' he observed. 'Must've been something drastic . . . ' He paused, and eyed me carefully up and down. 'You didn't *sit* on it, surely!'

He was making me miserable. I'd fought with it to get the leg loose. 'Why shouldn't I sit on it?'

'They're not for sitting on, they're for looking at.' Then he threw back his head and laughed heartily. His son joined him.

Amelia and I watched solemnly.

Eventually, he controlled himself. 'What you've got here,' he pronounced, 'unless I'm very much mistaken, is a walnut side chair, cabriole legs, carved knees and claw and ball feet. Walnut. Nice wood to work. Chippendale. Probably around 1780. One of these fetched over ten thousand at Christie's last year.'

'Pounds?' I whispered.

He nodded. 'Though of course, with the restoration work . . . it could cut that down a bit. It depends.'

I swallowed. 'Depends on what?'

'Have you ever wondered why this sort of thing is still in existence? The modern stuff – how long d'you think that'll last? But this is two hundred years old.' He slapped it. 'Solid as a rock. It's the joints, you see.'

'Joints?' I must have sounded like an idiot.

'What hold it together. You make a wooden chair nowadays, what joints d'you use for the legs and the frame? I'll tell you. Mortice and tenon. A tongue on the one going into a slot in the other, and you depend on the modern fancy glues to hold it there. But these people – they only had fish glue or hide glue. So they played a trick. Cunnin' lot. They didn't do a nice, easy slot, all parallel sides. No, they opened the slot out at the back. So the tongue would wobble around in it. But they cut two wedge shapes in the end of the tongue, and they put a wedge of wood in each cut, just a bit too big for it. Then they glued it up and they hammered it in, and the wedges opened up the tongue, inside the slot, and when it was all set nothin' on earth'd get it out. It's called a double-wedged tenon.'

I was grateful for the lecture. 'I never knew that.'

'The point is, you see.' He was explaining to Amelia now. 'If the joints in this chair are like that, then I've got to destroy the leg to get it apart, and with a new leg in it – well, it cuts down the value.'

'To what?' I asked cautiously.

'A couple of thousand, say.'

'It's lost eight thousand pounds, just for a loose leg!' I almost shouted.

'If my work's noticeable.'

I was beginning to understand the point of the lecture. A good job on the leg by himself might save me eight thousand. A rogue? Or a man so delighted with his work that he was willing to share his joy with us?

'What d'you think, Kevin?' he asked the lad.

Kevin glanced at him, at us. 'Plenty of wood at the top o' the legs, plenty in the frame. Probably double tenons. Plain.'

'Maybe you're right.' Askew scratched his head, and glanced at me. 'Got any more of 'em?'

'Eight in all.'

He whistled gently towards the shavings on the floor. 'If you're interested in selling, I could put you in touch with somebody. Porter and Matthews, just off the old market. Pair o' crooks, but now you know what you've got you could play 'em along.'

'Friends of yours?'

He cocked an eyebrow at his son. 'Friends d'you reckon, Kevin?'

'Not as I know.'

'Y're too damned right, beggin' your pardon, ma'am.' He explained to me: 'I made a reproduction mahogany and cherry-wood drop-leaf table for them, and they sold it as genuine Chippendale.'

'Does that trouble you?'

'It could get back to me. I'd lose my reputation. And who put you on to *me*, if I might ask?'

'Now let me see. Oh yes. His name's Latchett. Detective Inspector Latchett.'

'Ah, I see.'

'He's a friend.'

'I'm sure he is. Here, Kevin, you get back to your work. The gentleman wants to talk, kind o' private.'

He nodded towards the yard, and we led him out into it. He seemed to fit himself between us, rolling along placidly, pacing along the lines of sheds. Once out in the open he produced cigarettes, offered them, and we both shook our heads.

'So it's not the chair,' he said at last.

'It was an excuse to see you,' I told him frankly. 'But I still want it repairing.'

'You'll get as good as I can give it. If you had to find an excuse, that means you're not the police.' He nodded to himself, cupping the cigarette and drawing deeply on it.

'I'm not,' I said.

'And the lady?' He smiled at her.

'My wife. We're simply interested in helping out a friend. You wouldn't know him. I thought we'd come along and try to wheedle some information from you.'

'About what?'

'Linda Court.'

'Oh Lordy me! Not that again! I told that Inspector Whatever-it-was all I know. Why drag it up again?'

I couldn't see how I could possibly explain why. While I was thinking about it, Amelia helped me out.

'Until somebody's arrested and tried for it, everybody involved is sure to be uneasy. You don't strike me as uneasy, though, Mr Askew.'

'Well that,' he said in triumph, 'is because I'm not involved.'

We had reached the end of one alleyway between the sheds of wood. We turned the corner and started back along the next.

'Why d'you say that?' I asked.

'Look, you oughter know. I've got one o' them useful things called an alibi. Didn't your inspector mate tell you? I was on a stage. In front of a lot of people. Police Sergeant, I was. Rotten part. Do I *look* like a policeman?'

Strictly speaking, he would not have made the height regulation. 'I'm sure you rose to it. But you weren't on stage until nearly eight o'clock.'

'Don't mean anything. I was there at six, same like everybody else. Orders from Knowles. Boss-man Knowles. We were all there early. Ask anybody. And if y' think I could've sneaked out an' killed that girl . . . ' He was sounding annoyed, as he'd be to find a knot in the middle of a prime piece of wood.

'The inspector assures me you have a perfect alibi,' I told him. 'It's motives I'm after.'

'Then you go an' scour the town, mate. You'll find hundreds.'

'No doubt. But it's yours I'm interested in.'

'Aw, come on!'

131

'She threatened you, I believe.'

'Little bitch. Heard me talkin' in the dressing room one night. A bit pressed for money I was, and a feller was after his bit . . . '

'Nearly everybody's pressed for money, some time or other.'

'It was temporary. I was doing a job for the old Colonel. Forrester. A Regency rosewood side cabinet he'd brought in. Finish that, and I'd be in the clear. As I am now, if y' wanter know. But she heard. Said the news might get around, with a bit of encouragement. See what I mean? I just couldn't *afford* to have debts called in – '

'Now hold it,' I put in. 'You'll pardon me, but you're not exactly big business. Steady turnover, work in hand I noticed, and . . . ' I gestured around. ' . . . and plenty of stock. Where's the money pressure?'

He stopped, pulled his ear with finger and thumb, the two other fingers holding the cigarette, and grinned at me. 'You don't know a *thing*, do you? This business, you know nothing.'

'Very true. That's why I'm asking.'

'Well – you see – I'd bought a tree.'

'A tree?'

'An elm. Pretty rare, that. Cost a fortune, the whole tree.'

'You'd bought a whole tree? But heavens, man, you only use bits and chunks and lumps.'

'But you have to *pick* the bits out of the large sections, to get the grain right. Listen. The tree gets cut into planks. Not trimmed. The edges are left, bits o' bark an' all. We stack 'em. In these here sheds. Say I've gotta match two pieces, four feet by one. Match wood and the grain. Then I have to use two planks next to each other in the stack, and maybe select just two central lengths. This stuff round you – my dad bought some of it, and his dad some of it. The timber I've bought over the years, Kevin'll use that. This elm – oh, don't you see! – it'll be precious when it's weathered, when Kevin's lad's working on it. A man in this work's gotta lay out money, for his kids and his kid's kids.'

'I see.'

Amelia was looking round her in wonder. This wasn't timber, it was a life's work, a family's treasure.

'And Linda Court threatened it?' I asked quietly.

'Tried.'

'Lucky for you she died, then.'

132

'Wasn't it!'

'You'd have killed her for that elm, wouldn't you?'

He dropped his cigarette end and ground it under his heel, paying particular attention to it. Then he looked up at me, and there was no twinkle in his eye now.

'I do believe I would.'

'If you'd had the chance?'

'Yes. Chance is a fine thing.'

We were heading back towards his workshop.

'You won't take any chances with my chair, will you?' I asked.

'I'll try not to. Mind you – if you make me too nervous, my hand might slip.'

I slapped him on the shoulder, remembering that saw blade. 'You're not the nervous type, Mr Askew.'

We exchanged phone numbers. He said give it about a month. I agreed to do that.

'Oh, by the way,' I said, as we were about to leave. He paused, suspicious. 'You didn't say . . . what was it Linda wanted from you?'

'Not money.'

No, it wouldn't be money. She was not the type, and he hadn't got any. The pressure she'd been exerting had been based on his lack of the ready.

He didn't go on. I pushed him gently. 'Something you were reluctant to supply or do?'

'I think we'll leave it there.'

'All right. As you wish.'

Which only made him suspicious. 'Something I couldn't deliver, even if I'd wanted to.'

'Then she was on to a loser.'

Amelia was already strolling towards the gates. I moved to follow, and took one pace.

'Knowles wouldn't ever have listened to me.'

I turned back. 'Knowles?'

'It was absolutely ridiculous.'

'In what way did she want you to influence him?'

He shook his head, opened the door behind him, and it slammed on any comment he might have made.

Amelia was sitting in the passenger's seat when I slid behind the wheel. She waited patiently while I stuffed my pipe, and when I turned towards her she smiled and asked:

'Back with us, are you?'

'I was thinking.'

'About all that lovely money hiding away in the dining room?'

'No, no. Right at the end, he pointed me at Knowles.'

'He also mentioned the other two, Porter and Matthews.'

'But this was different. Deliberate. He needn't have mentioned his name at all. But Ian Knowles . . . he's about the only one who *couldn't* have got away for one minute that evening.'

'He wasn't on until nearly eight o'clock. The same as Mr Askew. Neither of them was in the first act.'

'Yes, but Knowles, he was the director. Dozens of people would've been pestering him. Knowles just couldn't have got away.'

She tapped my knee. 'It's your own theory – or Ken's, I can't remember which of you – but you're both convinced it had to be somebody who was *waiting* for Linda at the park. So come on, Richard, don't go all fanciful. Where's this old market he mentioned?'

'Want to go for coffee first?'

'I don't see why not.'

We went for coffee. Over it, we chatted emptily until eventually we set off to see Llew Porter and Clive Matthews.

13

'Do you know what we're supposed to be doing?' Amelia asked, as I skirted the site of the old market, wondering where I could park.

'Haven't the faintest idea.'

'Then why don't we simply go home?'

I wondered how to answer that, but it's no good trying to concentrate on ideas when you're confronted by the very real problem of parking space. The old market hall had been called the Agri when I was a youngster. Short for Agricultural Hall. As it had backed against the canal, it was, so rumour had it, infested with rats. We used to play there, running through the rows of stalls and nicking apples. I never saw a rat. The old building had been knocked down, and a brand-new office building erected in its place. Council Offices. The open, outside market, which might have been left as a useful parking space, was now the decorative, landscaped frontage for the office block. There wasn't a rat in sight.

Nor parking space. I had to go to the multi-storey behind the Hartley building, from which we walked back.

Totter's Close was still much as it had always been. It was too narrow for motor vehicles, and in case anybody thought to try it there were concrete bollards each end. You walked. Or rather, you hobbled, because the surface hadn't been looked at since the Prince Regent came to unveil that wretched green statue in the square.

The shop occupied by Llew Porter and Clive Matthews did not advertise its presence. It lurked. You got the impression that it was an exclusive club, to which only the knowledgeable had access. It was the only place resembling a shop, or even inhabited, in the short lane, a flat-faced and blank, apparently leaning front, with two bow windows relieving its architectural collapse. There might have been the original rotting oak beams in its structure, but it was too shadowed for me to be certain.

I peered through the windows. There seemed to be a dim light somewhere in the back. I put a hand to the door, and it opened with a ping. We moved tentatively into the gloom.

The unwelcoming interior reminded me that I'd not answered Amelia's query as to why we didn't go home. I said softly, as not to disturb too much dust: 'It's an old police principle. Keep annoying people, and something could break.'

'What is?' she asked, having forgotten her question.

At the rear, a bead curtain was swept aside. A light switch was fingered, and a transformation took place. It was all very clever. They had concealed lights on all the walls, in a display area much larger than the windows had suggested. The contrast between expectations and reality was calculated. We were in a clean and carefully displayed layout of a vast collection of what could be called junk or beauty, depending on your inclinations, with every smaller item displayed in all its grandeur on furniture so manifestly ancient that it just had to be priceless.

135

'Can I help you?' our host asked.

Amelia left it to me. She simply stood there, allowing her eyes to take it all in.

'I'd like to speak to either Mr Porter or Mr Matthews.'

'I'm Llew Porter. My partner's busy upstairs.'

'Then perhaps you can help me. We have a rather dull room at home, and we were looking for something to brighten it up.'

'Anything in mind?' he asked, moving forward, smiling, teeth perfect, poise magnificent.

This was Llew Porter, who'd played the part of the private detective in the play. He had presented it gay, and thereby annoyed Gail Martin. The implication was that he *was* gay, but I couldn't see any sign of it. Hadn't expected to. I can see no reason why a homosexual should appear more effeminate than a woman. The fact that Porter looked like six feet of slim but lethal hoodlum, with a face Bill Askew might have hewn from a chunk of his best oak, meant nothing. The fact that he made no affected movements of hands and hips, and had a firm baritone voice, also meant nothing.

The fact that I'd swear he lowered one eye in Amelia's direction did. It nearly earned him a fist in those perfect teeth.

'We were thinking,' I suggested, 'of a mahogany and cherry-wood drop-leaf table, possibly Chippendale.' I hoped I'd remembered Askew's description correctly.

Apparently I had, because I'd put in a good blow after all. He blinked. His smile disappeared. He managed to say: 'If you'll excuse me a moment . . . my partner may be able to help you.'

He retired behind his bead curtain, and I thought I heard a very distant buzzer. Or it could have been the hum of voices.

With a swish and a clatter of beads he reappeared. He had recovered his poise.

'My partner does the buying, and I do the selling. He might just know where to locate such a table . . . '

'I understood you had – '

'So while you're waiting, perhaps . . . ' He gestured embracingly. 'Maybe you see something that might interest you.'

He turned. His partner had appeared behind him, posed in the curtain and draped with beads.

'The gentleman was asking – '

'I heard.'

Clive Matthews, I knew at once, was the brains of the partnership. He was the expert on antiques, who could spot a Hepplewhite at a hundred yards and value it at twenty, deduct fifty per cent by the time he reached it, and be offering you twenty-five per cent as a bargain before you had time to blink. He was the quiet and apparently naive one on the back row at auctions. Matthews, for all his bluff and cheerful appearance, was the deep one, the jovial amateur with the incisive brain.

As he advanced on us there was no sign of joviality. I was going by his rotund and placid belly, by his red fat face and his twinkling eyes. He would be adept at chuckling. At the moment his mouth was too firm for a chuckle, but he apparently could not control the twinkle.

Without glancing at him, Matthews spoke to his partner. 'Didn't we sell the Chippendale?'

'Our information,' I said, 'was that you still had such a table.'

'Information from where?'

'A restorer in town here. Name of Askew. But he didn't describe it as a Chippendale. He said it was a reproduction.'

'That was how we sold it, and he knows that.'

'I must have misunderstood him. He's repairing a chair for me. That's genuine Chippendale, apparently. Kind of bowed legs, and ball and claw feet.'

'With a fretted back?'

'Well yes. Now you mention it.'

'Walnut?'

'Mr Askew said so.'

A change had come over him. Now he really did beam, his stomach seemed to vibrate, his hands parted in a gesture of fulsome comradeship.

'Have you got any more of them?'

'Eight in all.'

He had to glance aside to hide the avarice in his eyes. 'Now . . . I might be able to find a customer for those. If you're thinking of selling, of course.'

'They want to brighten up a room,' put in Porter, a little forcefully, I thought.

But of course, he wanted to sell. All this talk about buying was stealing his limelight. Thinking of which, I realized we were still a long way from the subject we'd come to discuss: Linda Court.

My technique was slipping. At one time I'd have led in smoothly without the join showing. Amelia came to my rescue. She hasn't my patience, and she'd thought of a lead-in.

'It's a very big room,' she said. 'You could put on a play in it, if you wanted.'

'Provided there's only a small cast,' I qualified. 'Say four men and one woman.'

Matthews lifted his head. 'Sweet heaven!' he shouted. 'You're the bloody police.'

'No we're not. Do we look like police?' Amelia is five feet four inches. 'I only wanted to ask about Linda Court.'

They glanced at each other. Matthews turned back to us, spreading his hands. 'Well, why didn't you say?'

I was beginning to wonder that myself. There had been so much opposition, though, to every move I'd made, that a bit of co-operation for a change was unexpected.

'We've got nothing to hide,' Porter said eagerly, now eyeing Amelia with open interest.

'Of course not,' she assured him.

The two men were both, I'd have guessed, in their early fifties. Past their bloom, if they'd ever had one, but with the petals hanging on with desperate tenacity.

'What about Linda?' Porter asked. 'Just don't expect any praise from us.'

Matthews included us both in one wide smile. 'What would you like to know about dear Linda?'

'The sort of person she was – that sort of thing.'

They glanced at each other. Porter led off. 'A self-satisfied and over-sexed bitch. Begging your pardon, ma'am.'

'Granted,' she said. 'We know that by now.'

'We also know,' I added, 'that she spent all her spare time interfering in people's lives, trying to get something on them she could use.'

They nodded.

'Is that what she did with you two?'

'Tried,' said Porter. 'Didn't get very far.'

'Met her match,' Matthews agreed. 'Shall I tell them, Llew? Shall I?'

'Why not.'

So he did.

'It's like this – two chaps living together, it gives people the wrong idea. A few years back, and there wouldn't have been any dirty thoughts, but with this new permissive nonsense it gets to be a bit of a pain. We've got our own friends. We play it cool, like. Going along nice and comfortable, and who comes along but darling Linda, who's got only one idea in her sweet little head: how can she make trouble? And she decided – how shall I put this? – decided I must be the straight one of the pair, and could be worked on.'

'You can see her game,' Porter plunged in, not intending to be left out of it. 'Lovely young woman, Linda was. Sexy. You know. Clive can tell you.'

'She was not really my type,' said Matthews distantly. 'I know what I go for, and she wasn't it. Be that as it may, we had to send her packing with a flea in her ear. So . . . we kind of drew up a plan. She was coming here one evening, expecting I'd be waiting for her. We were supposed to be going out for a meal, then back here later. But . . . well . . . I was well away before she was due . . . '

'Clive visits a widow lady the other side of town,' Porter confided.

'Never mind where. The fact was that Llew was waiting for her, and took her up to the flat to wait, and because she was curious, and because Llew's got quite a technique when he needs it, he got her into bed to prove the point, and they were still there when I got back the next morning. What set her running was that we both laughed our heads off at her, and she never came near us after that.'

Laughed? I wondered about that. There had been distant pain in Matthew's eyes when he'd spoken of the laughter.

In a few more years they'd be a pair of old lechers, I decided. 'But it was a close-run thing?' I asked.

Matthews blinked. 'How d'you mean?'

'She was an experienced and mature young woman. She would know how to handle you – either or both of you. But there was something behind all this, wasn't there? I mean, she wasn't just having her bit of fun – she was after something, wasn't she?'

'After me,' said Clive Matthews, with a touch of pride.

Porter seemed embarrassed. He glanced at his partner. 'Well, not really, old son. It was me she was pressuring. Behind your

139

back. She came here, once or twice, while you were away. She said she would break up our partnership.'

'She couldn't. Just couldn't.'

'Oh yes, she could. Admit it, you're a fat fool, and everybody loves you, but you've got no idea with women. Admit it.'

'Gloria ... ' He gestured vaguely towards the other side of town.

'A nice, safe widow woman, who's happy to see you from time to time. Once a month, say. But women ... healthy and virile ones ... normally you'd run a mile. With Linda, though, it was different. Believe me, my old mate, you were ready for the chopper. And by heaven, if I didn't do what she wanted she was going to chop.'

They were no longer aware of our presence. We watched quietly. Matthews was standing stiffly erect. 'I don't know what you mean.' His voice was pained.

'She'd have split us up, with you dreaming about all sorts of romantic and passionate futures, and then she'd have laughed in your face and left you flat. That's why I had to do something drastic.'

'Something drastic like getting her into bed?'

'It was difficult for me, Clive, but I was thinking of you. And Clive, you did laugh. You laughed till you cried.'

'Yes. Till I cried.'

They stared at each other, then Matthews thumped him on the shoulder. 'But it's for the best.' Then he spoke to us hollowly. 'But she died. We were on stage when she died.'

'Yes,' Porter agreed. 'And that's the end of it.'

That being its end, I cleared my throat. 'You said, Mr Porter, that Linda wanted you to do something for her.'

'Oh ... that!' he said airily. 'I couldn't help her there.'

'Couldn't or wouldn't?'

'Couldn't, really. I've got no influence with Ian Knowles, and even what I do know ... ' He shook his head. 'It'd never have forced him into doing what *she* wanted.'

By heaven, but she'd been a busy woman, putting on pressure here, there and everywhere. No – that wasn't quite right. The devastations she had spread around her had been mostly instigated in a sense of fun, and it was only in these two instances, Askew and now Porter, that she'd tried to use it towards a serious end: to put pressure of some sort on Knowles. Knowles. Everybody was prodding me towards Knowles.

'And what do you know about Ian Knowles?' I asked.

'As though I'd say!' And his eyes told me he would not.

I looked at Amelia. She looked at me. I shrugged and she pouted.

'Then we'll say good day,' Porter murmured, smiling, sliding past us to hold open the door.

'Nice to have met you,' said Matthews brightly.

As we walked away, I could swear I heard them laughing.

Amelia didn't speak until we were in the car. 'Did you believe all that, Richard? Two such unpleasant men, I don't believe they'd know what the truth is.'

'They work together, have done for years. They pick up on each other's themes, and develop them. Heaven knows what's true and what's false, but one thing's clear. It all hinges on Ian Knowles. Linda seems to have got everybody she met into a right state, but apparently she failed with Knowles. He said himself she tried to pressure him over a little affair he'd had, but he called her bluff. So she was after something stronger she could hit him with. She wanted something from him, or wanted him to do something for her, and it meant a lot to her, judging by the trouble she went to.'

'The trouble she went to that week, with those visits to the police station?' she asked.

'And that's the damned snag. A lot of trouble working on her acquaintances in the drama group, all of it aiming for Ian Knowles . . . that's one thing. And a lot of trouble working on the story of her blasted car and her coat and her shoulder bag . . . that's the other. Two batches of concentrated and determined effort, and what one has got to do with the other I just cannot see!'

'You will, Richard, you will.'

'Will I? Ha!'

She was silent for a while. I was so annoyed with my lack of clarity on the situation that I couldn't get my pipe going.

'Richard?' she said quietly.

'Umm?'

'Isn't the main trouble the alibis these people have?'

'It is.'

'That they couldn't – not one of them – take time out from the play to wait for Linda, in the park?'

'Well, that *is* the point.'

'But . . . between them they might have done it. One relieving the other. She'd made so many enemies – '

'A conspiracy? Oh no! No!'

'Why not?'

'People do conspire together, yes. If I found myself another woman, we might conspire to do away with you.'

'If I didn't get in first.'

'But we'd be equally guilty. A conspiracy in this way . . . oh, I can't see that. They'd know who actually did it, you see. They couldn't live with that. Oh no . . . never.'

'It was only a suggestion.'

'Good enough to keep in reserve, to fall back on if we're desperate.'

'And haven't we reached that point, Richard?'

'Not until after I've seen Knowles.'

'Do you really think he'll tell you anything, when the others wouldn't?'

I had no answer to that.

14

Before I started the engine I gave some thought to the problem of Ian Knowles. I could see no way in which I could exert any psychological pressure.

'I could thump him a bit,' I thought, quite surprised to hear myself saying it out loud.

'I'm not having that.'

'Why not? Not being a copper any more has its compensations.'

'You're a fool, Richard.'

I laughed. 'How about popping into his place for lunch?'

She pursed her lips. 'You couldn't thump him there, with all those people watching.'

I didn't laugh at that. She'd seemed serious.

'I can take you where we can get a good cheese and pickle sandwich. A pub. Suit you?'

'Just fine.'

'And there's always a chance we'll meet Ken there.'

'Then that's where we'll go.'

Not wishing to offer any provocation, I didn't use the police yard this time, but went directly to the multi-storey park just beyond it. The Rose Of Picardy doesn't possess parking space. I settled her in the corner of the snug and fetched two plates of sandwiches, a pint of bitter, and half of lager.

This being a haunt of the police, the sandwiches were cut at a generous thickness, for large appetites. Amelia eyed hers with interest, but not dismay. I pointed out to her the men I recognized from the old days. None of them came near, or even glanced in our direction, the word having filtered down. Richard Patton was not welcome in their town.

We sat quietly, Amelia working her way through the sandwich. I still hadn't thought of any way to tackle Knowles. The idea of simply packing it in and heading home was beginning to appear attractive.

'Here he is now,' said Amelia, jerking me to attention.

I looked up to catch Ken's eye. He raised his eyebrows, I pointed to our glasses and shook my head, so he came to our table with his usual.

'Glad I've bumped into you,' he said. 'You're looking lovely as ever, Amelia.'

'I feel worn and tattered.'

'I'm not surprised, with this oaf dragging you round town.'

'You don't know what we've been doing,' I told him.

'Don't be so sure of that. Tell me, though. Are you getting anything? Anything at all. I *need* something, and quickly.'

I told him nearly all about our perfectly legitimate activities, but what I'd found amusing left him cold. He stared at his beer as though trying to hypnotize it. When I'd finished, he lifted his head and looked directly at me. His eyes were heavily pouched and red. He looked exhausted.

'You're being pointed towards Knowles,' he decided.

'Exactly my impression.'

For a moment he allowed that subject to lie dormant. He said

143

hollowly: 'This morning we had a conference. Donaldson's room.'

I nodded. 'About the case.'

'I don't know how much longer Donaldson can keep going,' Ken went on, his voice low. 'I don't think he's slept for two days. He wants an arrest. Any arrest. And right now. Just crazy. And I think he's already pushed his brain too far. He's getting mixed up, Richard. So help me . . . several times I thought he was talking about the wrong case. *Your* case, Amelia. He's got to have some-thing, anything – '

I put in quietly: 'Any ideas he's got on that, I can shoot 'em down.'

'But he's not rational. Oh Lord, never mind that. We've got two murders here, Linda's and Marjie's. He's convinced they're linked.'

'And you're not? I thought we'd accepted . . . '

'Oh, I'm not arguing with him there. Two murders, and we're after one murderer. Richard, we did a back-check on that trip that Rupert Martin made to Saudi Arabia. His plane *was* due to land at around 11.30, his original booking. But he switched flights. Delib-erately. He could've been back home at eight, and, because his wife was acting at the theatre, he could have waited for Linda to arrive home. Then waited in the shadows while she did all that business to rig the hot-wiring . . . and what *that* was all about, God alone knows . . . and then he could have killed her.'

'Neat, simple and tidy,' I agreed. 'But it's got no backing, Ken. No motive at all. And all the rest of the tangle, what Linda did – or rather, what she didn't do and lied about – that isn't in any way relevant to Martin.'

Ken merely nodded and nodded, urging me on to the end of it because he knew all that. 'But I explained about Donaldson. He's not prepared to get involved with side issues. What the victim did or didn't do isn't of interest. She was there, in that cul-de-sac, and she was killed.'

Amelia sat back, so that she could keep an eye on both of us at the same time. We weren't in dispute, but Ken's voice had an edge to it. He was exhausted, and was indicating he wasn't prepared to continue to argue with Donaldson. It was Donald-son's case – let him stew in it.

'Motive?' I asked casually. 'Or is he dispensing with that, too?'

Ken's lips twisted into some sort of a grin, then he buried it in beer and came up for air to remark: 'There could be something. We've had a team around town with photographs. The two of them had been seen together. Rupert Martin and Linda. Evenings together. Now . . . isn't that interesting!'

'Don't tell me she'd got something on him, too.'

'Facts, Richard. I'm sticking to facts. We now know they were at least acquainted. I went to see his wife – Gail Martin – and she'd remembered she'd introduced them, a year or so ago. She'd been trying to get him vaguely interested in the drama group. Even vaguely would've been a big advance. But he didn't go to any of the other meetings. He hates the theatre, no getting away from it. Particularly the amateur theatre. He told her the pros at least had an excuse for posturing, and exposing themselves to ridicule on a stage, because they had to eat. But there was no excuse for amateurs, except for a feeling of self-grandeur. She describes him as a very old-fashioned stick-in-the-mud. Gail Martin: strange woman, Richard. As cold and distant as a mountain peak.' He paused, smiling at his own flight of fancy. 'But I think she knew something. Or felt it. I could see it in her eyes. Scared stiff. I think *she* believes he did it. Did them, rather.'

'It seems to me you've got enough there to have him in for questioning.'

'That's the general idea. But he's disappeared.'

It hung heavily between us. The snug seemed suddenly very quiet, as though everybody was listening. But when I glanced round, nobody was paying any attention to us.

'Exactly what d'you mean – disappeared?'

'He was supposed to be in Aberdeen today. He's something to do with pumps, though what that's got to do with Aberdeen – '

'Oil pumps, Ken. The oil industry.'

He nodded. 'I get it. But the company he was supposed to be visiting tell us he hasn't turned up.'

'He's heard you're after him.'

'I don't see how. Anyway, he was supposed to fly from Birmingham, but his booking wasn't taken up. His car's not in any of the airport car parks. It's a yellow Austin Princess, so it'd stand out. The Brummagem police did a check for us. No car.'

'Hmm!' I said.

'Poor man,' Amelia commented.

'He's probably a murderer, love.'

'You don't know that. Now he's hunted. On the run.'

'Hardly that,' Ken told her. 'We can only keep a general look out for him, at this stage. Wait, and he'll turn up. Sure to.'

If he was so sure, why did he grimace, and make angry jabbings towards his mouth with a cigarette?

'And there's Tony . . . ' he admitted, not looking at us.

'What about Tony?' I managed to make it casual.

'When the meeting ended, Donaldson asked him to stay behind. It was timed just right. I was already out in the corridor, so I could hardly turn back. I waited out there. It wasn't long. Five minutes. Then Tony came out, and I don't reckon he saw me. Shut the door all careful and quiet after him, and walked right past me. White. Even his lips. He looked at me, but didn't see me. I called after him, but he just marched on, and when I got into my room I saw him driving his car out of the yard. Richard, he was on duty. I'd got things lined up for him, and he knew it. You know what that means . . . '

He stared at me in agony, searching for some sign that it wasn't serious. I could offer nothing. It *was* serious. Tony would be considered to be in dereliction of duty. I didn't suppose he cared. I didn't think I'd have cared, if Donaldson had thrown at me anything such as the theory Ken had outlined. Yet how could Donaldson have done such a thing, when the conference had been discussing the possible guilt of Rupert Martin?

'Ken,' I said, 'it's possible Donaldson called Tony back in order to point out another possibility.' Ken would have realized what I'd been thinking. I was only hunting for something more acceptable.

'Such as?'

'He could simply have taken him off duty and sent him home.'

'He'd have told me, and Tony's not at home.'

'Home figuratively. Anywhere out of the way. Donaldson probably told him that Martin, if he killed Linda, probably killed Marjie too. So Tony would have a personal involvement, and you know damn well you'd have taken him off, yourself, when you thought about it.'

'I did think about it.'

'Well then!'

146

'Christ!' he said violently, thumping the table. 'D'you know how that used to irritate me? This "well then" of yours!'

'All right, Ken. Sorry.'

'There can't be any possible reason for Rupert Martin to want to kill Marjie. Not one. And I was going to tell Tony that. And now we've got Tony on the loose. And where d'you imagine he'll be?'

'Hunting for Martin.'

'You don't seem to damn well care.'

'Of course I care, Ken. Listen . . . you've got a lot of men out looking for Rupert Martin. What chance d'you think Tony's got of beating 'em to it?'

He was silent. I hadn't really offered any comfort, he was only tired of arguing about it.

'That terrible young woman,' said Amelia, tossing it into the silence. 'All this trouble she's caused! Men are such fools. Time and time again . . . '

'It's sex, love. Number one motivation for violence.'

'Nobody ever fought over me,' she said, I thought wistfully.

'I would,' I assured her.

'Oh . . . you!'

I don't think Ken had heard a word of this diversion. He lifted his head and spoke with deliberation. 'Richard, do me a favour, will you.'

'If I can.'

'Go home. Drive away from here and go home. Everything's flying apart in all directions, and Donaldson doesn't care who gets hit. I don't want anybody hurt. Anybody else, I mean. Marjie was enough for me. So go away. It's not a healthy place to be. Do I make myself clear?'

'Perfectly. But how can I? As things stand.'

He sighed. He hadn't expected much co-operation from me on that issue. 'If that's how you feel . . . you can have my car.' He reached in his pocket and tossed the keys on the table. 'I'll use an official one. Use my car for whatever trouble you want to get yourself into. Then Amelia can drive herself home . . . '

'Now you listen to me – ' began Amelia.

'I don't want you within thirty miles of Donaldson,' he told her. 'Whatever this damn fool of a husband wants to do, I want you out of it.'

'You can't force me!'

'I can plead. On my knees, if you like. In here. But get away from this town, Amelia, please.'

'Ken,' I said easily, 'she's my wife. And if you think I'm going to let her out of my sight for one minute – '

'For God's sake, what do I have to say!'

We now had attention, and the snug was quiet. Heads were turned and glasses were poised.

I leaned towards him. 'You have to say nothing, Ken. I'm going to do what I can to help . . . I don't know how. But what I *can*. Amelia's going to be with me. Is that clear? Ken, are you hearing me?'

'I just wanted to know,' he muttered.

'Sure you did. And I understand how you feel. But help me along, will you? Go on, Ken. I'm not going to queer anybody's pitch.'

He tried to smile, a pitiful failure.

'I'll get 'em in,' I said.

He nodded and I went for beer and lager, taking my time over it. I could see Amelia talking to him quietly, her hand over his on the table. They both looked up as I returned.

'He wants me to go and visit Cath,' Amelia told me.

'Go if you wish, my dear.'

'I promised we would, afterwards. Didn't I, Ken?'

I sat down. 'After what?'

'You know. Everybody's been pointing to Ian Knowles, and you won't relax till you've seen him. Isn't that right?'

'Sort of.' I might not be able to relax afterwards, either.

Ken groaned. 'One damn thing after the other. Now it's Knowles.'

'I've got an idea there's something there, Ken. In fact, I know there is, if I can only winkle it out. Linda was trying to force Knowles into doing something for her. She tried, and she didn't succeed. She was after something stronger to hit him with. Now . . . if I knew what *that* is, I could use it myself.'

'Don't you dare!'

'No, no. Listen. Short of violence, I've got to have something more subtle, even if it's blackmail. So . . . Ken . . . anything you know about him, which I might be able to use – how about it?'

'There's nothing,' he said flatly.

I took a deep breath. 'Ken, you're not understanding me. I've got friends involved here, Tony and Marjie . . . and you, damn it. So I couldn't dodge out of it if I wanted to. But I'm telling you this – if I have to go to that place of his in the middle of rush hour and break it up, I'll do it. If I have to break *him* up, I'll do that. But I'm going to find out what Linda wanted from him. Do I make myself clear?'

'Now Richard!' said Amelia. 'Quietly, now.'

'I'll tell you what I know,' said Ken resignedly. 'And if you can get anything out of it, then that's up to you. But we've got nothing on him. Nothing. Heavens, you've met him. Remember? Years ago. He had a break-in, and beat 'em off, all on his own.'

'I remember.'

'He was a toughie, then. Nobody put a finger on what was his and got away with it. Violently possessive. And that's the word for him – violent. But it doesn't show. Only when somebody tries to do him down. Then he goes wild.'

'There've been incidents?'

He shrugged. 'Some. But it's been getting worse. His violence, I mean. It all seems to have happened since he got married. Six or seven months ago, that'd be. After your time, Richard. You might remember her. Hester Green as was. The daughter of old Andrew Green who's got that mill the other side of town. Went on to leather goods forty years ago, and made a fortune. A bit of a drab, poor Hester, everybody said, but there was the money, you see, and she was pushing thirty and hadn't seen anything she fancied. Then she went to that place Knowles runs . . . ' He snapped his fingers impatiently.

'The Vortex,' I offered.

'Yes. That's it. She met Knowles there, and he was apparently what she wanted, and the place was going bust, so . . . Daddy had a word with him, and a marriage was arranged.'

'Sounds like you wrote it, Ken. You can't possibly know – '

'Gossip. I'm quoting gossip. But what I do know is that Knowles has been like a wild animal since then. Look aslant at his wife . . . whoo-hoo! They were eating out one evening – '

'He runs a restaurant, Ken.'

'So what! Probably couldn't stand the food there. They'd driven out to Morgan's Point – you know it – that fancy place I couldn't afford to glance at, and they were sitting there quietly when a chap . . . oh, twenty-five, hard as nails . . . this feller walked past on his way out and said something unpleasant to Hester. Richard, it was simply a mistake. He'd mistaken her for somebody else. But he didn't get a chance to apologize. Knowles followed him out to the car park, and put him in hospital. We'd have had him for assault, only this chap didn't want to press it. That's the sort of thing. He just loses control. Touch him, and he fights.'

'There's more?'

'More incidents, yes. But it always comes out as self-protection. A pub – on his own this time – somebody spills beer on him, and finds himself on his back in seconds. Other times . . . somebody scratched his car in a car park. Broken jaw.'

'But that wouldn't be self-protection.'

'The other one swung first. Or so Knowles claimed. The other driver couldn't remember. You don't want to come up against Knowles, Richard.'

'Linda was willing to risk it.'

'Do I have to remind you she's dead?'

'But it wasn't Knowles, Ken. Anything else?'

'Something. But we couldn't connect it up. Two muggers, one with a knife, stopped a man in a dark sidestreet in town. September, this was. But the victim fought back . . . it *sounds* like Knowles. One ran off. The other one . . . well, their victim went wild, or so the story goes. Finished up in hospital with a broken rib and a broken wrist, and a mess of a face. And *that* was just like Knowles. And he – well, he had five stitches put in his arm the next morning. Said he'd put a fist through a pane of glass. So we couldn't pin it on him. But that would've been grievous bodily harm, Richard, and you know it. It went way past the point of self-defence.'

Amelia was staring at him with big horrified eyes. It was the way Ken was telling it, his flat and technical delivery, with not a scrap of emotion in it.

'Where was this?' I asked.

'The narrow lane by the old market. Totter's Close. Know it?'

I kept all emotion from my voice. 'Yes, I know it.'

'So you can see why I don't want you tangling with him.'

'You know, Ken, I can see no need for violence, even if I do have a word with him.'

'Of course not,' Amelia agreed.

Ken eyed us with suspicion.

'Any objection if I have a look round for Tony?' I asked.

He smiled, heaving himself to his feet wearily. 'I've got men out, looking for him. But you can't do any harm there, I'm sure.'

We watched him out before Amelia spoke. 'Which first? Tony's place, or that restaurant?'

I looked at my watch. It was too early for The Vortex. They would still be serving lunch. Besides, I was more concerned about Tony.

'Tony's, I think. How is it that you always know what I'm thinking?'

'You're like an open book.'

'One of these days you might read the wrong page, then where will you be?'

'I'll turn down the corner, then you can't get away.'

And, laughing, we went to pick up the car. But beneath the banter, we both knew, there was the unspoken fear that something could, at any time, take one of us away. I wondered whether this persistent terror afflicted all married couples.

No, not all, I decided. Only the lucky ones.

15

There was a police car waiting just beyond Tony's place, with two people in it. I paid it no attention, but parked openly opposite Tony's drive. His car was in it, nudged up as far as it would go against the garage.

I said: 'I'm sure he's not here, but I'll make the necessary motions. Shan't be a minute.'

I got out and walked up to the front door. There was a knocker and a bell-push, and I considered both, but I was aware before I reached them that there was a special emptiness about this house.

I can't remember how many thousands of times I've knocked on doors. After the first few hundred or so you get a feel for what's beyond that specific door: fear, trepidation, terror, panic, relief. And with some there is an emptiness, the vacancy of

151

non-occupation, the heaviness of an undiscovered death, or the casual placidity of a temporary departure.

At Tony's there was that special emptiness of a house from which the life has been drained away.

I did not even touch the bell-push. I knew Tony had probably not been inside since Marjie died, living in his car and on his feet, existing. But now his car was left on the drive. I knew where he'd be, but made a show of using the knocker and bell-push. Peered through windows. Walked back to the car, to find one of the two officers from the police vehicle leaning against it and chatting with Amelia through the side window.

He looked round as I approached. 'Oh, hello, Mr Patton. Didn't recognize you.'

"Lo Colin. This is Colin Drew, my dear. My wife, Colin. You didn't stick it in the CID then?'

He shrugged, grinned, fingered his moustache to show me how new and attractive he thought it. 'Too much waiting around, sir, like now. But they've drafted in the uniform branch for this one, and it's back again to waiting.'

I slapped him on the shoulder. 'Don't let it get you down.'

'He's not here.'

'So I gathered.' I walked round and got in behind the wheel. 'See you again.'

I backed into Tony's drive and then drove back the way we'd come, except that I took the first left, right, then left again, and very shortly we were running along with the high wall at our left.

'Is this Manor Park?' she asked.

'It is. If you feel like stretching your legs, I'd like to take a walk.'

'You think that's where he is?'

'Sure to be. Marjie died there, though that wouldn't be the draw. No ... I know what he's doing. The same as Marjie. Waiting. Staring at that spot were Linda met her death, and trying to imagine it. No, recall it. Like a backflash on the screen. I know what it's like when you're waiting. You get this idea that if you wait long enough the images will creep back and replay it for you, then you'll know the truth.'

I drew in outside the five-barred gate. She got out and had a look at it. There was a single strand of rusted barbed wire, which I hadn't noticed before, along the top rail.

'I'll never get over there.' She was wearing a brown tweed skirt with her russet cardigan.

'We'll try.'

'I can wait in the car.'

'I'd rather we weren't separated.'

She managed it by tucking up the skirt in her hands while I steadied her, then she jumped down beyond the nettles.

We began to walk up the path, which was just visibly tramped through the grass, towards the bridge. As we approached it, I noticed she slowed. When we were on it, she spotted the broken rail.

'Is this where Marjie – '

'Yes. Usually there're masses of ducks and geese around. They're probably at the other end of the lake today.'

'A pity.'

'In the early morning, the Canada geese fly off in V formations to the lake in the North Park. It's a grand sight – they're quite low over the centre of town. Then they come back at sunset. People take their kids to North Park, to feed them, that's why they fly there.'

'Then why do they fly back at sunset? Why don't they just stay there?'

'Hadn't thought about it. I suppose it's because they lock the gates at North Park at sunset. They'd be locked in if they left it too late.'

'Ho!' she said. 'Funny.'

But it had distracted her from the broken rail in the bridge. We were approaching the narrow path through the undergrowth. It was a fine afternoon, the sky clear, but with a heavy cloud layer low in the west. If it had not been for the seriousness of our purpose, the walk would've been pleasurable.

We picked our way through. It occurred to me that Amelia had not been in the park before. I was explaining about Forrester's grand design when we forced our way through to the cul-de-sac.

Here the light was not so good, with no sight of the sun. I walked the length of the tarmac surface and looked round.

'That was where the car was,' I told her. 'The passenger side was hard against the hedge. Linda's home is beyond that hedge. The car was parked as though she'd driven from the main gate, which is straight back up the hill, and through the park.' I gestured up the slightly sloping roadway, which, in daylight, gave a very much less romantic impression without the streetlights. 'And as if she simply drove past her own entrance, and stopped.'

'And you think Tony's somewhere around here?'

'Yes.'

I'd been moving around, making it very obvious to any watcher who I was. There were a thousand places he could stand quietly and wait. Banks of rhododendrons, I now saw, packed the open spaces beneath the trees, which were just sprouting their spring leaves.

'Then give him a shout,' she suggested.

'It's private property, so we don't want to draw attention to ourselves. No – if he wants to speak, he'll appear. If he doesn't, we'd never be able to find him.'

'Then it seems to have been a bit of a waste of time.'

'Yes.'

There'd been no life in her voice. The setting depressed her. I could see she wanted to leave, yet I had an uneasy feeling I would be leaving something undone. But I couldn't think what. I went back to look at the position where I'd backed the Stag beneath the trees, but in daylight it all looked different. Not so menacing, and with not so much cover as I'd thought at the time. But I couldn't detect any tyre tracks. Further along, I did, but these were not wide enough to have been the Stag's. Here the rhodos were riotous, set well back beyond the grass verge. I followed them in. There was a yellow Austin Princess parked inside them.

I went back and fetched Amelia. 'Come and look at this.'

We stood together and looked at it. The glass was misted with early-morning damp, which the clinging, heavy leaves had prevented from dispersing. I told her not to move, and walked to it carefully, taking a looping approach. There was a possibility that footprints could be important.

The doors were locked. The misting on the glass was external, and I rubbed free a small circle on the driver's side window. There was nobody inside.

I stood, looking round me. The surface was ideal for footprints, and I could see where he'd walked away from it, small feet, the shoes with toes more pointed than I would choose. Beside my own footprints there were others, not mine. A heavier shoe. The

154

shoe a man might choose, whose work involved a lot of walking. Tony had stood there, and had found what I had found.

I circled back to Amelia.

'It's Rupert Martin's car,' I said. 'From the description.'

'Then where is he?'

'Say he heard the police had been making enquiries about him. He panicked, perhaps. If he had anything to panic about.'

'Isn't it clear, now, that he did?'

'Not clear at all. But suppose he wanted to give himself time. He would drive away from home. He would have to do that, because the police might come and ask about his car. His wife wouldn't be able to see which way he turned, from the house. This is a good place to hide it, and as he's supposed to be in Aberdeen, they'd look elsewhere for him.'

'Are you saying this to me, or just talking to yourself?'

I took her elbow and moved her out on to the tarmac. 'Both of us. Somebody's already found the car, you know, and the guess is that it's Tony.'

'Ah yes,' she said eagerly. 'I see what you're getting at. Mr Martin could have walked back to his house to hide away there, while the police look for him elsewhere. So Tony's watching the house, cut off from a phone or from his car radio, and can't get in touch . . . '

'Well yes. That would apply, perhaps, if Martin hid away in his own home. But he could well want to keep his movements secret from his wife. Don't forget, his involvement in all this would have to be because of Linda. He might not want his wife to know about that.'

'So why don't we walk up to his house – it isn't far, is it? – and see what the situation is. Tony could be there.'

'It's just up here, towards the top of the slope.'

I didn't tell her that Tony, if he was watching, would probably not reveal himself to us. His purpose was not to get to a phone and inform his superiors. His central motivating force was personal.

It seemed further than when I'd driven it. Then, I'd barely got up to third when I'd passed the drive entrance, and had caught that second's glimpse of Gail Martin's white face. But, approaching it on foot, I got the chance to look around. There was no relief either side to the heavy impenetrable spread of trees and shrubs.

155

Tony could be hiding anywhere, watching, chilled and hungry and thirsty. But stubborn. I did not call his name.

We walked in at the entrance to The Swallows, following the curve of the drive. Amelia lagged behind. Although our act of trespass had begun the moment we climbed the gate, in a private drive she felt it to be a more personal encroachment.

'I wouldn't like to live here,' she said, her voice disappearing into the oppressive silence.

Then we were in sight of the sprawl of bungalow, which, with its near-flat roofs and its artificial angles to break up the frontage, seemed an alien thing in its surroundings.

'And certainly not in that place,' she added, coming to a halt.

But I'd seen a pale face at one of the windows. It had disappeared at once. I murmured softly: 'Let's go a little further.'

Her Audi was parked along the drive. Both doors to the double garage were up-and-over, no doubt to demonstrate that the yellow Austin Princess wasn't there. It would not fool Donaldson, I was certain. He hadn't much evidence to level against Rupert Martin, but I could guess he'd be trying to persuade a JP to sign a search warrant. Then he would be through the house like a hurricane.

The front door opened. For a moment she stood in the porch, then she advanced on to the gravel and began to walk hesitantly towards us. She was wearing what seemed to be a short housecoat, though its exotic pattern, vaguely oriental, gave it a heaviness that would make it uncomfortable to be lounging about in. It came to her knees. She had on slacks, and on her feet sandals. Her hair was untidy, and if she was wearing make-up she'd made a mess of it. I was forcing myself to maintain the smile I'd mustered up, but it was an effort. She had changed terribly, the flesh seeming to have fallen from her cheeks, leaving them hollow. She appeared to be squinting, though she was not facing brightness; the clouds were massing behind me to darken the sky.

'My husband is not at home,' she said distinctly, in a tone she had rehearsed, with dignity and rejection combined.

'It's Richard Patton, Mrs Martin. I've brought my wife. Just for a peep at the house. I admired it so much, but it was dark when I was here – '

She managed to raise her head, though her smile was empty. 'Oh yes. Hello, Mrs Patton. Do look round if you wish.'

'Thank you,' said Amelia. 'It was just a general impression . . . '

'And while you're looking round,' Gail Martin went on, her eyes beseechingly on me, 'you might just look through the shrubbery. It's your job, isn't it?'

'Not really. Why the shrubbery?'

'I'm sure I've seen somebody lurking in there.'

Gail Martin had an eye for lurkers, a special affinity for them. It was she who had first noticed Marjie walking in the park.

'Surely not, Mrs Martin,' I said cheerfully. 'Not in daylight. Anybody with an eye on your property – '

'I don't want intruders.' She clamped her lips together in fierce determination. 'You don't think it could be the same woman?'

Oh dear me! I thought. 'I shouldn't think so. I'll tell you what . . . ' I drew close to her, lowering my voice in conspiracy. She smelt of stale lavender water. 'We'll walk out of here, openly, and then I'll hide. You won't be able to see me, I'll be so careful. And I'll watch. How will that do?'

'Oh!' She put a hand on my arm. 'I'd be so grateful.'

'So don't you worry.'

As we turned away, I saw that her face had set in intense concentration. It was clearly an effort for her to marshal each consecutive thought. Feeling her eyes on our backs, Amelia and I walked stiffly out of the drive, and turned back again down the slope.

'You deceived her,' she whispered.

'Reassured her, I hope.'

She thought about it, then suggested: 'More than likely she did see somebody.'

I nodded. 'Tony perhaps. Or even her husband, creeping round to try to find out what's happening. Or maybe nobody. This seclusion's all very well, but when you're so quiet and remote it leaves you wide open to intruders. On her own – and I gather she's spent long periods like that – she'd begin to imagine things. Now she'll be able to imagine me, not visible, but guarding.'

'Hmm!' But she wasn't happy with my small deceit. 'You described her as younger. You said she could be taken for being in her late twenties.'

'Did I? Well, she *looked* younger. Make-up, perhaps. And now . . . it's all coming too close to her. Ken said it. He said everything was beginning to fly apart in all directions. That's what's happening to Gail Martin.'

She was very silent all the way back to the car. She slammed the door and settled into her seat.

'Richard,' she said, in her decisive voice, 'I never want to go inside that place again. It's perfectly hateful.'

'I'm sure the park itself is a pleasant place. It's people who give it the atmosphere. Shall we go and get a pot of tea and some sticky cakes? It should fill in the time before we visit Knowles at The Vortex.'

'He won't be serving dinner until much later.'

'So it'll be just the right time to catch him unoccupied.'

Simply to change the mood, and to introduce a touch of nostalgia, I took her to the narrow little café where we'd first sat facing each other across a table, and first began to learn about each other. That process is still going on. She is still capable of surprising me. At the café door she caught my arm, stopping abruptly.

'But we can't go here!' she cried, as though I might be dragging her into a den of vice.

To me it was a special memory, which I cherished. 'Why not?'

'The tea was terrible.'

'So it was. I'd forgotten. There's another place, further up the arcade.'

'Then let's go there.'

The other place, further up, was more spacious and more modern. It boasted fast service, because you did it yourself. We found a quiet corner. The tea was just as bad. It's not that I have an objection to teabags, it's the nasty bit of string attached to them.

'Richard,' she said, pushing her cup away, 'we should not have come back to this town. *You* should not. A few days, that's all it's taken, and you're drifting back into your old life. The old Richard, the hard and determined policeman, he's taking over again.'

'It's how I was when we met,' I protested.

'But you've been improving, dear. Softer, more thoughtful and understanding. But now . . . look at the way you treated that woman. You were unsympathetic. And don't try to deny it.'

I'd opened my mouth, but shut it again.

'I hate this town,' she told me with quiet intensity. 'For what it's done to you. Hate every stone and paving slab, and all the feet that walk on them ... '

'Here, now –'

'I could not have entered that other café, Richard. I want one place that I can treasure in my mind. Enter it now, and it'd take on the same tawdry and unpleasant odour of the rest of the town. You've got to leave me one tiny item of pleasant memory.'

Told you, didn't I! Still learning.

'We'll go home,' I decided. 'Right now.' I hadn't realized how deeply it had affected her.

She reached over and grabbed my wrist. 'No. You don't understand. Leave me that memory and you can have the rest. It's coming to an end, here. I can feel it. Let's stay for the end.' Her forehead puckered, then she produced the impish smile I hadn't seen for ages. 'And then you won't have anything to hurl at me when we get to the shouting and throwing things stage.'

'I was never good at throwing,' I said glumly.

'Idiot!'

We went to rescue the Granada from its parking meter, so lost in our own thoughts that we didn't realize the foolishness of it before we walked past The Vortex on the way.

She eyed the frontage without enthusiasm. 'It doesn't look much.'

'For all I know, the food might be splendid. But we didn't come here to eat. Remember?'

'I bet it's not even open.'

'Then we'll go round the back and climb over the cabbage stalks to get in. Come on, let's get it over.'

My hand was already on the door, and I'd felt it move. I pressed firmly against it, held it at full swing, and she walked in beneath my arm.

16

The interior was brighter than when I'd seen it last. There were more lights on, white ones. It detracted from the mystery of a meal, deprived it of enchantment, but this hour was not one for mystery. It was break time.

Three of the far tables were occupied. The waiters and the chef and his cooks were sitting there, discarded crockery from their own meals on the tables, and with playing cards being dealt between them. I wondered whether they ate first and got the best, or had to manage with leftovers from the previous session. Then I became aware that Knowles wasn't amongst them.

He spoke from the kiosk to one side of the entrance. I had not noticed him in the shadows there. It is movement that attracts attention, and all that was moving was a licked finger counting the fivers and tenners.

'I'm sorry, sir, we're not open yet. First serving at eight.'

'I wanted to speak to you, Mr Knowles. Privately. I thought this would be a good time.'

He'd given us no more than the flick of a glance. Now he leaned forward, closer to the glass. I could clearly detect his expression of disgust.

'Oh, it's you.'

'A few minutes,' I suggested. 'I know your time's valuable.'

He didn't answer, but came out from the kiosk door, locked it behind him, and slipped the keys into his trouser pocket. He was wearing his dinner suit, less the jacket. All very smart, with a gold watch on his wrist, and cuff-links to match. Standing together, I could see that he was about my own height, though slimmer. But there was power in his shoulders. I assumed he would be shaving before eight. His dark stubble was already noticeable. Perhaps he covered it with make-up, though.

'This is my wife,' I said.

His bow was habit. 'I'm pleased to meet you, Mrs . . . what was it? I'm sorry.'

'Patton,' I reminded him. 'Have you decided?'

'Decided? Decided what?' He was impatient. Leaving all that lonely money uncounted was grieving him.

'Shaw,' I said. 'The next play. Or perhaps Ibsen or Chekhov? When I last saw her, your leading lady could well play a tragic part.'

'You came to ask *that*?'

'No, no. But she's very good when the character's mood fits her own.'

'For heaven's sake!' Which, I guessed, was a concession to Amelia's presence. 'If you want to book a table – '

'No, thank you. I've been talking to people around town. I'd like to consult you on the conclusions I've been coming to –'

'You get the hell out of here! I've heard what you've been asking, and nobody's told you a thing.'

'They phoned you?' I found myself a little surprised at that.

'I've got friends. They don't know anything.'

'I can put two and two together,' I said with mild confidence. 'We're already attracting attention, so can't we go somewhere more private?'

'What's so special that it needs privacy?' He stuck his hand in his pocket and jingled the keys.

'Totter's Close,' I told him, getting tired of playing around.

The jingling stopped. The hand was withdrawn, clenched. For a moment I wondered whether he had the keys in his fist, in which case I would have to allow for having them thrown in my face. But he opened his hand, using it to gesture, and managed a smile to back it up.

'Shall we go into the kitchen?'

He preceded us, and held back one of the two swing doors, producing a second, though this time mocking, bow as we went through.

I had never been inside the kitchens behind a restaurant, and you can catch only glimpses through the swinging doors. But I'd heard disquieting reports, when five-star names had been bandied about disparagingly. This, therefore was a revelation. It had been cleaned down and prepared for the evening. Stainless steel predominated, and gleamed beneath the strip lighting. Knives were laid ready on formica counter surfaces. Pots and pans and saucepans, spotless, were poised ready above cold gas burners. The cookers showed not one suggestion of burned fat.

I stood and stared. Amelia took a deep breath and let it out slowly. Surprisingly, Knowles laughed.

'We don't need inspectors. My wife calls from time to time. She's a regular tartar.' He said it with subdued pride.

He had taken up a stance beside one of the counters. Close to his hand lay a row of butchers' knives. Abruptly, his mood changed.

'So what's this about Totter's Close?'

He was moving too fast for me. I had wanted to lead into it, producing a steady progression of proof. I was also disconcerted that Amelia, fascinated with the place, was moving away from me to one side, when I'd wanted to keep her behind me.

'Suppose we start at the beginning,' I suggested. 'It's all about Linda Court.'

'As though I hadn't guessed!'

'Everywhere I go, whoever I talk to, it all seems to come back to you, Knowles. Linda was trying to force you into doing something for her. You can short-cut it all, if you like. Just tell me what it was she wanted you to do, and we'll be on our way.'

'Drop dead!'

I hadn't heard that for ages. I sighed, and began moving towards him. His fingers played with one of the knives, I hoped absent-mindedly.

'My impression is that she tried it once, and you called her bluff.'

'Impression!'

'Something about a woman you were playing about with, and your wife wouldn't have been happy to know about it.'

'Keep my wife out of this,' he said quietly, but something unpleasant had happened to his eyes.

'I'd like to. But you took a big risk there, my friend, from what I've heard about Linda.'

'And what've you heard?' he asked, lifting his head. 'Friend.'

'That she was a right little bitch. Not the sort who'd hesitate to carry out a threat. So you took a risk. If, as I rather gather, your wife means something to you, then you were sticking your neck out when you threw Linda out of the play.'

'Big speeches now,' he said with contempt. 'And don't light that bloody pipe in here.' I'd taken it from my pocket without conscious thought. 'You don't know about that little episode, do you? Only what you've been told. Well, here's how it was. She challenged me – deliberately played a part in a ridiculous, tarty way, when the character was a serious and frightened woman. She knew it was a challenge, but so did I. And d'you know what, friend? She didn't want the part. Oh, don't tell me I'm crazy. That was what I thought at the time. Sure, I called her bluff, but I didn't expect her to back down. Not Linda. A wildcat, she could be, a right terror.'

162

I considered how this left me. I'd thought I understood Linda, yet he was speaking of her as having backed down. I shook my head. Amelia was examining a set of saucepans, I noticed. I tried to rationalize.

'If you managed to call her bluff, then she'd realize she hadn't a strong enough hold on you. An affair! Perhaps she knew your wife wouldn't care tuppence about that.'

Instantly he was poised like a street-fighter, his eyes hard now, his shoulders braced.

'Didn't I tell you . . . '

'I'm sorry,' I said smoothly. His attitude had supplied the answer. 'My information's all wrong, it seems.'

'Information!' he sneered. Then he laughed, a harsh and cruel sound. 'Gossip from the town bitches. What do *they* know! I'll tell you. Shall I tell you?' As though the truth could be painful to hear.

'I'd be pleased to hear.'

'Hester!' he said softly. 'You haven't met her.' Then his eyebrows shot up. 'You haven't been talking to *her*?' I shook my head. 'As well for you,' he went on, grudging the lack of motive for killing me on the spot. 'People say she's plain. Nothing to look at. They haven't really looked. You have to really look at Hester. There's something special there. You've only got to dig. I keep digging. There's more gold coming to the surface every day.'

I glanced at Amelia. She was watching Knowles with renewed interest. From him, this was poetry.

'We met here,' he said. 'I asked her out for a drink. We talked. She knew who I was, and my reputation. It didn't matter. I knew about her money. That didn't matter, either. And don't you sneer at me, mate.' I hadn't been. 'Everybody sneered. But I *like* her money, and what it brings. After she'd tarted this place up a bit, I started earning money myself. I bring it in, and I spend it. On her. Hester means everything to me. I think I mean something to her. She calls it security. I don't understand that, with the money she's got. But that's what she says. So when I tell you Linda was threatening to inform Hester, you'll know what it meant to me. But I called her bluff, and she backed off. A minute before I would've done. That's why I say she wanted to lose that part. I don't know why, and that's the truth. And if that's all . . . '

163

'No, it's not. Linda knew about an affair. If your wife means so much – '

He interrupted harshly. 'It started before Hester, damn you. I had to shake the other one off. It takes time. You oughta know that.'

I nodded, though I'd never had that sort of trouble. 'But since then – nothing?'

'No secrets from Hester now.' He said that with modest pride.

'Not even one?'

For a moment his eyes flickered, then he smiled and his confidence returned. 'I'm a talker,' he explained. 'Hester's a listener. Sits there, smiling quietly to herself, and I talk. Well . . . I found out . . . it's not like the odd bit of tumble in the old days.' He extended his hand and wiggled his fingers. 'You know – it didn't matter what you told 'em. But when you're married, it gets difficult. All this business of trying to remember what you said before! It's too much'f a strain. So I tell Hester the truth. 'Seasier. An', y' know, it's cosier. I can relax. You wanna try it sometime, matey.'

I'd noticed that, in talking about relaxing, he'd slipped into street vernacular. I promised him I would. 'Sounds a good idea.' Then while he was still relaxed, I asked: 'But I bet you didn't tell her what Linda was trying to get you to do.'

The fingers that'd wiggled, now fell back on the knife handle. 'Y' think I'm crazy?'

'So there *was* something. And what did Linda, having failed by threatening you over the woman friend, have in mind for the second go?'

He moved his shoulders, but it was not aggression. 'You tell me! She never did.'

'Perhaps she knew about Totter's Close.'

'What about it?' But his eyes had wandered from mine.

'As I said, I've been putting one or two things together, Mr Knowles – '

'An' making five?'

'There was a mugging in Totter's Close. Two people. They seemed to've got the wrong victim, because he fought back. Fought too well. One of them ran away, and the other finished up in hospital.'

'Where do I come into this?'

164

'It sounded like your form . . . no, wait.' I held up my palm. His anger was simmering again. 'The premises of Porter and Matthews are in Totter's Close. They live above the shop, and sometimes Matthews is away. Porter could've seen something that night. They never traced the man who did all the damage. It's possible Porter could identify him. If it was somebody he knew. Such as you.'

'But he ain't said he saw a blind thing!'

'Possibly he's scared to. Or doesn't want to get involved. But if I drop a word to a friend of mine in the police, they'd go and have a word with Porter. Pressure him a bit. And if it got to court, they could subpoena him, Knowles, and he'd have to go as a witness. He'd be what they call a hostile witness. It means they can cross-question their own witness, and force him into telling the truth, or he'd be committing perjury.' This was stretching the law a bit, but he wouldn't know that.

'You finished?'

'There's not much more. I believe Linda was trying to make Porter go to the police and tell them what he'd seen. Or make him promise to. So far he hasn't said anything. Maybe I'll be able to say it for him.'

'Do I get to say anything?'

'You can tell me what Linda was trying to force you into doing.'

'You can just forget that.'

'We're not talking about a slap on the wrist from the magistrate, you know. This is grievous bodily harm. It carries a prison sentence.'

'You bloody amateurs, you know nothing. Nothing!' he shouted. 'Self-defence. I saw a solicitor. He says it was self-defence.'

'It went far beyond – '

'Then what's this? What's this then?' He was fumbling with a cuff-link at his left wrist. He freed the sleeve and pulled it up. 'What d'you think this is – a pin-prick?'

On the inside of his left arm he had a healed seven-inch wound. The stitch marks were still visible. He jabbed it towards me. 'Go on, have a good look. What's that but evidence of self-defence?'

'It's contributing evidence that you've been in a fight.'

165

He appealed to the ceiling. 'Sweet Jesus! What do I have to say?'

'You can tell me why you haven't gone to the police and made a statement, if you're so sure you can plead self-defence.' Yet I felt that it wasn't the police he was afraid of.

He looked down at his hand on the counter, and at the knife so close to it, then glanced sideways at me, weighing his chances. He had a good brain, linked to the aggressiveness and self-protective instinct of an alleycat. In other circumstances, he'd have been a successful top executive in business. But he had a weakness. Such men, trading on their strengths, always have something to hide, and they conceal most jealously their weaknesses.

'You don't know much about it, do you?' he asked, this in itself being a concession.

'Clearly not.'

'I'll tell you. Get you off my back. But if I hear it's got around, I'm coming after you, Patton. Wherever you hide.'

I inclined my head. 'Agreed. There's no reason it should.'

'I was taking a shortcut through Totters' Close. About midnight, it was. We close late, here. They must've been in one of the doorways, two of 'em. I heard the movement and looked round. There was just enough light – one of 'em had a blade. I caught the light on it. The little un. Y' have to think fast an' act fast. I decided – take out the big oaf first, then I could concentrate, on that bleedin' knife. One good left to the guts, and that was it for Lofty, who ran off. So it was me an' the runt. No contest, except for the knife. But the little bugger went wild, kickin' . . . feet an' knees an' teeth . . . an' that soddin' blade. Hardly felt it, to tell the truth, when it sliced me arm. Just the warm blood. But everythin' went. No more science – you know. Put the bastard down, that's what y' got to do. Ten seconds, an' that was that. Lyin' there, not even a whimper.'

'Busted ribs,' I said, trying to remember. 'Broken wrist. Face bashed in.'

'Yes.' It came out as a hiss. His face was dark with hot blood and the memory. 'I was worried. Yeah . . . worried. Flicked on my lighter to have a look. Then I went and phoned for an ambulance, and got to me car an' sat a bit, tied up the arm, and went home.'

'So?' I asked. 'What's new in that – except your viewpoint?'

166

'Nobody told you, then? It was a girl, damn it, a girl. I'd beaten up a seven-stone slip of a girl, who turned out to be seventeen.'

'Ah!' I said, and Amelia cried out from the side: 'A girl!'

I glanced at her. She was waving a two-pint saucepan, as though caught up emotionally in the violence he'd been describing. She clearly had not understood the significance of what he'd admitted. To have beaten up a girl, whatever the provocation, would disgust him. He would certainly not have dared to admit it to his quiet and admiring wife, who saw him as a woman-protector, not a woman-beater.

Yet to me . . . yes, to me he could afford to admit it, in fact might be eager to. Certainly it would've been the first time it'd been said, his guilt not shared but confined. And guilt would be a novel, even destroying, emotion to him. He was glad to reveal it to someone who would understand. The modern generation would scoff at his ancient philosophy.

When I looked back at Knowles, he was nodding and nodding at me. We were two kindred souls.

'So that was something you lied to your wife about,' I said with confidence.

'Yeah. Sort of.' He held up the knife. 'Told her I'd slipped with one of these. They're very sharp,' he informed me meaningfully.

'It therefore follows,' I went on, ignoring the knife, 'that if Linda could've pushed Llew Porter into saying he would report you for it, you'd have quite a bit of trouble explaining it to your wife.'

'Sort of,' he admitted. His voice was very low. Everything was suppressed, his expression, his cat-like tension.

I took a deep breath and went on: 'And you wouldn't have been able to refuse doing what she wanted you to do.' I spread my hands. QED, as we used to say at school. I spread my feet also, just an inch or two, in case I needed a rapid take-off.

In the silence I heard somebody say: 'Twenty, and see you.'

'Don't tell me,' he said softly, 'that I'd got a good motive for killing Linda, because I know I had. I'd have done it, too, if it'd got to the point. But it didn't. Somebody else did it first.'

'Which means you're the only one who knows what she was after,' I pointed out.

'And I ain't gonna say.'

I considered whether it was worth taking it on. I didn't know

167

with any certainty that Knowles had anything important to reveal. It was only an instinct, perhaps based on the fact that he was so determined to hide it. I decided to take the risk.

'But I think you'll tell me. Otherwise I'm going to drive straight from here to the gatehouse and tell your wife . . . '

'Richard!' Amelia screamed.

The knife had come up. I was already moving, but a blur in the corner of my eye distracted me. Amelia had thrown the saucepan. Her aim was not accurate; it flew through the space between us, closer to me than to him. The knife dug a scar in the counter surface, and the saucepan crashed into piled crockery at the far side. He was panting, but then I had his wrist and he grimaced. The knife fell from his fingers. Behind me I heard the double thump of the swing doors and a voice with a foreign accent called out: 'Boss! You in drouble?'

'Get out of here!' he shouted, and again I heard the double thump. We faced each other, both breathing hard.

'Easy,' I whispered. 'Don't be a damned fool.'

'You go near my wife . . . '

'No. An empty threat.'

I felt him relax. It all died as rapidly as it had flared up. He hissed his compliance, and I released his wrist. He shook himself, then bent to retrieve his cuff-link, which had finished on the floor.

'What,' I persisted, 'did Linda want you to do?'

I heard Amelia whimper, but I didn't dare to glance in her direction.

I had called it an empty threat, but Knowles knew it would remain so only if he decided to co-operate. The issue couldn't have been very important now, not compared with his marriage. Nevertheless, he showed me his teeth, to indicate he wasn't pleased.

'Oh, you're a beauty, you are!' he said in disgust. 'All right. I'll tell you. But if it gets back to Hester . . . I told you I was prepared to kill Linda. I meant it. Are you sure you want to hear this? It could be your death warrant.'

'I want to hear it.'

He smiled while he said it, waiting for my reaction. 'She wanted me to go to Rupert Martin and tell him I'd been having it away with Gail for over a year.'

'Oh!' I said. I considered it, and moved it round in my mind.

168

No flashes of inspiration relieved the darkness. 'Why?'

'How do I know?'

I thought I saw a possibility, and cheered up marginally. But more definitely I realized why he hadn't wanted even to admit that. 'She'd really got you by the short and curlies, hadn't she! If you didn't do what she wanted, your wife would find out you'd beaten up a young girl, and if you did, it'd probably get back to your wife, which would be just as bad.' I grinned at him. 'And had you?'

'Had I what?'

'Been having it away with Gail Martin?'

'Are you bloody crazy? That stupid, frigid creature! She'd been messing around, trying it on, but I wasn't playing along. Don't you understand?'

'Beginning to.'

'Good. I'm very happy for you. Now get outa here – they've gotta get things moving.'

'And so have I, friend, so have I.'

'And remember . . . ' His finger almost touched my nose. 'Go near my wife . . . '

'I've got no reason to. Shall we go, my dear?'

But Amelia was already standing by the swing doors.

He watched silently as we left. In their corner, the poker players sat rigid, their eyes urging us out. The rain in the street was refreshing, and cooled my brow.

'I had an idea it might rain,' I said. 'We'll have to hurry if we're not going to get soaked. Cut through the new shopping precinct and the arcade, and we'll get some cover.'

I got her moving fast enough that she couldn't start a discussion in the street. It wasn't until we reached the car that she found time for words.

'What a terrible man! So violent.'

'It was a display, to convince himself. He's losing the drive of it, though he doesn't realize that.'

'Very subtle,' she said, quietly sarcastic.

'Logical, my dear. That mugging upset him. He's not the sort of man to go along with this equality lark. Striking a young girl, and doing it so brutally, isn't in his book at all.'

'Self-defence. She had a knife. She was the attacker.'

'In law, perhaps. Not in his personal code of behaviour. His wife's taming him, and he likes it. He'd kill for her, and *she* likes it. But if she tames him too much, he'll lose his appeal for her. Ironic, isn't it! He knew that if she found out what he'd done to that girl, he'd have lost her.'

'So he had a strong enough motive for killing Linda.'

'Yes. What a pity he wasn't able to be there, waiting for her to get home. There's one thing certain, he wasn't her killer.'

'Does that mean you know who was?' she asked suspiciously.

'Not really. But I think I can guess why. We'll have to get back to Manor Park. I've got to get hold of Rupert Martin, before he makes things worse.'

'You think that's where he'll be?'

'I'm banking on it. If I can't find him I'll have to explain it all to Donaldson, and you know how thrilled he'll be about that. And I've to hope they'll get to Tony in time.'

'So why are we sitting here?'

I was reluctant to say it, because she doesn't like being left out. 'I was wondering if I'd better run you along to Cath's first.'

'Don't be ridiculous.'

'You know you can't stand that park.'

'More than anything, I hate you chasing around and getting yourself into trouble.'

'Yes.' I smiled at her. 'Thank you for the saucepan, by the way.'

'I missed.'

'All the same, it served its purpose.'

'I was aiming at you.'

I turned the ignition key, the starter motor drowning my comment.

17

'I could do with a word with Ken,' I commented, having continued to clear the situation in my mind.

The wipers were lashing vigorously, attempting to clear the glass, but I could still barely see enough to drive.

She asked if I could remember where she'd hidden her folding umbrella. The rain was really lashing down now.

'Look under the seat,' I suggested. 'I need to know whether Tony's been contacted, and I'll look a fool if I search for Martin when they might have got him at the station by now.'

'Phone them, then. Yes, it's here.'

'They'll have orders not to speak to me.'

'If you ask me, you won't be able to do much searching in this rain, anyway.'

The spray was dancing high from the road surface, catching rainbows from the streetlights. Plumes of water were being sprayed by approaching traffic, and anything over 20 mph was impossible. Pedestrians were darting across the street from one possible shelter to the next.

'Let's get there first, then see what the situation is,' I said.

It was now 7.30, but already as dark as midnight. The rain roared on the roof.

I was aware, long before we reached the gatehouse, that something was going on. The wall was running along the far side of the road, and I was still half a mile short, but nevertheless I'd already spotted two police cars parked at intervals. The park was under siege. What did they expect? That somebody would make a break for it by climbing over the wall? In which case, who? Tony Brason or Rupert Martin?

I slowed even more as we came in sight of the entrance. Through the downpour it was difficult to see what was going on the other side of the road, but several cars were spread around the gatehouse opening. Quietly, I coasted in, edging my nearside tyre over the kerb, so as not to cause an obstruction and thus draw attention to myself. Cautiously, I lowered the side window. The rain was slanting the other way, and I got only the benefit of a few bounces.

All the same, I was spotted. A uniformed officer, heavily caped, walked across the road to me and leaned against the roof.

'You can't park here, sir.'

'Is Inspector Latchett available?'

'Yes, sir, but I don't see . . . '

'Come on, Colin, we've already met once today. It's Richard Patton.'

'Yes, sir, so I see. All the same, will you please move on.'

There was abrasion in his voice. I spoke with sympathy. 'Tricky, is it?'

'You wouldn't believe! I've just got to ask you to move on.'

'I need to have a word with Inspector Latchett.'

'He's sitting in with the Chief Inspector. How can I possibly – '

'Try, Colin, try.'

Rain ran from the peak of his cap and on to my lap. In the end, he nodded. More of it ran. 'I'll try.'

I watched as he headed back across the road. With the window still down, I could see more clearly than I had through the windscreen. A large, dark car was parked half across the entrance, and another one, which I recognized as Ken's, was parked nose-in, to absorb the other half. This was a technique I knew. Ken's car could back in or out to allow other vehicles access, once it had been checked that they had a valid right to entry or exit. Colin walked to the large car. I saw a rear window move down, and Colin bend his head. There was a glimpse of Ken's face, pale against the rain, as he looked across to me. After a few seconds the door opened.

I turned off the engine, which I'd left running in case we were forced to depart rapidly, turned the lighting down to sides, wound up my window, and reached back to release the lock on the rear door. And waited.

The door opened, and Ken slid inside. It slammed, and I turned, releasing my seat belt to give me more room.

'What the hell're you doing here, Richard?' He was in a savage mood, his knuckles white from his grip on the back of my seat.

'I need to get inside the park.'

'In no way will you get in there. Oh, for God's sake, why don't you go home!'

'What's going on, Ken?'

'Donaldson's got a warrant for the arrest of Rupert Martin.'

'And you're all waiting for him when he finally drives home?'

'That's the idea,' he said, tensely weary.

'What if I tell you he hasn't left?'

'I wouldn't believe you.'

'Why not?'

'It's one of your tricks. Donaldson got a search warrant, too. We've been through the house.' His anger seemed to ease, and he tried persuasion. 'Richard, I'm up to here with Donaldson. He's sitting there like a ghost, waiting, fading away in front of my eyes. Nothing I say penetrates. So go home, please. I've got more than I can handle as it is.'

'Tony. Any word of Tony?'

'No.'

'He's looking for Martin, too, you know. Can you imagine what'll happen if he finds him first?'

'I can imagine.'

'Then shift your car, Ken. Let me through. I think I know where I can find Tony. The rain'll drive him out.'

This was very unlikely, and if Ken hadn't been under such stress he'd have realized it at once. Tony was not the type to surrender to a bit of discomfort, though the rain might soak through to his underpants.

Ken said: 'I don't know where it'll drive him, and I don't care any more.'

'Yes you do. I'm talking about Tony Brason. I've been digging out some facts, Ken, and at last I think I'm in a position to help him. But I need to find him first. Not have him picked up by your lot and carted away for Donaldson's attention. I want to get into the park, and I'll do it if I have to drive round and walk in the back way.'

'We've got it covered,' he said flatly.

Donaldson had finally got through to him and dented his self-esteem. Ken was talking like a man beaten into submission. I couldn't think what to say to him.

There was a tapping on my side window. I wound it down.

This I had not expected. Donaldson was standing outside, as though it could have been a calm, dry evening. He was wearing a light mac and his strictly correct hat, rain pouring from his shoulders. He was stiff, holding it all in, struggling for control of the situation when he had already lost it.

'I thought it was you!' he said in disgust. 'Why are you talking to this man, Latchett? Patton, I ordered you out of my town.'

'So you did,' I agreed evenly.

'So why are you here?'

It was his calm assumption that he could order my movements that angered me. 'I don't want to teach you your job, Donaldson,' I told him briskly. 'But I'd just like to remind you that you're *Detective* Inspector Donaldson. So why aren't you detecting? An ordinary –'

173

'How dare you!'

'An ordinary constable could've sorted this out better. Get away from my car, damn you.'

It was getting like two schoolkids blustering at each other. I hoped he would go. I wished I was in a position to leave, myself.

'I'll have you arrested – '

'In another minute,' I told him, 'I'm going to open this door and get out and give you a bloody good excuse. You'll be flat on your back . . . '

'Richard!' Amelia whispered, grasping my arm.

I'd just about had enough of Donaldson. Very nearly I came to the point of shaking her off violently. But not quite.

He must have realized he couldn't push me much further. He looked past me. 'And you, Mrs Patton . . . I have unfinished business concerning you.' He was ignoring me completely. I was no more than a faintly buzzing annoyance in the background. Now he had Amelia to torment. But he was uncertain. He was talking as though searching for the correct tone.

'Not unfinished, Mr Donaldson,' said Amelia firmly, leaning forward to look past me.

'I am sitting in my car,' he complained. 'Alone, since Inspector Latchett sees fit to come over here and chat. And I have hours. I can expect that. Hours.' Despair edged its way in.

I had the door unlatched, but he put his hip against it. Standing, he was able to exert more pressure than I could. He seemed not to realize that his action was petulant and immature.

'Perhaps you'd care to come across, Mrs Patton,' Donaldson suggested, now all fatherly attention. 'There's so much to talk about.'

I growled deep in my throat, and Amelia touched my arm. 'Richard, it's all right.' She sounded confident, but I could detect a tremor in her voice. It was not all right, and she knew it.

'I'll kill him.'

'Don't be ridiculous. I'll go and talk to him. No, it's my decision. It'll do no harm. Be sensible for once, Richard.'

Ken had his hand clamped on my shoulder. He whispered: 'I'll be there.' He was still trying to rescue the situation.

'No, Ken. I'll be there myself.'

'But wasn't there something you wanted to do?' she asked softly.

Amelia had her door open. She was unfurling her umbrella,

glancing at the sky, like a woman wondering whether to go shopping. She was offering me my chance, by distracting him.

Ken understood, and whispered in my left ear: 'The keys are in the ingnition. Help yourself. But make it quick, Richard, or I may have to kill him myself.'

I removed the pressure I'd been exerting on the door. To me, it was an admission of defeat. Donaldson stood back. Amelia walked round, and I do believe she smiled at him. Ken thrust something over my shoulder. It fell into my lap.

'A radio,' he said softly. 'In case you need help.' Then he climbed out of the car.

I needed help, right at that moment, for control and for rational thought. For my heart, which was jumping about violently. Ken had meant: in case he had to recall me urgently.

Donaldson took her arm. He actually put his hand on her! I was nearly out of the door, but swore violently and held on. I watched them reach his car. He held open the rear door for her, and when she was inside he walked round to the other side. Ken had caught up with them, and glanced back for a second, then he got into the front, behind the wheel.

I slipped the radio into the side pocket of my anorak, and waited two minutes. Then I got out into the downpour, locked the car door, and walked unhurriedly across the road. Rain lashed my face. I reached Ken's car, opened the door, slid inside, and gave it full choke because I didn't know how long it had stood there. The engine awoke at the first touch of the key.

'Heh!' somebody shouted, but I was already moving.

I heard running feet, but I was up to second gear and accelerating fast up the slope.

The trees closed around me. Now it was really dark, Forrester's decorative streetlamps being smeared by the downpour. On full main beams, the rain was caught in front of me like a curtain of silver strings. It seemed that the car had difficulty in forcing its way through, which was ridiculous, but it wouldn't move fast enough for me. I had to see whether the yellow car was still there, where I'd last seen it. If it was not, I could think of no action I might take.

I breasted the peak of the rise. Briefly, the headlights danced in the tops of the trees, then they were down again, fighting through the rain barrier. I knew when I passed the entrance to

The Swallows, but I couldn't see it. I was having difficulty holding a line on the flooded tarmac surface.

I calculated I was a hundred yards short of the drive to Judge Hope-Court's residence, and began to slow. The brakes wouldn't hold, the drums being swamped. I edged over on to the grass verge, feeling its soggy surface begin to absorb the speed. The outer edge of the headlight beam fell on movement, on the opposite verge. I swung the nose over, just before the car came to a halt. Now the beam fully revealed what was happening.

Two men were fighting.

I jumped out of the car and began to run. I could recognize Tony from the set of his shoulders, and the light also caught a flash of beard. Tony had his hands round Rupert Martin's throat. He was shaking him loosely, like a wet dishcloth. I shouted: 'Tony! No!'

There was a lighter flash as he turned his face, then I took him at a dead run, shoulder down into his side. It broke his grip, but Martin was flung spinning away. We fell heavily, sliding, and I held on while Tony tried to fight his way free.

'It's me, Tony, you stupid bastard!' I gasped. 'Leave him. Leave him. He didn't kill her.'

He got to his knees, knuckles digging into the mushy turf. His face, streaming and muddied, was distorted with fury and effort. I didn't think he understood.

'He didn't kill Marjie,' I shouted into his face.

He shook himself, and fought his way to his feet. For a moment he was unsteady, his feet spread, then he reached down to help me up.

I was winded, and had to bend over for a few moments. My ears were buzzing. I dimly heard him demand: 'Then who did?'

'For God's sake!' I gasped. 'You've had all day to think about it. I was going to ask you.'

We went over to have a look at Martin. He was on his knees, doubled over and retching. We helped him to his feet. He was a mess, his natty suit now hanging on him soggily. Like Tony, he had no coat. Shudders were running through him, and he was trying to choke out words. But only groans emerged.

'Certainly not him,' I said. 'Let's get him into his car.'

Tony glanced towards the headlights. 'Why not yours?'

'It's Ken's. D'you think he'd want you two in it?' Or me, come

176

to think of it. I was covered with mud all down one side, and my face felt stiff with it.

'No,' he agreed. 'The other one, then.'

'Let's see where he keeps his keys.'

Martin was hanging between us, a sodden wreck. We slapped his sides, and located the keys in a jacket pocket. Even inside, the pocket was wet and cold. I lifted them out, and handed them to Tony.

'Take it easy,' I told him. 'It's soft ground back there.'

He whipped rain from his face with the back of his hand. His hair hung lank over his forehead and ears. His eyes caught a gleam from Ken's headlights, and the shadows were carved heavily round his mouth.

'Can you handle him?'

I said I could. Martin was now managing to croak a few words, but they weren't intelligible. Water ran from his chin when I lifted his head.

'How's your throat? Can you swallow?'

'Maniac!' He wheezed. 'God, it hurts.'

'He's bringing your car out. We'll have the heater on, and you'll feel better. We could take you home, if you like.'

'No!' It came through with more resolution. I felt his fingers digging into my arm. 'Not yet.'

I heard the engine of the yellow Princess burst into life. The lights came on, the heads blinding us on main beam at first, until Tony flicked to dip. The engine note became more purposeful as the tyres dug in, and the beams jigged, tossing our shadows around. But then it settled, and the nose emerged from the shrubbery. Tony eased it beyond the grass verge, and turned the nose uphill. He obviously believed Martin would want to be taken home.

I called out: 'Leave it ticking over with the heater on.' Tony slid out of the car and came over to us.

'We're going to make a right mess of that lovely interior.'

'Who cares! Get him in the front, Tony. You too. You both need the best of the heat. Suit you, Mr Martin?'

He nodded, and wheezed something. When Tony tried to take his other arm, Martin struck his hand away angrily. 'Madman!' So I did it myself, getting him into the front behind the wheel, where he'd feel at home. The familiarity caught him firmly

177

enough to prompt him to turn the lights down to sides, which reminded me of Ken's lights. I'd have the battery flat in no time. I walked up the slope and put off all the lights, then went back.

Tony and Martin were in the front, with the engine on fast tickover. Already a little heat was making itself felt. We left one door open a fraction to operate the interior light, and I settled in the back.

Martin managed to say: 'The glove compartment.' He gestured across Tony's lap. 'Cigarettes.'

'They'll kill you,' I told him. 'That throat . . . '

But Tony had found them. Martin fumbled one out, then, hesitantly, he offered one to Tony, who gave a bleak smile but shook his head. There was nothing in Martin's attitude to suggest a feeling of guilt, but the very fact that he was not raving in fury at his treatment by Tony was an indication that he knew his actions were not exactly rational. There was a resignation in the slump of his shoulders. The time for a settlement was facing him.

Giving him time to settle his thoughts, I reached for my pipe. It was broken. A tip for you – don't smoke a meerschaum if you want to get into a fight, they're only clay.

Martin lit up and drew in smoke deeply. He coughed and spluttered, and clutched at his throat, but when he tried it his voice was better.

'I'm having you in court,' he told Tony, but it was really no more than a comment.

Tony grunted. I could smell his wet trousers warming up.

'Suppose you tell us,' I said from the back, 'what all this has been about?'

'Why should I?' He was strong enough for defiance.

'Because there's a road-block at the gatehouse, and a chief inspector is waiting for you with a warrant for your arrest.'

Martin was rapidly regaining his control. He drew on his cigarette and blew smoke at the windscreen. Already the glass was steaming up inside. I turned down a window a few inches.

'On what charge?' he asked at last, using his mature executive voice.

'I believe for the murder of Linda Court. Which probably means for the murder of Marjorie Brason, as well.'

'Ridiculous! Who's this Brason person?'

'This is her husband, sitting beside you.'

178

Martin darted a glance towards Tony, who bared his teeth at him.

'So,' I suggested, 'before we take you there, why not tell us why you'd hidden your car away and then spent all day hiding in the trees.'

'I have not spent all day hiding in the trees, as you put it. I had lunch with Colonel Forrester. We talked, we played some chess.'

'But he must have known the police were at his gates!'

'Forrester would hardly accept that there could be a murderer amongst his residents,' said Martin drily, so drily that it set him off coughing again.

When he'd finished, I went on: 'But nevertheless, you hid your car, when you were expected to drive to Birmingham and fly to Aberdeen.'

'You know so much!' Now he was strong enough to venture into sarcasm. 'But I knew, you see. I have friends. I heard the police were making enquiries. I was . . . well, afraid and con-fused, I suppose. I needed time to think. I drove away from home . . . ' He stopped, then half-turned, so that he could bring both Tony and myself within the confines of his fears. 'It was so . . . unacceptable that I should be accused of harming Linda. The last person . . . I'd have given my life for her.' He stopped again. Tony and I glanced at each other. There was complete blank surprise in Tony's eyes. 'I drove away,' Martin continued, 'because I didn't want to worry my wife. She involves herself so deeply in my life, you see. Every movement has to be accounted for. I couldn't . . . just couldn't . . . tell her I was in trouble. She is very possessive. She would want to possess the trouble, too. But it was something I knew I had to face on my own. It was mine. So I drove out of the gate, but to here. I had to have time to think, and . . . ' He hesitated, tossed his head, then lowered his eyes. 'And I couldn't, of course, go to Linda's funeral. So I came here. Where she died. I often come here,' he admitted.

Tony cleared his throat. A fellow sufferer. 'I know what you mean. She was close, eh? Mighty close.'

Martin turned on him fiercely, as though Tony had challenged his right to it. 'I'll listen to no criticisms!'

'Not intended,' Tony assured him.

'You were referring to the fact that I'm a married man.'

'Not at all.' Tony's voice changed. I thought he was handling it

179

well, and sat back, leaving him to it. 'Tell me about Linda,' he suggested easily, confidingly.

I thought at first that Martin was not going to reply. He took out another cigarette, but then replaced it. There was an element of decision about the action.

'I was introduced to her at one of those drama society meetings. I hadn't wanted to go, but my wife can be very persistent. Linda seemed at first somehow unreal. But the whole bunch of them were unreal. The moment they entered the hall they seemed to discard their own personalities. It was fascinating, and somehow disgusting. You might not feel the same,' he conceded. 'Linda was the only one who spoke to me as though I was a person and not a weird character. So I asked if I could see her again, away from that atmosphere. She was . . . was someone completely outside my experience. As – I suppose – I must have seemed to her. I am not a fool. Not completely unworldly. I knew what she was and I'd heard about her lifestyle. But we met, and met again, and again. I wanted to . . . to discover her. Does that make sense? And she me. We uncovered . . . well, excitement in each other. I don't know about her, but I also discovered aspects of myself I hadn't dreamed existed.'

He stopped, looking around, perhaps expecting to see superior smiles at his naivety. But, for me, it was too damned acceptable for smiles, and I was trying to control my sympathy. The man was completely at a loss in the modern world, yet somehow, with his awakened romanticism, admirable.

Tony said: 'I know exactly what you mean.'

'Yes. I believe you do. But there I was, wanting her more and more, longing for her when we were apart, but beneath it all I knew what she was, and had been, and that she was the best actress they'd got in that group, and me trying to persuade myself that what I saw in her eyes and in every gesture was real and true. Damn it!' He thumped the wheel with his hands. 'I can't even *tell* it right. It was far, far more than I've said. My wife . . . I do not like to speak in this way about my wife, but it has to be said . . . my wife has not always been warm. I believe she felt this, and that she might have been – what is the word? – more compliant. That's not it. But you know what I mean. Certainly, over the past year or two I've felt her possessiveness growing, as though she realized she might lose me. Though of course, that was not a valid

180

possibility. And yet, with Linda, I began to believe it might be so.'

Tony waited a moment, then said: 'Linda led you to believe there could be some permanency in your relationship?' He'd been caught in Martin's formal style.

'More than that,' Martin said softly. 'Linda wanted me to divorce my wife, and marry her.'

And then I understood. Linda had been throwing her sexuality around for so long that it had become a boring game. In her mid-twenties, she'd realized it was time for a more solid existence. Rupert Martin had offered that. Who knows, she might have seen something exciting in him. Certainly he would be far removed from her usual experience of male contacts. So she'd decided she wanted him, not, I suspected, as she'd wanted the others. She had come face to face with a genuine passion. From that moment of realization, nothing would have stopped her.

For the first time for some minutes I spoke. I had knowledge that wasn't in Tony's possession.

'And was there a barrier to divorce?' I asked.

'I'm afraid there was.'

'A religious barrier?'

He turned to face me. 'I am not a religious man, though I understand religion has its comforts. People of religion run their lives by a set of rules that have been laid out in front of them. From time to time they break them, and there are provisions for that, too. But non-religious people have to frame their lives within their own personal set of moral laws. And as they're their own, they can't be lightly broken. A conscience is very unforgiving, don't you find? So marriage, to me, is a very special contract. I find . . . I found it was very difficult to consider breaking it.'

'But you might have been persuaded into breaking it?'

'I don't know what you mean.'

'If it was shown to you that your wife, Gail, had already broken it, say . . . '

'How could she have done that?' He was genuinely puzzled.

'By committing adultery.'

'I . . . wouldn't believe such a thing. Nonsense.'

'Even if the man with whom it had happened came to you and admitted it?'

181

In the dim light within the car I couldn't read his expression accurately. But his voice, when he spoke, was thick with emotion. 'You know something.' It was an accusation, not a question.

'I know that Linda was trying to arrange that. It was not true, but you would've accepted it. Wouldn't you?'

He shook his head violently, but he whispered: 'Yes.'

'So at least you now know the truth,' I told him gently. 'Linda loved you so much that she went to a vast amount of effort to bring that about. She was trying to put pressure on a certain man to force him into claiming adultery with your wife. But she didn't succeed.'

Abruptly he turned from me, burying his face in his hands, his forehead on the rim of the wheel.

Tony and I looked at each other. He shook his head. I sat back and waited. The engine was now overheating and racing. Tony reached across and switched it off. The heater motor was roaring, a fact that seemed to penetrate to Martin. He turned it off. Full silence rested inside the car. The air was humid and stank of wet worsted. The roar of rain on the roof asserted itself.

'And she did all that for nothing,' Martin croaked at last.

'In what way – for nothing?' I asked.

He raised his head and spoke to the now-cleared windscreen. 'That week in Saudi . . . it was different. I had time to get out on my own for once, and see the sights. I was surprised to find that I wanted to. And it's different there, I discovered. Something I hadn't realized: the women, they are treated as inferior beings. It set me thinking. My wife has always thought of *me* as an inferior being. She owned me. With Linda, we were two people. Equal. I'm nearly twice her age. But equal. So suddenly, in Saudi, I discovered that I'd made up my mind. I changed my flight back. I sent Linda a cablegram. Meet me . . . meet me here!' He gestured frantically. 'I came early, to meet her, and to tell her that I'd decided on a divorce, and I found her dead. I found her dead!'

He flung open the car door. I thought he was going to run away from it, but he only needed air, wet and cold air. He was gasping for it.

'I found I couldn't touch her,' he said on a sob. 'My brain didn't seem to be working. In the end, I left her and went home. Home! My wife . . . Gail . . . came in at about midnight. She was drunk. How she drove home I don't know. I went to bed. She was – *that*

182

night! – she was warm and wanted me. But there was nothing I could offer her. Or she me.'

When he seemed not to want to go on, I said quietly; 'And in the morning, then you decided Linda ought not to lie there.'

'I thought it could've been a nightmare. I took the dog out early. But it was all so stinkingly, filthily true.'

'The dog,' I said. 'It died.'

His head jerked round in surprise. 'What? Yes. She died. She was very old. She died. Everything I loved was dying around me.'

'But you managed to continue with your life.'

He shot me an angry glance. 'What else was there to do but go on dragging along with it?'

'And all this while you must have suspected . . . ' I deliberately didn't finish it.

'I suspected,' he choked, 'that my wife had found out about Linda and me, and killed her.'

'But surely that couldn't be so,' I said. 'The police are satisfied that at 5.30 Linda was visiting the police station, reporting her car stolen. Your wife was at the theatre at six, and there until midnight.'

'Do you mean this? Is it true?'

'Why d'you think there's been no arrest, Mr Martin? Anybody who had any sort of motive for killing Linda has been checked. Not one of them could have waited here to kill Linda at the time she would have reached home.'

'Oh,' he said emptily.

'There's an interesting sequence of events.'

Tony spoke heavily. He'd been quiet for quite a long while. 'I don't think Mr Martin would be interested in that.'

'But I'm sure he would. He might even want to make a comment or two.' What I meant by this was that Martin, in the context of what Tony was about to say, might have some comment to make that would clear the issue.

'You mean the hot-wiring?'

'And what led up to it.'

'Well, if you think so, Mr Patton,' said Tony. 'But I warn you, there's a weakness in that marvellous theory of yours.'

'Then let's hear it, Tony, weakness and all.'

So Tony told it. Martin had only one comment to make, but it

183

did clear up one minor point I hadn't quite accepted. When Tony explained that the week of visits to the police station probably explained why Linda had deliberately allowed the lead in the play to be snatched from her, to give her the time to do all that, Martin spoke up gruffly.

'No. You're wrong there. It was to please me. I asked her not to take the part.'

After a moment's pause, Tony continued, to its end on the Saturday.

18

'So you see,' Tony finished, 'the hot-wiring, all done wrong, proved that it'd been done after the car was driven here and parked just past the drive.'

Martin had been silent, listening carefully. He was a good listener, and would give all his concentration to anything he undertook. He was, however, slightly impatient. 'But I can't understand this. Linda did all *that* herself? But why? Whatever for?'

'I don't think we decided on a reason, Tony, did we?'

'No. It wasn't relevant at the time.' He explained that to Martin. 'The hot-wiring theory was only meant to reassure my wife.' He twisted round to face me again. 'But I've been thinking about it, Mr Patton.'

'I thought you would.'

'There's a snag or two in it.'

'Is there? Let's have 'em then.'

'The fact that the bonnet was broken open, that's a snag.'

'And the letter,' I suggested.

'Yes. The letter.'

'What letter?' Martin demanded.

Tony looked to me to carry it on, but I said: 'No. You Tony.'

'It was your theory, that hot-wiring business.'

'And now, it's your turn. You carry on and chop it to pieces, Tony.'

184

'*What* letter?' Martin demanded.

'I received a letter, signed Linda Court, sent that weekend, but it arrived too late. She was apparently asking for help.'

'But you see!' Tony pounced in, talking half to him and half to me. 'Whatever Linda was doing – even if she was only trying to draw attention to herself because she thought she was in danger – she was achieving nothing by sending that letter. Nothing to help. It'd take ages to filter back to here. So it was weak, Mr Patton, as far as your theory was concerned. She took too much trouble for so poor a result.'

'Granted,' I said. 'So the theory was also weak. But what about the broken bonnet catch?'

'You know all this,' he said suspiciously.

'You've got something in mind, Tony. Let's hear it. The broken bonnet catch . . . '

'You're leading me in again!' he said harshly. 'Just like you did before. Lead me on, then tear into me and make me sound a fool.'

'But now it's you destroying *my* theory.'

'I don't believe it.'

'Then carry it on. Find out.'

I was tossing him a challenge. He'd matured since I'd seen him the first time. Then he'd been over-eager, anxious to seize on any theory that would exercise his mind. When I'd offered it, he'd been too anxious to be able to see the trap. Now he should have been sufficiently experienced to match wits with me, to offer the challenge to me and carry himself forward on his own self-confidence.

Perhaps there'd been a lift to my voice, the hint of a trap. He reacted violently, his previous hurt still controlling him.

'Find out your bloody self!' he shouted. Then he opened the door, clambered out, and slammed it behind him.

I was outside no more than a second later. The slam of my door sounded like an echo. We stood, one each side of the car, with the rain bouncing from the roof between us.

'Stop acting like a fool, Tony.'

'You know you've got it all worked out!' he accused me. Then he turned on his heel.

'Don't you walk away from it!' I bellowed at his back. 'I can't do this myself.'

He stopped and turned his head. 'You're lying.'

185

'Tony, there's a theory. You *must* have heard it. A theory that you could have done it. You knew Linda, and you killed her . . . '

'And Marjie? he cried wildly. 'Go on. Tell me I killed Marjie!'

'Tony, listen. I know you. I wouldn't accept you could kill Marjie. But I don't *know* you didn't. Not as you do. I can't clear it out of my mind and throw it away, and it confuses me. But you know the truth, so you can. It doesn't even exist for you. So you can concentrate on what is the truth. You must have *thought* about it. Tony, please! The broken bonnet. What does it mean?'

'You know damn well.'

'So . . . you say it. Get back in the car and say it.'

He ignored that suggestion, but advanced and put his hands on the roof of the car, like a gangster about to be searched for weapons.

I felt he offered me something. I smiled, and he said, talking to the rain, hoping it would wash clean his precious thoughts: 'Why would Linda need to break open the bonnet of her own car?'

'Because she didn't know where the bonnet-release knob was,' I suggested.

'In her own car?'

'It's possible.'

'She knew,' put in Martin suddenly.

We had forgotten Martin. His voice emerged in a dead tone from the open window, in the region of my waist. 'She knew where it was. We were out driving. She drew in to a garage. It was her car we were using, mine's too noticeable. She asked them to check the oil, and reached for the bonnet release without even looking. What *is* this about breaking open the bonnet? She wouldn't need to do that.'

'Not if she knew,' Tony said, his thoughts now flowing free. 'Not even if she wanted to help with the impression that her car *had* been stolen. How could it have helped? It'd be obvious to anybody that any thief would've had to open the door somehow or other. And once in, there was the bonnet release, waiting to be used. But damn it, damn it . . . ' He thumped the roof of the car, 'I can't see what it *means*.'

'But we're progressing,' I said encouragingly. 'We're now certain she knew where the bonnet release was. If we take it in sequence, perhaps . . . '

Tony was now so involved with the progression of logic that

186

he'd forgotten his suspicion of my intentions. His hair was plastered to his head and the rain dripped from his nose and chin, spraying from his lips when he want on with it. He seemed unaware of the rain, so drenched with it that it was an insignificant trifle. I had a hat and my anorak, but I was feeling it. I was praying he'd make a move towards retreating into the car, but his excitement carried him forward.

'Right! Right! We know the car had been driven here, and the engine was switched off before the hot-wiring was rigged.'

'That wiring would've stopped it, anyway.'

'But in order to do the hot-wiring – to get into the engine compartment – the bonnet was broken open. But *why* force the bonnet, if the release was available?' he asked himself.

'To make it look good?' I suggested. 'If the idea was to fake a car theft, perhaps it'd look even better with the bonnet broken open, too.'

He threw up his hands. 'Don't you understand! What was done was exactly what Marjie had been explaining to her – except that she got the connections wrong. Marjie didn't say anything about broken bonnets. In fact, she explained how the car door could be opened, and then there'd be no *need* to force the bonnet.'

'It wasn't part of the effect, then?'

'Couldn't have been.'

'Then what?'

'Oh Lord, I don't know! Yes I do. Because it *had* to be done.'

'You mean the bonnet had to be forced open in order to do the hot-wiring?'

'One followed the other. One was done so that the other could be done.'

'Well all right . . . Then why should force have to be used to open the bonnet?'

He stared at me in infuriated disgust. 'Oh, come on! It was you who always said: get a clear mental picture. Well, I've got one, and I don't have to imagine it. I saw it.'

'That's where you've got the advantage of me.'

'I was on the scene. Wasn't I! Part of the team. I saw just how it was. The way Linda was lying, half inside the door, it would've been impossible to *reach* the bonnet release from outside.'

'But you're now saying the bonnet forcing and the hot-wiring were done after Linda was dead.'

187

He must have thought my grin was derisive. He said forcefully: 'Must have been. It's the only thing that makes sense.'

'Then – by whom?'

'Somebody else.'

'But you're saying – '

'Why not?' Now, in spite of the cold rain and the chill of his wet clothes, his face was flushed with mental effort. 'Why not!' he repeated. 'The way the car was, it would be impossible to get into it to reach the bonnet release. Linda was dead, and the hot-wiring had to be done. This somebody else thought it had to be, because Marjie had explained about it. It *had* to look as though the car had been stolen. And that means . . . ' He took a deep breath, then blew out a gust of steam that the rain hammered through. 'It means that the woman who came into the station nearly every day that week couldn't have been Linda Court.'

'No?' I said.

'And it explains that letter, too.'

'Yes,' I agreed. Does it?'

He paused for thought, and then went on:

'There was a whole week used in creating the impression that she was Linda Court. That's a lot of work. The letter added to the illusion. Or was supposed to.'

He was panting, having worked hard at it.

'The letter,' I said. 'Did you see it, Tony?'

'I saw it.'

'There was something strange, but now I understand it. Although it was dated November 14, the sender wrote that the car had been stolen again *today*, and 'Saturday' was added in brackets. Why? The fourteenth *was* Saturday. If Linda had sent it, she wouldn't have needed to add: Saturday. To her, it wouldn't have mattered. But to the person who did send it, it mattered a lot. The impression had to be maintained that it *had* been written on the Saturday, when Linda was alive to write it, when in practice it was probably written and put in the postbox on Sunday, when Linda was dead.' I sighed. 'It was just a touch of gilt on the lily.'

'This lily of yours being the whole impression that Linda was alive when she walked out of the police station!' he cried.

'Which leads to . . . '

'Of course. At 5.30. Good Lord, yes. At 5.30 the illusion was

188

that Linda Court was alive. That means – it has to mean – that she was dead. Already dead, Richard.'

'An alibi,' I said with satisfaction. 'An alibi for anybody who could demonstrate a lack of opportunity after that time. It means that any one of those people at the theatre, with their tight little alibis, could have killed Linda *before* 5.30.'

'But . . . the hot-wiring!' said Tony in dismay. '*That* wasn't done before 5.30, because Marjie hadn't explained it before then.'

'Yes.'

'You know!' he accused.

'I can guess. What about this? The murder done, Tony, before that final visit to the station to see Marjie, and right at the end of it Marjie explained how a car could be stolen, in spite of there being no keys – which were at that moment in that person's hands. Think of it, Tony. There must have been panic. She'd never heard of hot-wiring. But this was an amateur, an amateur murderer and an amateur at pretending to be a car thief. It wasn't known that it would *still* look like a car stolen by hot-wiring if the wiring wasn't there. A genuine car thief would take it away. But she couldn't know that. So she thought it had to be done, and be seen to have been done. Such a stupid detail, and it's the thing that's tripped it all up. It was more gilding of a lily that was already full-blown. She didn't know that – it had to be another woman, of course. There would be just time before the do-it-yourself shops closed to get a length of wire and two dog clips. But not time to go straight there . . . no, come straight back here . . . ' I gestured behind me. 'And get it done. Because the cast had to be there at six. But there was a gap, during the second act and the interval, when it *could* be done. Just. She told me – she actually told me herself – that she left the theatre, too nervous . . . Oh yes, she'd be nervous. Didn't she triumph in the last act, playing the part of a tense and nervous woman?'

Tony stared at me across the car. We were talking within feet of her husband. I was glad we weren't in there with him.

Tony said in a hushed voice: 'To kill her, she waited here, if necessary most of the afternoon, probably in her car, parked along the cul-de-sac – that explains why Linda's was parked against the hedge. Linda pulled in, seeing the car in her lights.'

'Would it have been dark?'

'Yes. I'd think. This'd be about 4.30. Dark enough. She knew –

the wife knew – about Linda and her husband. She'd realized it was serious. Linda got out of her car. There were words. Linda turned away . . . '

The engine woke into full song at the touch of the key. I shouted. 'Hey!' But the roof slid away beneath my hands. He raced through the gears, wheels snaking and screaming for grip, raced away from it, though there could be no escape. We ran a few yards. But there was nowhere for him to go, with a barrier at the gatehouse.

We stopped, side by side, panting.

Martin was still accelerating as he neared his own drive. A shadow flitted out from the shrubbery, a white face turned towards his lights. Hands were raised. She stood at the edge of the tarmac, took a tentative step forward, waving again.

The car seemed to buck. It swerved towards her. The edge of the bonnet caught her and whirled her high, tumbling over the roof. Then she was lost in the darkness behind it.

The car had run part way on to the soft verge. He lost control and swerved the other way, ploughed into the opposite verge, and the nose plunged into the shrubbery. The sound of the crash drifted back to us. There had been a tree in there. One headlight still flared into the bushes.

We ran. Tony plunged ahead. He paused and bent down. I still hadn't reached him when he raised his head and called out: 'She's dead, Richard.'

We both ran to the car. Martin hadn't had time to fix his seat belt. Blood was pouring from his face, and I didn't like the way the steering wheel was pressed into his chest. The engine had stalled, and there was no sign of fire, so we didn't touch him.

As I watched, one eye flickered and his lips moved. I told him not to move and we'd get help, then I used the radio and explained to them at the gate what had happened. The radiator hissed.

I told Tony I would stay there, and that he should walk down to the gate. 'No.' I changed my mind. 'Go back to Ken's car. It'll be quicker. Tell Donaldson . . . '

'Tell him there's been another murder?' he seemed confused. 'I saw him swerve, Richard. He swerved towards her.'

'Did you? I wouldn't say that.'

He sighed. 'No. Of course not. Then tell Donaldson what?'

190

'Everything. Linda's death, and Marjie's. Yes, Marjie's, you fool. It would only work for Gail if she and Marjie never met again. And Marjie had taken to walking in the park. Tell it all to Donaldson. It's *your* theory.'

'Yours. You know that.'

'It was yours. Besides, he wouldn't want to hear it from me, and I *did* promise him a constable. Get going, Tony.'

I stood and watched him drive past me, and already cars from the gateway were heading my way, and the howl of an approaching ambulance was cutting the night apart.

Ken climbed out of an official car, gave the scene a quick glance, and began issuing orders. He came over to me. 'Richard . . . '

I handed him his radio. 'There's a woman, lying dead, just a hundred yards down the hill.'

'I'll see to it. I want to talk to you, later.'

'Some time, yes. You know what you told me – go home. That's just what I'm going to do.' He'd turned away. 'Tony knows it all,' I shouted after him.

I stood and watched while he sent a car along to look to Gail's body, then waited for the ambulance, waited for them to cut Martin free, waited for a word with them. They said they thought he'd live, but I wasn't sure he would be pleased about that. Then I began to walk towards the gatehouse.

Donaldson's car was still parked there. Two men were in the back, one of them Tony. Amelia was where I'd expected her to be, waiting in the Granada.

I said: 'Slide over, love. You do the driving. Home.'

She did. I got in the passenger's seat and put my head back. The rain still pounded the roof, but it wouldn't drown out the distress in my mind.

'I've broken your Christmas present,' I told her miserably, trying to justify, to her, my distress.